KU-520-218

Meet Me in San Francisco

SHANA GRAY

HEADLINE
ETERNAL

Copyright © 2018 Shana Gray

The right of Shana Gray to be identified as the Author of
the Work has been asserted by her in accordance with the
Copyright, Designs and Patents Act 1988.

First published in Great Britain in 2018
by HEADLINE ETERNAL
An imprint of HEADLINE PUBLISHING GROUP

1

Apart from any use permitted under UK copyright law, this publication may
only be reproduced, stored, or transmitted, in any form, or by any means,
with prior permission in writing of the publishers or, in the case of reprographic
production, in accordance with the terms of licences
issued by the Copyright Licensing Agency.

All characters in this publication are fictitious
and any resemblance to real persons, living or dead,
is purely coincidental.

Cataloguing in Publication Data is available from the British Library

ISBN 978 1 4722 6003 1

Typeset in 11/14 pt Minion Pro by Jouve (UK), Milton Keynes

Printed and bound in Great Britain by CPI Group (UK) Ltd, Croydon, CR0 4YY

Headline's policy is to use papers that are natural, renewable and recyclable
products and made from wood grown in well-managed forests and other
controlled sources. The logging and manufacturing processes are expected to
conform to the environmental regulations of the country of origin.

HEADLINE PUBLISHING GROUP
An Hachette UK Company
Carmelite House
50 Victoria Embankment
London EC4Y 0DZ

www.headlineeternal.com
www.headline.co.uk
www.hachette.co.uk

I've been to San Francisco twice. The first time was with my mom back in 1998, and we had a 5.4 earthquake! I fell in love with the city, as did she. Two scenes in this book are based on our adventures. The cable car ride and Muir Woods. My mom was an adventurous lady and it's clear she passed her wanderlust on to me. I lost my mom in 2012, miss her so hard. This book is dedicated to her.

Doris. XO

Acknowledgments

A special thank-you to Louise, Kate, Kristin, and all the people that touched MEET ME IN SAN FRANCISCO. Without you, it wouldn't be the book that it is.

I'd also like to give heartfelt thank-you to my long-time friend Kerstin Kelly. She shared with me all the details of her sky-diving adventure she did with her daughters, Alexandra and Lauren. Sadly, Lauren is no longer with us and Kerstin is a huge advocate for mental health. She sends this message to all, 'Make a Mental Health First Aid Plan with everyone you love because you never know when a perfect storm can happen to you. Your life matters! The world is never better off without you!'

Meet Me
in San
Francisco

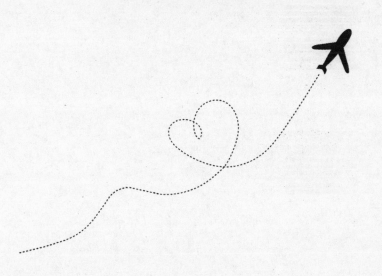

Chapter 1

March 11, 2018 23:49

L: Hey, sexy.

C: Hey, hot stuff.
Sorry for not saying goodbye.
Had to rush to catch my flight.

L: No worries ;)
I'll always have the family size stall in
Vibe to remember you by.

C: And the panties you refused
to give me back.

L: Darling, I framed those.

C: Hahaha
C: You're joking, right?

April 2, 2018 18:17

L: In the meeting from hell. Save me.

C: Sorry, also in hell. I love my kid,
but her soccer games get loooooonnggggg.

L: Soccer, nice. I played lacrosse as a kid.

C: I bet you had all the cheerleaders
swooning for your sexy ass in high school.

L: I stopped playing much in middle school.

Dad felt I should focus on other things.

What position does your daughter play?

C: Jilly's a striker. She gets her
athletic talent from my ex.

C: I prefer bedroom sports. 🐻

L: You're a MVP in my book.

April 5, 2018 22:04

C: I can't believe you just sent my
daughter all this expensive sports stuff
without asking me first.

C: I really want to pack everything up
and send it back to you.

C: But Jilly is over the moon.

C: So I'll swallow my pride for her sake.
But don't do it again.

L: That's not all you swallow.

L: Shit, no, sorry.

L: I'm drunk.

L: Celia?

April 11, 2018 9:46

C: You can't just throw money at a
problem to make it go away.

L: You got the flowers?

C: Yes.

L: Did you also get the card that said I am an
utter git who should never drink and text
and that you are an amazing, sexy, caring and,
hopefully, a very, very, very forgiving woman?

C: Yes.

L: OK.

C: Anything to do with my kids goes
through me first, got it?

L: Yes, ma'am.

C: If we ever hook up again,
you have to call me that.

L: YES, MA'AM.

April 22, 2018 14:37

L: Been a while since I heard from you.
L. Everything OK?

C: Yup. ;)
C: Just been working on a project.

L: Oh, wanna share a bit of your first draft?

C: Nah, still a work in progress.

May 1, 2018 7:15

L: Quinn says hi.
L: He peeled himself away from
Bonni long enough to visit.

C: Shhhh.
C: Still night-time here.

L: Whoops, sorry. Forgot about the time difference.
L: Want me to have coffee delivered?

C: No.
C: Yes.

L: Yes, ma'am!

May 9, 2018 22:11

L: So did Colin get a part in the play?

C: I can't believe you remembered he auditioned.
His father certainly didn't.
C: And yes, he did. One of the older kids got Peter Pan,
but Colin's playing Michael.

L: Awesome!
L: When is it? Maybe I can use the jet to come see it.

C: Really?
C: You're gonna fly across the country to
see an elementary school play?

L: If you ever get around to telling me when it is.

C: May 12th & 13th.

L: Shit, I can't. Dad found some Asian investors
he wants me to meet with.

C: No worries.
C: It was a nice thought, tho.

June 2, 2018 17:03

L: Just checking in.

L: Ready for summer vacation?

C: Yeah.

L: I bet the kids are looking forward to no more school.

C: Yeah.

L: Everything OK? You seem a little off.

C: No.

L: What's going on?

L: Celia?

C: Can't talk about it.

L: I'm here for you.

L: C?

L: Are you ghosting me?

Chapter 2

'Whoever said being a single mom was easy can kiss my ass.'

Still in cotton sleeping pants and a tank top, with her hair piled up in a messy bun, Celia wasn't sure she'd be able to get the house in order fast enough so she could escape into her writing, accompanied by a nice cup of Earl Grey and a shortbread cookie.

She hated a messy house. It drove her nuts, but lately she couldn't stay on top of it. So now she found herself in the kids' bathroom, picking up their jammies, scraping dried toothpaste out of the sink and cleaning a toilet used by a little boy who still hadn't quite figured out how to aim.

God, she loved her kids. More than anything. But damn, they could create a disaster zone out of nothing.

'I shouldn't be so hard on them. They're just kids, after all.' She was talking to herself. Was that a sign of insanity? No, that was when you kept doing the same thing over and over, expecting a different result. Celia didn't want to be one of those moms who insisted on having an immaculate home, one where you could barely tell children lived there. She didn't. But she also didn't think it was too much to ask that towels were hung back up on the bar rather dumped into a pile on the floor.

She swept up the musty-smelling towels and pajamas into a laundry basket and started to tackle the toilet. Wielding the toilet brush, she scrubbed viciously, taking out her anger at her ex-husband on the porcelain. Today – today of all days – he pulled this shit. The past few months had been excruciating. He'd been a complete asshole and her bank account was running low. And, now, being served with court papers before she'd even had her first cup of coffee was the icing on the cake.

The only thing she had to be grateful for was that the kids were at day camp and would be picked up by their dad later. She didn't have to hide how incredibly pissed she was. Celia gritted her teeth at the frustration welling inside her and flushed the toilet with a slap of the handle. Today should've been a good day.

Celia pushed some hair out of her face with the back of her hand. Okay, yes, Jilly and Colin were spending the weekend with her ex because Dickhead was getting remarried. He hadn't even waited until the ink was dry on their divorce decree before he was shacking up with the floozy he cheated on her with. But she wasn't going to be bitter. She wasn't going to be angry that he was showing his true colors. It wasn't her nature to hold grudges or to wallow in self-pity. No matter how much she deserved to.

She sighed and stretched her back. Dropping the toilet brush into her cleaning pail, she began to spray the shower with bleach and thought about her original plans for a kid-free weekend. She'd been determined to get at least another five thousand words in on her new book, and then she was going to treat herself to the latest superhero movie. Watching buff men throw punches in tight clothing was a sure-fire mood-lifter.

Coughing a little from the bleach fumes, she pushed open the window, allowing the dry heat of the California air to come wafting into the room. Beginning to scrub the tiles of the shower, she snorted. Some of her author friends would post things like this on Facebook or Instagram. The glamorous life of a *New York Times* bestselling author.

Celia's heart jumped, remembering the thrill that had raced through her last night when she found out that her first book was now a bestseller. After she and Frank separated, Celia had begun supporting herself by taking whatever freelance writing gigs she could get. It was mainly magazine articles, a few blog posts, and poetry for greeting-card companies. But after a wild night in Vegas she'd been inspired to write an erotica novel. Sales had been slow at first but, as word of mouth spread, it began climbing the charts.

And she couldn't tell a soul because Dickhead would be a dick about it. Of that, she was sure. She wrote, and did all her social media, under a pseudonym, to keep her author life under wraps. Not even her best friends knew. Still, having a bestselling novel was worthy of celebration, so she had planned to splurge on Chinese for dinner. But those plans were before she'd been served with those court papers.

She couldn't believe he was taking her back to court to reduce her child support and alimony, as well as to increase his visitation rights. It just boggled her mind.

Stepping out of the shower, Celia looked around the bathroom. Toilet, sink, shower, check. Floor . . . not so much. It had rained before Jilly's last soccer game, and her darling eldest child must've worn her uniform into the bathroom before taking a shower. When she was still married, they'd had a housekeeper, and Celia missed her more than she ever missed Frank. Her fantasies these days consisted of being able to hire someone else to clean up after her children, but every penny she had went to bills, which now apparently included paying a lawyer. The latest money from her book sales wouldn't come in for a while and in the meantime . . . well, in the meantime . . . she'd make do.

Feeling sad and depressed as her plans of a movie and Chinese food faded away, she made quick work of scrubbing the floor. Grabbing her cleaning pail and the laundry basket, she dropped them in the hallway outside the kids' rooms and decided to shower the bleach smell away.

A few minutes later, wrapped in a towel, she left her clothes on the floor (she'd pick them up before the kids got home) and padded down to the kitchen. Her little townhouse was just enough for the three of them. Money was tight, but she could make ends meet. Things would be so much easier if the asshole would just pay up his fair share of child support, though. The man was a highly respected cardiac surgeon, but God forbid he give a crap that Jilly needed new cleats. He was such a cheapskate. If it hadn't been for Landon . . .

She shook the thought away. Letting the days slip by and not replying to his texting had probably sealed the fate on them. It wasn't like she'd intended it to happen. She liked him soooo much – still did – and memories of their fling warmed her on lonely nights, but she was just getting so damn depressed about things and trying to be happy was coming awful hard these days. Celia plugged in the kettle and stared out the window into her little backyard, elbow propped on her hip as she chewed her middle finger, imagining that she was flipping the bird at her ex.

The doorbell rang and she jumped. She clutched the top of the towel and spun around with her legs spread wide, and her other hand reached out as if to ward off the devil himself.

'Who the hell is that?'

Gone were the days when, as a kid, everybody loved it when the doorbell rang. It meant visitors. Mom always had a cake ready, Dad had beer in the fridge and the coffee pot was ready to perk up some liquid goodness.

Not anymore. No one expected or wanted doorbells. They were the most dreaded sound going.

Celia tiptoed out of the kitchen and down the hall, out of sight of any windows. She knew where all the blind spots were in her house. She made a point of knowing them, in case of situations just like these. As a single mom with two kids under ten, you could never be too careful.

The doorbell ringing switched to pounding, like fists were thumping on her door. Her heart jumped into her throat. Could it be the police? Only police banged like that. What if something had happened to her kids?

More pounding.

More hesitation.

'Celia, for crying out loud, open the fricking door!' Celia relaxed. She knew that voice. Running to the door, she unlocked it and flung it wide.

Celia could barely believe her eyes. Her best friends, the sisters of her heart, were standing on her front porch. 'Oh my God, guys! What the hell are you doing here?'

'Girl, what's with the towel? Always running around in a towel.' Fredi elbowed her way past Ava and Bonni and took Celia into a big bear hug. Fredi was not the sentimental type so Celia hugged her back fiercely, appreciating the support.

'I just got out of the shower. I was cleaning the little monsters' bathroom and felt all gross myself,' Celia replied.

'Yeah, and that's disgusting,' Fredi said, making an *eww* face and stepping back.

Bonni nudged Ava inside and pushed the door closed, locking it behind them, ever the cop. Ava laughed, tugging on Celia's wet hair. 'You're going to get me all damp, but I don't care. I need a Celia hug.'

Celia found herself swept up into another hug, and then Bonni joined in. Celia just let herself hang in their arms as they squeezed the breath out of her. 'Oh guys, you have no idea how good it is to see you.' She was close to tears.

Fredi patted her on the shoulder before going to investigate the kitchen. 'Mmm, I need coffee.'

Ava took Celia's hand and they congregated in the kitchen. Celia found herself sitting in a chair at her battered kitchen table while her friends bustled around the room. Fredi found her Keurig and picked through her remaining pods to make coffee for her and Bonni. Ava went right to the cabinet holding the mugs, taking out four before grabbing two tea bags. Bonni poured hot water from the kettle into two of the mugs and then went to the fridge and pulled out the milk and the half and half.

Celia felt her chin tremble. 'What are you guys *doing* here?'

Ava carried over the mugs of tea and placed them on the table for her and Celia. She pulled out a chair but, before sitting in it, she rested her palm on Celia's face for the briefest moment and gave her a soft nod. She whispered, 'It'll all be okay, sweetie.'

'We're here to save you.' Bonni sat down across from her, and Celia looked at her friends. To her horror, tears pricked at her eyes, and she swiped her hand over them.

Ave jumped up to grab a box of tissues. 'Aw, honey, no tears. We knew you needed some cheering up.'

'H–how did you know?' Celia sniffed, taking a tissue to blow her nose.

Bonni spoke. 'Landon told me you'd been sounding kinda down. I noticed it too. So we conspired. We knew you'd be kidless so we thought it was the perfect time to run away with you.'

'C-conspired? What are you talking about?' Celia added a little milk to her tea and stirred it with a slightly shaking hand. She was happy to hear that Landon had been talking to Bonni about her. It meant she was still on his mind, and a tiny little spark of happiness flared inside her. After their last long conversation they had texted back and forth on a somewhat casual basis. They had bantered, flirted, but she was too off her game to fully enjoy it. She'd been too damn low, worrying about the demands of her ex, and threats, that she rarely paid attention to her phone anymore. Plus, she was on a huge deadline that she wasn't able to explain to anyone yet. Life was so complicated sometimes it was annoying.

'We're kidnapping you,' Ava burst out, and Bonni gave her a narrow look. 'What's the big deal? We're here. She's coming. That's that.' Ava shrugged her shoulders.

'You coulda eased into it a little more gently,' Fredi said over the rim of her coffee mug, leaning against the counter. 'Or you could check your phone more often, Cee.'

Bonni adjusted herself in her seat. 'Cee, hey, look at me.'

After gazing at Ava and Fredi, still unable to comprehend what was happening, Celia turned her attention to Bonni, who reached out and put her hands over Celia's.

'We're worried about you. You've lost your zazzle, your spark. You've been getting more and more worn down since Vegas. So we're scooping you up and we're heading off to San Francisco and then to Quinn's family vineyard in Napa.'

Celia shook her head, the logistics overwhelming her. 'Uhm, I can't. Mom's away and I promised to keep an eye on her house. And I should stay close in case the kids need me. Plus, I have no clean clothes.' She looked at her friends. 'It's Thursday, laundry day.'

'Laundry day is a thing?' Fredi asked. 'Who knew?'

'Ya, it is, so I don't have to do it on the weekend and can just spend time with my kids. I'm so happy to see you guys! But I can't just take off.'

'Wow, you are in a bad way,' Fredi said, shaking her head.

'What do you mean?' Celia was beginning to feel more ruffled now, and ready to push back. She couldn't just drop everything and go. She was a mom, she had responsibilities!

'The Celia we know would already be upstairs, packing, and then be out the door before anyone else, make-up on, dressed to kill. Ready for an adventure.' Fredi put her mug down and a hand on the table. She leaned into Celia, cupping her chin with her other hand. 'You need rescuing, and we're here to do it.'

'The kids—'

'Are with their dad until next week,' Ava reminded her. 'Remember, they're in his wedding party, and we found out all the details. He'll be keeping them for a bit before the honeymoon.'

'You have? Oh, wow. Uhm, I – I don't have enough cash—'

'That is all taken care of, and there's no room for argument,' Bonni was quick to say, in her stern-cop voice.

Celia was quiet and considered what they were telling her. She had enough food in the fridge to make the kids' lunches when they got back, and her next manuscript wasn't due to the freelance editor she'd hired for another three weeks. Plus, her lawyer's billable rates were crazy on the weekend, so it would be better to wait until Monday to discuss the new court papers. Sure, the house was a disaster area, but it wouldn't crumble if she skipped vacuuming for one week. She looked at her friends' beaming faces and felt Celia the Mom start to get pushed aside by Celia the Woman.

'A long girls' weekend? What exactly would be the plan?' she asked tentatively.

Ava cheered because she'd known Celia long enough to understand when she was giving in. Fredi began to tidy up the kitchen in preparation for their departure while Bonni answered, 'I have a car outside. We're going to drive up the coast and do whatever we feel like along the way. We'll crash tonight in San Francisco and then, tomorrow, head up to a vineyard that Quinn and Landon's family owns. We've got it all organized, made the necessary calls. Frank is aware.'

'You told him!' Celia was stunned they'd called him.

'I did,' Bonni said. 'You know I won't take any bullshit from him, but I was polite, told him you would be with us for a few days, and he passed along a message for you to have a good time.'

'I don't believe it.' Celia looked at her skeptically.

Bonni shrugged her shoulders. 'Unlikely, true, but he did.'

A slow smile curved on Celia's lips and a tiny little glimmer of excitement sparked inside her. 'Okay, then. I'll go pack whatever's clean.'

Fredi rolled her eyes. 'Oh, please. You're talking to your former college roommates. You'd have to skip doing laundry for two months before you ran out of clean clothes.'

Celia stood, clutching her towel at her chest, and Fredi continued, 'Yeah, and get dressed too. Towels are not socially acceptable attire for a road trip.'

Fredi's snark rolled off Celia's back because she was hit with a giant wave of excitement at the thought of leaving her troubles behind for a little while. 'Oh my God. A road trip! I so need a road trip.'

Ava jumped up and threw her hands in the air. *'Rooooad-ddddd trippppppp!* Look out, San Francisco!'

Celia dashed up the stairs, narrowly avoiding a stray piece of Lego as she left her friends in the kitchen. This was going to be the best kidnapping ever!

Chapter 3

'I don't know how you managed to pull this off. Especially with my mom on her trip to Tuscany.' Celia sat in the back seat of Bonni's rented Mustang convertible and yelled loud enough for her friends to hear. 'I think she's hoping to find an old wreck of a chateau that she can renovate and then some hot young number will come along and sweep her off her feet.'

The girls all laughed and Bonni called back as she drove, 'I know the movie you're referring to. Maybe ladybugs will land on her.'

'That doesn't sound all bad, you know,' Fredi, sitting next to Celia, said, her eyebrows raised. 'I'd put up with doing a little home renovation if it means I wind up with a young Italian stud in my bed.'

Ava nodded in the passenger seat, her hair flying around her in the wind. 'I can see the attraction.'

Bonni laughed. 'Oh, please, Aves, you'd rather he sweep you off your feet than bang you against a wall.'

Waving her hand dismissively, Ava replied, 'A good hero could do both.'

'You guys are crazy. Didn't you see that movie? There were snakes in the bedroom, bats in the belfry, no water. No guy is hot enough to put up with that crap.' Celia shivered.

Ava shook her head. 'You say that now but, if you meet the right guy, your tolerance for "crap" will go up.'

'Aww, come on, Ava, not every woman finds a Mr Right. You're such a dreamer,' Fredi scoffed.

Celia met Bonni's eyes in the rear-view mirror as Ava and Fredi re-started a very old argument.

'I can't believe a woman who designs wedding dresses for a living can be so cynical about love!' Ava exclaimed.

'When you have as many repeat customers as I have, you learn that "happily ever after" really just means "happy for right now",' Fredi shot back.

Celia shook her head. 'How in the hell did this convo go south so quickly?' She saw Ava open her mouth to reply and kept talking, 'Anyway, you guys are awesome for kidnapping me. I swear single moms should have a special holiday in the year.'

Ava pouted a little before her usual sunshine nature took over again and she offered support. 'A single mom needs more than one holiday in the year, honey.'

'Aww, thanks, sweetie.' Celia leaned back.

There was a beat of silence, and Celia's gaze wandered to her friends. Each of them was so different, but they were so tightly knit as friends they almost felt each other's emotions. In the driver's seat, Bonni's dark hair was pulled back in her usual ponytail, the wind whipping the strands around her. She shot a quick smirk to Ava, and Celia fancied she could see Bonni's cop façade just melt away. Her heart swelled with love for them all.

'I'm glad you didn't fight us on the kidnap plan.' Fredi repositioned their purses between them.

'I'm glad too! And, I do admit no kids, no drama, just us, sounds wonderful,' Celia replied.

Fredi snorted. 'No drama? Since when is there no drama where we're concerned?'

Bonni laughed and looked at them in the rear-view mirror. She pointed at Celia and scolded, 'You're the drama queen. It follows you wherever we go!'

'Hey, how am I the drama queen?' Celia exclaimed, then pursed her lips at Bonni.

Ava twisted in her seat to raise an eyebrow at Celia. 'Remember when you were pregnant with Jilly and I flew out to meet you in Los Angeles, and we were having dinner when you saw that guy you were *so sure* was a celebrity?'

The problem with staying friends with the same women for over a decade is that they knew everything and they never let you forget it.

Celia airily said, 'That was merely pregnancy hormones. I couldn't be held responsible for my actions. Those cops even agreed with me.'

Fredi snickered and, smiling, Ava pushed her hair out of her face as the wind blew the auburn strands around. The sun caught the color of her hazel eyes and made the green flecks even more vivid.

Bonni lifted a shoulder and Celia could hear the grin in her voice. 'See, somehow, it finds you.'

Celia was starting to feel more relaxed as the time went by. More like herself. Being with the sisters of her heart, her Sassy Squad, was the absolute right choice to make. She raised her face to the sky, so blue it almost hurt her eyes. The warmth of the sun beat down on her skin and she felt happy. A deep, heart-clenching happy. She only hoped she could hang on to the feeling.

The wind tugged at her long hair and she didn't bother to tie it up. So what if it got all tangled up in a mess? She was a California Girl and used to the wind, sun and surf. Before they had the kids, she and Frank used to surf together early in the morning, before he had to head to his residency at the hospital. It had just been them and nature, two young kids wildly in love and in sync on the water. When had they lost that? Ruthlessly shoving the thought aside, she inhaled deeply, forcing her muscles to relax. She was determined to enjoy her kidnapping, dammit! 'This is just wonderful.' She flung her arms wide.

'I can't remember the last time I was in a convertible.' Fredi reached up to grab her long curls. She braided and wound them up into a tight bun, securing it with a hairband. 'My hair is going to be a rats' nest tonight.'

'This is the best,' Celia said. 'Another girls' weekend away, and in San Francisco! There's so much we have to do. Visit Haight Ashbury, go to Ghirardelli's, and—'

'Celia, stop! No planning. We've got some sorta definite plans, remember,' Bonni interrupted.

'Oh, yes! I simply can't wait. Bring on the wine. Nothing sparkly either – ugh,' Celia said.

'We have to stop and grab a bottle of Jack. Just in case,' Fredi informed them.

'Oh, Fredi, you and your Jack,' Celia teased. 'We're in wine country, baby!'

'Damn right, me and my Jack. He's the only dude that doesn't talk back or make things suck. I'm quite happy with Jack being the sole man in my life.'

'We're going to drive along the coastline. I'm sure we'll pass a liquor store along the way.' Bonni turned her head so they could hear her.

'It's a beautiful day,' Ava answered. 'Maybe we can stop for a seafood lunch somewhere.'

'That would be awesome,' Celia said. With kids and not a lot of extra cash, the only place she ever ate out these days was McDonald's. A fresh lobster roll would be divine.

'I can't wait to sink my bare feet into the sand and have waves splashing up against my legs.' Ava raised her arms in the air. 'This is just glorious. I think I could get used to living by the ocean.'

'I'm thinking we stop in Monterey for lunch and then head back out on the road. Unless we see something that catches our eye along the way,' Bonni said.

'Sounds like you've got this all planned out,' Fredi replied.

Celia slid her phone out of her bag to check the time. Her kids were still in school so she wouldn't hear from them for a while. Almost against her will, her finger tapped open her text messages. Landon's name was near the top, and she opened their thread, rereading his last text. He had started this whole weekend in motion. 'Bonni, did you know the Bryants had a vineyard before now?'

'I just found out recently. You know, the family has so many properties around the world and a vineyard in Napa Valley just happens to be one of their many holdings,' Bonni yelled above the wind.

'That's just plain *wow*,' Celia said. She knew Landon's family was wealthy, but imagine owning a vineyard and having it be nearly an afterthought . . .

'Can you believe it?' Ava said, swiveling in her seat again. 'We're going to a vineyard! What better place for a busy single mom to take a break than a fancy vineyard?'

'You're right. I'm just a little depressed these days,' Celia admitted. It was the closest she'd come to saying just how low she'd been feeling, and she wouldn't say another word. Now was not the time to get into it or drag her friends down.

'Aww, honey, I know it's tough. I can't believe he's actually marrying her.' Ava was always the one to try to empathize. 'I mean, I don't want to slut-shame—'

'Oh, I'll do it,' Fredi said. 'Once a cheater, always a cheater. Her inevitable heartbreak is what she deserves for sleeping with a married man.'

'Fredi!' Ava exclaimed, twisting to slap at Fredi's knee.

'Oh, I don't really care about that. I mean, I care for the kids' sake, but our relationship . . . It's just that . . . well, oh, I don't know.' Celia drew in a sharp breath and threw her hands up into the wind as if to halt the thoughts. 'Enough of all that. Let's have some fun.'

Fredi looked at Celia and pursed her lips. 'With Bonni in charge of the car, we're just passengers along for the ride. A crazy ride, by the look of it. Is your seatbelt on tight?'

Celia giggled. 'You know, right now, that's absolutely perfect for me. I don't really wanna have to be making any decisions at the moment. But hey, drive safe, Bon-Bon, you have precious cargo back here and my kids are expecting me home alive.'

'I'm a cop. I know how to pursue a fleeing vehicle, how to shake a tail, and I can certainly get us to the vineyard in one piece,' Bonni stated, and met Celia's gaze in the rear-view mirror again. Celia batted her eyelashes at her and Bonni just shook her head, smiling.

Fredi nodded and leaned over. 'I hear you, sister. I'm glad to be leaving behind those bridal bitches.'

'You really need your own studio, you know.' Celia nodded, her eyes wide and knowing. 'You're far too talented to be wasting away underneath the restricting pressure of that cow of an owner.'

'Don't insult cows,' Fredi said, adjusting her sunglasses.

They all cracked up at Fredi's snide remark. Celia's heart swelled with love for her friends. 'You guys are too much,' she laughed. Still, even though she appreciated what they were trying to do, the problems she hoped she could leave behind continued to lurk in the back of her mind. It wasn't easy to forget the alimony, the child-support legal suit her ex had dropped on her. How was she going to pay for costs and still be able to keep her head above water? But she refused to think about it now. 'Thanks, girls. You're the best kidnappers a woman could ask for!'

Celia sat back and shoved her worries away once more. Instead, she lapped up the fantastic feeling filling her from being with her friends and having a fun weekend ahead of her. Dare she hope there might be grape-stomping in her future?

Looking down at the phone she still held, she wondered if Landon might be in her future as well. She realized now that she wanted to see him again. It had been hard to balance everything – the writing, the kids, the fight with her ex – and maintain a bright and cheery text convo with Landon. The last thing she wanted was to be miserable to him and that was part of the reason she'd just sort of let it slide. But he'd been persistent, continuing with the easy-going messages that held a teasing tone and had in fact carried through her low moments. Now she wished she'd been more responsive to him.

Chapter 4

Celia watched the scenery pass and enjoyed the spectacular views around each bend in the road. Even though she lived in Southern California, she couldn't get enough of the sea, the coastline scenery, the salty tang. It was nice to just sit and not have to think about anything. Let the drama of her ex and the looming custody fight just melt into the background. Time enough for dealing with it later.

'Oh, look! Can we pull off here?' Ava pointed her finger.

Celia craned her neck to see and drew in a gasp. 'Oh, wow, stunning. Yes, can we stop?' she echoed.

A row of cars had pulled off on the shoulder of the road and beyond was a wonderful view of the sea and a beach below.

'Maybe there's a parking spot.' Bonni slowed the car down and turned off the highway into a widened area where cars had been parked wherever they could be. 'It's not looking too good.'

'Oh, there's a guy coming out. Just up ahead. The red car.' Celia released her seatbelt, rose up and stood behind Ava's seat, hanging on to the headrest.

'I see it,' Bonni said, and wheeled the Mustang into the tight spot. 'I suggest you put your purses in the trunk. No point carrying them down to the beach, and it's asking for trouble if you leave them in full view in the car.'

The women piled out of the car and Bonni popped the trunk. Celia dropped her purse beside the other bags, took off her shoes and placed them in as well. Going barefoot was her favorite thing to do.

'Time for sand between your toes.' Celia was the first down the path. She ran like a child and, if she'd had a sand pail and a shovel, she'd have been swinging it like she didn't have a care in the world. Celia sprinted down the last bit of the path, carefully avoiding rocky outcrops. She couldn't wait to get down and dip her toes in the water.

'Careful, guys, the path is a bit rocky,' she called over her shoulder, then finally she was on the sand. She waited at the bottom for the rest of them as they picked their way down the path.

'Oh, wow, look at this beach!' Ava exclaimed, running across the sand toward the surf.

'I do love turquoise water. It's so pretty, but usually a shit ton warmer than this,' Fredi noted.

'I bet the sunsets here would be fantastic,' Bonni said. 'We should keep an eye out when we're on the drive back on Monday for somewhere to stop and catch a sunset over the ocean.'

'That would be wonderful,' Celia agreed. 'If we're lucky, there won't be a cloud to be seen and we can have a beautiful sunset, watch the sun sink below the horizon, painting its wonderful colors of pink, purple and fiery orange across the sky.'

'You really are getting romantic with your words,' Ava said, and gave Celia a nudge on the shoulder. 'How are you doing with your writing? Published anything recently? We want to hear all about it.'

Celia hesitated for a brief moment, still not willing to share her news, as it was too dicey as far as her ex-husband was concerned. Her friends had long supported her freelance writing career, always buying up every magazine her work was featured in, but even though she trusted her girls, she just couldn't risk anyone knowing about her bestselling erotica novel. It had been less than twenty-four hours since the book had charted, and she was dying to share the news, but she couldn't. Not yet anyway.

'It's so busy with the kids, but I write whenever I get the chance. I've started dictating too, so I can write in the car, doing laundry, cooking. And I take my iPad everywhere, you know that.'

'That's awesome. I'm really proud of you for reinventing yourself after the divorce,' Ava praised. 'But dictating? How does that work?'

It made Celia feel good to have her friend acknowledge her efforts. 'I turn on the microphone on my phone and dictate into an email or other app program. It gets the words out and then I have to edit and clean them up later.'

'Wow, that's truly dedication.'

Fredi and Bonni were right behind them and had overheard their conversation.

'So what's next on the publication front? "The Latest in Ska Music?" "Hidden Gems: Antique Stores in Southern California?" Oh, I know, "How to Win in Vegas!"' Fredi said.

'We all know Bonni was the big winner in Vegas – although you scored pretty good in that nightclub, Celia!' Ava teased.

Fredi hooted approvingly and fist-bumped Ava. Bonni picked up a handful of sand and flung it at her friends, who darted backward, squealing.

Celia watched her friends play and felt so bad that she was unable to share her big secret with them. Telling her friends now about her career as a romance author might put them in a difficult position, as she wasn't sure yet if she'd have to disclose the potential income from her book to the courts. Celia would do whatever her lawyer advised, of course, but until then she wasn't going to risk putting her friends in a position where they would have to perjure themselves. As soon as this lawsuit was done, she'd be able to shout it from the rooftops.

'Come on, guys. Keep walking. We need to get our ion cleanse from the sand,' Ava said.

'Ion cleanse?' Bonni looked skeptical.

'Of course. Walking barefoot in the sand is like an ion cleanse. Positive and negative energies between your feet and the sand draw all the toxins out,' Ava explained earnestly.

Celia exchanged looks with Fredi and Bonni. Fredi said, 'For someone who is so no-nonsense when it comes to money, you are such a sucker when it comes to everything else.'

'I've never heard of such a thing,' Bonni said. 'Sounds like voodoo stuff to me.'

Ava crossed her arms and tapped her foot on the sand. 'It's not! I read an article about it. People feel better by the sea and after walking on the sand. Don't you remember how good you feel walking on the sand with the water breaking around your feet? You naturally breathe deeper, relax and are at one with nature. Check it out. Come on and try it.'

Celia was willing to try anything right now, so she followed Ava down to the surf and waved for her friends to follow. Fredi had her head bent to her cell phone and Celia knew she was googling it. Bonni trailed behind them a little reluctantly.

'We're already in the sand. Wouldn't we get the same benefit if we just did the "Running Man?"' Bonni said, still skeptical.

'Seriously, Bonni, believe me. You'll feel a hundred per cent better. Just let the toxins flow out of your soles.' Ava was insistent.

'I love the beach and rarely get to stick my toes in the sand these days,' Celia said. 'Whether I'm leaching toxins or not, I'm getting a mood-lift just being here with you guys.'

Fredi tilted her phone to Celia, showing her a study debunking the benefits of ion cleansing. Celia shrugged and tilted her head meaningfully. Fredi rolled her eyes and sighed. Pocketing her phone, she said, 'Okay, well, let the cleansing begin!' She raised her hands in the air and twirled around. 'Come on, sand, do your thing!'

Ava huffed, and Celia knew she was a little bit offended that they were making a joke out of it. 'The heck with the lot of you. Be impure – what do I care?'

'Speaking of impure, Celia, how's it going with Landon?' Bonni asked her, and Celia glanced up from the water. Bonni waggled her eyebrows and Celia smirked.

'I don't know what you're implying. We're merely friends.'

Fredi hip-checked her and she stumbled a little further into the water. 'Friends, right. Friends with benefits, maybe.'

'Just because we had sex once doesn't mean we can't also be friends,' Celia replied primly.

'When Quinn went to visit him, he said Landon was never far from his phone and every time he got a text he immediately read it. I wonder why . . .' Bonni teased.

'Quinn has a big mouth.' Celia smiled to herself, kinda liking that Landon had enjoyed hearing from her so much. That meant she was still on his mind, much like he had been in the back of hers. She tapped the pocket holding her phone, tempted again to text him. Celia waded further into the surf, which was quite wild. The waves crashed on the rocks just offshore and sent up a tang on the wind. She tipped her head back and breathed in the sea air, deciding on a change of topic.

'We're all going to be sunburned and salty. Remember that time we went down to the Gulf of Mexico for Spring Break?'

Fredi sighed longingly. 'Warm water, white sand, and very hot, very drunk frat boys. We didn't pay for a single drink.'

Ava wandered back their way, her usual smile back on her face. 'I thought the water here would be warm like that, but it's like a knife has cut off my ankles. Holy crap!'

'We had fun, didn't we?' Fredi hooked her arm through Ava's.

Bonni moved next to Fredi while Celia took a quick selfie. Bonni said, 'It was great. That was our first or second Spring Break?'

'It was our first.' Celia walked out of the water and stood beside Bonni. The four of them, arms linked, stared out over the waves. 'The second one was Mexico. Man, that was even crazier.'

They fell silent, contemplating the past. Celia continued, 'Can you imagine? All those years ago we were just babies, and now look at us.'

Fredi agreed. 'I know, right? Country girl Ava is now in the big city, commitment-phobe Bonni's shacked up, and Celia's got two munchkins and a mighty fine man on the hook.' Reaching to pinch Celia on the forearm, she said, 'You hussy, you.'

Celia knew she should protest against the idea that she was keeping Landon dangling, but she sighed. After Frank, having a man in her life who remembered events in her kids' lives, who took the time to send them presents, who had coffee delivered – it was amazing. She felt a brief moment of blinding happiness thinking about Landon. 'I'd be his hussy any day.'

The girls laughed. 'Now, that's an admission,' Bonni said.

Flushing, Celia started to head back to where they had parked the car. 'I guess it is. You know, he's a really sweet guy.'

Ava dragged her feet against the sand, presumably still cleansing. 'You don't have to tell us. Considering he and Quinn come from the über-rich, they are remarkably down-to-earth compared to some of the clients I have to deal with at work.'

Fredi groaned. 'Tell me about it! The wealthy bridezillas are the *worst*.'

Ava and Fredi traded horror stories as the group slowly wandered back up the beach, picking up shells and stones that caught their attention. Celia spotted something sparkly, half buried in the sand. She reached down and grabbed a rock, shaking the sand off it. Colin had developed a fascination with geology, and this would be a great souvenir for him.

Peering over her shoulder, Ava said, 'Wouldn't it be awesome if that was a diamond? And it was worth millions? Or someone lost it, and there's a big reward? Or—'

'Aves, romcoms are called fiction for a reason. It's just a pretty stone,' Celia said. Her friend looked disappointed and Celia felt a pang. She used to be a lot more open-minded, a lot more willing to go along with Ava's whimsy, but now she only felt that part of herself when she was with her kids. Even with her friends, it was hard to reconnect with the wild and impulsive person she used to be.

Bonni checked her watch. 'We should get going.'

'Yeah, I'm getting hangry.' Ava was hot on Bonni's heels as they made their way up to the car.

Celia hung back. Rolling the stone in her palm, looking at the way it glinted in the light, she felt that old urge to be spontaneous. Tucking the stone away, she pulled her phone out of her pocket and texted Landon: *tnx for getting me kidnapped.*

Almost immediately, she saw the dots indicating he was writing a reply, but her phone was snatched out of her hand.

'Hey! Who are you texting?' Fredi asked, startling Celia. Fredi ran away, with Celia's phone held high over her head.

'What are you doing? Give it back!' Celia took off after Fredi as she sprinted toward the path.

'Landon says "you're welcome" with a kissy emoji. Oh, yeah, Celia's gonna get some!' Fredi called out.

'Dammit, Fredi! Give me back my phone or, so help me, I will plot a horrible revenge,' Celia shrieked. She increased her speed when she saw Fredi typing, disastrous visions floating through her head, but although Fredi was short, she was speedy. Ava and Bonni stood by the car, making no move to intercede on Celia's behalf. Finally, she reached the car, panting, slapping at Fredi. Fredi fended her off for a moment and then, with a satisfied 'There,' she handed the phone back to Celia.

Celia was afraid to look, but she had to know.

> C: thx for getting me kidnapped.
>
> L: You're welcome. 😊
>
> C: Really looking forward to seeing you, hot stuff.
>
> L: Yes, ma'am, sexy. ;)
>
> L: Enjoy your time with your friends while you can. I've got plans for you.

Slumping against the car, Celia fanned herself at how Landon's words made her rather hot and bothered and watched while Fredi accepted congratulatory high-fives from Ava and Bonni.

Chapter 5

They drove into Monterey, following the road along the water-front, past the beaches, little boutiques and foodie establishments. They all watched for a parking space and Bonni was the first to spot a Land Rover backing out of a spot next to the pier.

'Whoa, perfect timing. Bonni, you have the parking goddess on your side today,' Ava told her.

'Lucky for us! This place is packed. I thought we'd grab something to eat around here. I heard there's a lot of good seafood places,' Bonni said.

'Like that place?' Celia said, pointing.

'It looks really cool. Like an old cannery or something.' Ava climbed out of the car and hitched her bag over her shoulder.

'This is called Cannery Row. It would be neat to know the history here. Everyone got their purses?'

The women found a spot on a deck overlooking the beach and the sea beyond. The view was fantastic, but Celia needed a drink. Landon's texts had fired up her libido, but they had also reminded her of why she was on this trip to begin with.

She didn't really know how everything had gone off the rails so swiftly. So much had happened since her ex walked out it made her head spin. Yet, if truth be told, Celia had known in her gut that things were off. If her marriage had been solid, nothing could have gotten between them and ripped their relationship apart.

She supposed, in a way, she was thankful that it had happened while she was still in her early thirties and she hadn't given Frank too much of her youth. Her heart was torn to shreds for her kids, though. They didn't really understand why Mommy and Daddy weren't together anymore and she'd be damned if she was going to pull them down into her bitterness. He was still their dad and she'd never make them question that or cause them to feel like he was a bad man.

Only she would know that Frank was an asshole who was attempting to get her time with her kids reduced so he wouldn't have to pay her as much.

All these thoughts raced around in her head as she contemplated the cocktail list.

'Good Lord, I'm in the mood for drinking,' she murmured.

'When are you not?' Fredi pointed out.

Celia looked at her, confused, before she realized she'd spoken out loud. 'Right then, not only am I in the mood to drink, I'm in the mood to have a damn good time with my girls.' But her words didn't totally reflect how she felt.

She looked at the prices of the drinks and the food. Bonni had made it clear that Celia wasn't to worry about money, but she had her pride. If it wasn't for her kids, she wasn't going to accept handouts. If she was careful, she could use her credit card for a few treats this weekend. Celia had to admit, though, she missed the days when she could drop twelve dollars on a cocktail without blinking. How much money had she spent on booze over the years?

'Why are you shaking your head?' Bonni asked her, and Fredi elbowed her to snap her out of her musings.

She lifted a shoulder, determined not to bring her girlfriends' moods down to her low level. 'Just stuff, you know. Life. Dickhead. Money. The typical shit.'

'Aww, don't you worry, honey. It'll all work out. You just wait and see.' Ava, ever the optimist, always had something positive to say, and Celia loved her for it.

'I know, Aves.' Celia leaned over and squeezed Ava's hand. 'It'll all be good. You're right.' She let go and turned her attention back to the menu open in front of her. 'So what are we all drinking today?'

'Well, I'm the designated driver, so no booze for me,' Bonni said.

'We'll take care of you later.' Fredi nodded.

'There will certainly be enough alcohol where we're going! Is Quinn going to be there?' Ava asked Bonni.

'At the vineyard, you mean? Maybe. He's still settling in to Toronto, and then we'll be uprooted for the move to Atlanta or wherever, but he said he would try to come,' Bonni replied, flipping through the menu.

'I'm looking forward to seeing the place. Vineyards are one of my favorite settings for weddings. Not to mention the easy access to alcohol,' Fredi said, looking around for a server.

'But you don't like wine,' Ava reminded her.

Fredi raised a hand to flag a nearby waitress. 'Desperate times, make it work, beggars can't be choosers, et cetera.'

Celia shook her head. 'Only you would look at drinking wine as a necessary evil, Freds.'

The waitress came to the table and took their food and drink order before leaning over to crank open the table's umbrella. The sun was strong so it was quite warm on the deck and no breeze was blowing. With the umbrella up, Celia was in the shade, but Bonni and Ava had wound up in nearly direct sunlight. Bonni shaded her eyes with a hand so she could check her phone while Ava fanned herself with a flimsy paper napkin. With only a shared look, Fredi and Celia got up to switch places with their friends.

The women reorganized themselves and shifted chairs to get the perfect position at the table.

'Okay, girls, everybody settled now? Everybody got the right amount of sun? Nobody's gonna burn their delicate skin?' Fredi teased. Bonni flipped her off and Ava quickly shoved her hand down, gesturing to the kids at a nearby table.

'You sure can tell who's not from a sunny location,' Fredi said to Celia.

'I forgot to bring sunglasses. Why is it so damn bright?' Bonni complained. Celia delved into her purse and pulled out a baseball cap she sometimes wore at Jilly's games. She tossed it at Bonni and smirked when it bounced off her friend's face.

'I've got mine.' Ava pulled out the sunglasses and put them on, striking an overly dramatic model pose.

'Wow, you look just like Audrey Hepburn. So classic and beautiful,' Bonni told her. Ava flushed and dropped her hands to her lap. Once upon a time she'd wanted to be a dancer, but she became less and less comfortable being in the spotlight as the years went by. They had danced in clubs together, of course, but Celia had only seen her friend truly perform a single time, and Ava had been grace personified.

The waitress came back with a basket of cheese biscuits and another with fresh fried seafood. Practically salivating as the baskets were slid in front of them, Celia inhaled deeply and moaned with delight.

'This smells so yum.' She reached for a shrimp and dipped it in cocktail sauce before popping it into her mouth. 'Heaven. You kidnapped me before I got to eat breakfast.'

Another waitress came with a tray of drinks, setting a great big glass of iced tea in front of Bonni before distributing the rest of the glasses. Celia took a sip of her Mai Tai, enjoying the burn of the alcohol down her throat. Unlike when she was in college, she didn't drink much these days, especially not when she had her kids with her.

'How are Jilly and Colin, Celia?' Bonni asked, as she pulled off a piece of biscuit.

Celia selected another shrimp before she answered. 'They're great. Even though they drive me nuts.'

'I'd love to see them again. We'll have to work something out. Skyping is awesome, but I need to see them, to squeeze and hug them.' Bonni smiled at Celia, and it warmed her heart that her friend loved her children so.

'Are they excited about the wedding?' Fredi asked, fussing with her hair.

Celia shrugged. 'Oh, I don't know. I suppose it's exciting for them. It's different, and it'll be the longest stretch of time they've been with him since the separation, so it should be interesting.'

Ava nodded and inspected the shrimp she plucked from the basket. 'He'll have to be an actual parent now. Maybe he'll stop being a dick about paying child support.' She bit down on the shrimp with a bloodthirsty snap.

Celia stared at her friend and then just blurted it out. 'Frank's taking me back to court. He wants joint custody, like, alternating weeks, and to reduce child support and my alimony.'

Her besties erupted with various cries of outrage and shock. Their dismay on her behalf washed over Celia. All she felt was a wave of love. She could always count on them to be on her side.

'That effing bastard. I've dealt with some pretty stingy misers in my day, but he takes the cake!' Ava looked ready to find Frank and give him a beat-down. Fredi, on the other hand, would ambush him in a dark alley, and no one would ever believe a sweet southern belle like her would be capable of doing so much damage. But Bonni . . . she looked thoughtful.

Celia said sharply, 'Bonni, you can't tell Landon. Or Quinn. This is my problem and I'll handle it myself.'

Busted, Bonni looked vaguely guilty as she said, 'I bet their company is already paying a whole fleet of shark lawyers who'd munch Dickhead up like he was chum. I'm sure they wouldn't mind sparing just one—'

'I said no!' A hush fell over the table at Celia's exclamation, and she felt like shit for casting a pall over the day. She should have never said anything. Bonni cleared her throat and then returned to their previous topic.

'So, anyway. The kids.' She turned to Celia. 'Maybe they could come and visit me for a long weekend sometime. I'd love it.'

Celia felt a wave of gratitude. That was her Sassy Squad. They always had her back. 'They would love that. They always enjoy spending time with their Aunt Bon-Bon.'

'Then we'll plan it around their school schedule.' Bonni reached over and patted Celia's hand. Celia turned her hand over to give Bonni's a squeeze.

Ava casually changed the subject. 'I love patio time, and this is so awesome, being over water.'

'There is something special about the ocean,' Celia agreed.

'It has a mystique, a romance to it. So many treasures are buried deep under those waves.'

'Oh Lord,' Fredi moaned. 'It's the ocean. It'll take you down if it could. Under those waves are things that want to *eat* you.'

Celia giggled as the waitress showed up with their orders. Before she stepped away Celia asked her to take a picture of the four of them. They squished together around the small table, with windblown hair and slightly sunburned skin, smiling brightly at the camera on Celia's cell. Feeling her besties pressed against her, Celia knew that she had already discovered one of life's greatest treasures.

Chapter 6

After lunch, the rest of the journey flew by. Once they got to the hotel, they quickly checked in to their adjoining rooms. Celia dumped her suitcase next to the bed she'd chosen and wandered into the other room.

'I don't know about you guys, but I'm kinda wired. I'm not ready for calling it a day. We still have a whole night ahead of us.' Ava was chattering again.

Fredi raised a shoulder and tipped her head to the side. 'I could use a walk. We have been cooped up in the car most of the day.'

'Why don't we ride the cable car down to Fisherman's Wharf?' Ava made the suggestion, nearly bouncing on her toes with excitement.

'I think that would be awesome,' Celia agreed. 'If we only have one evening here before heading up to the vineyard, don't we have to make the most of it?'

'I'm brain-dead from driving all day, but I'm in. You just lead me around like I'm on a leash. I bet we can find some cool eats down there.' Bonni put her hand out. 'Take it. Lead me, I'll follow.'

'There'll be lots to eat down there. It's Fisherman's Wharf! But I want to change my shoes first if we're going to be walking.' Ava dug out runners from her bag and shoved them on. 'Ready!'

'Alrighty, then,' Fredi said, and she took on the role of sheepdog, herding her friends out of the hotel and down the street. A few minutes later the women were on their way to the Powell-Hyde cable-car station, which was around the corner from the hotel.

'There shouldn't be too much of a wait now.' Ava was optimistic.

'I'm kind of excited about this.' Celia was walking at her normal quick pace, pulling to the front of the group. She and Frank had been to San Francisco once, for some kind of boring medical conference, and Frank had flatly refused to play tourist, calling it 'undignified'. So Celia was looking forward to this, and not only because it also helped to distract her brain from thinking too much about her woes. 'There's the station!'

'The cable car is being turned around. Look how they do it.' Bonni pointed. 'That's so cool.'

The women rushed to the turnaround and watched as two men pushed the cable car around on what looked like a huge wooden turntable so that it faced the direction it had just come from. The car moved forward to the stop and the waiting crowd started to climb on.

'Come on, guys, let's hurry.' Celia rushed around to the other side.

'Jeez, Celia, they are not going to leave without us. I don't know why you have to rush around like green grass through a goose,' Fredi complained.

'Just hurry up – we want good seats.' Celia climbed up and

hooked her elbow around a pole in front of the row of shiny wooden slatted seats. 'This must be an original one. It looks old, but so well restored.'

'Do you really think so?' Ava asked, as she climbed up and found a place at the front.

'It would be cool if it was,' Bonni said, finding her own seat.

With Fredi being so short, she had a hard time getting in. 'Bonni, here, gimme a hand. I can't climb up.'

The girls laughed and Bonni reached down, easily pulling Fredi up into the car. 'See how the gym comes in handy,' she said.

'Whew, that was a treat.' Fredi was breathless, as were the others, from the dash to get on to the cable car.

Nobody said anything for a few minutes as they caught their breath. The gripman rang the bell and they were off down Powell Street.

'This is such a pretty street. Look at all the trees lining it, and the cobblestone between the tracks. I can just imagine what it looked like one hundred years ago.' Ava had a wistful look in her eye. 'I really had no idea San Francisco was so charming.'

The car sped along at a steady pace, picking up and discharging passengers at stops. The crowd was busy taking pictures as the tram carried on along the tracks and turned off Powell on to another road then made another turn on to Hyde Street.

'Oh, look, there's Lombard Street.' Celia pointed.

'That's crazy. Look how twisty it is,' Fredi said.

Tourists spilled off the sidewalks and on to the road so they could take pictures of the famous street.

'That's so weird, to see people taking photos of a road,' Fredi commented.

The car moved along, clanging and ringing its bell. Celia drew in a sigh. Boy, was she glad to be here with the girls, and thrilled they'd whisked her out of her house. She looked at them as they took in the sights and sounds of San Francisco. True friendship was being willing to fly across the country to kidnap a person.

Celia was beginning to feel San Francisco-y. The smell of the sea was in the air. As they went over another hill, starting to descend toward the bay, the view was breathtaking.

'Look, look! There's Alcatraz.' Celia hooked her arm tighter around the pole and leaned out of the car, stretching her other arm out so she could get a good shot with her phone.

'Celia! What do you think you're doing? Get back in here or you'll go splat out there on the road.' Ava grabbed her around the waist with one hand and Fredi with the other.

'Hey, I'm too delicate to be used as an anchor!' Fredi braced her feet against the pole in front of her and clutched the seats.

'She won't fall. She's a bit of a daredevil, if you ask me,' Bonni said, not looking the least bit concerned.

Celia threw back her head and laughed, her hair flying out behind her, and gave a loud whoop. 'I have to hang out of a cable car. Isn't that part of being here in San Francisco? You gotta live, you gotta be excited, you gotta do things that scare you a little bit.'

'Well, you're sure as hell scaring me. Get back in here.' Ava gave her a tug.

'Stop, you're going to make me lose my balance, and then I *will* go splat out on the road,' Celia said, pulling free. Fredi sat back in her seat with a thump while Ava crossed her arms and turned away.

There was something so freeing about not being the responsible one for a change. If either of her kids tried this, Celia would be livid, but it seemed perfectly safe for her. When she looked off to her left Celia gave a surprised gasp and yelled, 'There's the Golden Gate Bridge! Look, it's going to go out of range in a minute.'

'Damn, I missed it,' Ava said, and pouted for a second before excitedly continuing, 'It really was a good view from the top of that hill behind us. Did you notice how all the cars had their tires turned? I read somewhere that they could get ticketed if they don't. Ooooh, look there Swenson's ice cream. I've think I've heard of them. I think we're climbing Russian Hill now? And if you look over there, you might see the Coit Tower on Telegraph Hill. Oh, I wish I had gotten a cable-car route map.'

'Jeez, Ava, you missed your calling. Why be a financial genius when you can narrate cable-car tours instead? And, dammit, Celia, will you get off that pole? What happened to staying alive for your kids?' Fredi snapped, glaring.

Celia gave her a big smile. 'Can always count on you to tell it like it is, Fredi.' She leaned out a little more. 'Maybe I should just be a pole dancer. They make good money, right?' she asked, as she tried to swing herself out and around the pole. But she soon discovered it was a dumb move when she slid down the pole with a jolt, nearly losing her grip.

'For the love of God, Celia,' Bonni shouted, and lunged for Celia as she grasped at the pole with a small yelp. 'Get in here and sit your ass down. You're going to get us kicked off.'

'That was a bit scary.' Celia sat as Bonni instructed her, and she looked at her friends, eyes wide. 'My heart is thumping like mad.'

'I'm not surprised,' Ava said. 'That was really dumb.'

Celia nodded. 'I think I'll just sit here for the rest of the ride.'

'Good idea,' Bonni told her, although she still hadn't let go yet.

Fredi shook her head and tapped Celia on the shoulder. 'I'm going to remind you about this the first time Jilly does something crazy. You'll be all set to kill her for doing something hair-raising and I'm going to call you a big fat hypocrite.'

Celia made a face at Fredi's smug expression because she knew Fredi would do it.

'Okay, guys.' Ava sat down beside Celia. 'We kidnapped her to lighten her spirits, not to scare her about how Jilly is going to grow up to be exactly like her.' Ava patted her back condescendingly and Celia stuck out her tongue at her friend. Her precious baby was going to be a soccer star and she wouldn't have time to get into the kind of trouble that Celia had as a teenager.

The women were quiet for a little while and watched the scenery pass by. They snapped shots of all the buildings from famous films and waved at the cable cars that they met along the way as they went back up Hyde Street.

'You know, it really is amazing, the view from these hills. You can see how the water is pretty much on all sides of the city,' Fredi said, looking around and finally getting into a touristy mood.

The tram slowed to a stop and the gripman yelled out, 'It's time to say goodbye!'

All the passengers piled off and the women headed toward the waterfront.

'Fisherman's Wharf should be just down here. Maybe we can get something to eat there?' Bonni suggested.

'I thought you wanted to go to Chinatown?' Celia said, opening her phone to check her messages. There was a terse text from Frank, letting her know he had the kids. One of the few things they agreed on was that Jilly was too young for a smartphone, so she had a clunker of a flip phone for emergencies.

She'd call them once she got back to the hotel. Celia's gaze lingered on Landon's last message for a moment before she locked her phone and slid it back into her pocket.

Bonni shrugged her shoulders. 'It doesn't really matter to me, I suppose. We wouldn't be able to take the tram back up, though. We'd probably have to get a taxi.'

'Oh my God, I know what we can do. We can get Dungeness crab and clam chowder in a sourdough bread bowl,' Ava said with gusto. 'I mean, come on, we *are* in San Francisco – we need to have San Francisco sourdough, right? And Dungeness crab was made famous here. It's a no-brainer.'

'I kinda like that idea,' Fredi said absently, as she peered at a nearby woman wearing a ruched dress in a crazy bright pattern.

'I think I've died and gone to heaven,' Celia said with a mock-swoon, and gestured broadly to the left.

'What?' Bonni asked, immediately on alert. Her friend was such a cop sometimes.

'Over there, it's Ghiradelli Square. That means there's chocolate in the vicinity.' Celia started to walk in that direction, her nose in the air.

'What are you, a bloodhound? Sniffing your way to chocolate? Okay, then. Go find that chocolate, Lassie.' Despite her cutting words, Fredi was quick on Celia's heels. Bonni and Ava laughed, but they weren't far behind.

After nearly overdosing on the glorious smell of chocolate, they were strolling down Fisherman's Wharf with their purses stuffed with bags of chocolate and a few little souvenirs they'd bought in the shop.

'Can we get dinner now?' Ava asked, peering into her bag of chocolate and clearly having an internal debate.

Fredi was typing a note to herself on her cell but looked up to say, 'You nearly cleaned them out of free samples and you're still hungry?'

'Not all of us can survive on colors and the tears of models,' Ava shot back, defiantly unwrapping another chocolate.

'I'm looking up suggested seafood stands on TripAdvisor,' Celia said. She followed behind the others so they could keep her from bumping into anything. 'There's a bunch of them and they're all getting pretty good reviews and stars but, if you'd rather sit down and eat, we could do that too.'

'I'm actually enjoying walking along here. There's so much to see,' Fredi said.

'Sun's going to be setting soon. Maybe we can grab something and go sit somewhere to watch the sunset?' Bonni suggested.

'I like it!' Celia hooked her arm through Bonni's. 'By the way, Bon-Bon, thanks for saving my life back there on the cable car.'

Bonni snorted and then said, 'Ah, it was nothing. Just don't do it again. That was scary.' Bonni gave Celia a shoulder nudge.

'Don't worry, I don't plan on doing anything daredevilly again anytime soon.' It had been scary. Now that the adrenaline rush had worn off, Celia realized how foolhardy her actions had been. What if something had happened? Jilly and Colin would only have Frank. And she would just bet that he'd keep her friends far away from the kids, even though Bonni was Jilly's godmother. Celia had to keep her feet firmly planted on the ground, for her kids' sake.

As the women walked along the sidewalk they window-shopped. They stopped a few times for Fredi to take 'inspiration photos'. Considering that the last picture she'd taken was of a particularly bizarre teapot, Celia had no idea how her friend's mind worked. She was just hoping to see something jump out at her as a good souvenir for her kids.

They'd reached the end of the sidewalk when Ava stopped and refused to move. 'Feed me. Now.'

Ava was normally all sweetness and light, but the term 'hangry' had been invented to describe her.

'Okay, I say we grab something to eat at this place up ahead. And then go find somewhere to sit and watch the sunset.' Bonni pointed at a big sign saying 'EST 1927'.

'Wow, that place has been here over ninety years.' Celia was in awe. Her neighborhood was mostly desert and strip malls.

'Let's go check it out,' Fredi said, but Ava was already marching ahead, gracefully dodging pedestrians in her quest for dinner.

Celia felt her phone vibrate in her back pocket and waited until the others had lined up to order their meals before checking her messages.

It was a message from Landon, and her heart leapt in her chest. Her mouth went dry as she swiped open her phone.

L: Having a good time?

C: Yes! Exploring San Francisco. Aves now insisting on dinner, even though we ate way too much chocolate.

L: Sweets for the sweet. Nice.

Celia giggled. He could be so corny.

L: The kids okay with their dad?

And super sweet himself. She took her time to order before answering him.

C: Yup! Frank checked in and I'll call later.

L: Excellent. So tomorrow.

C: We're heading to the vineyard. Will you be there?

L: You're going to see me a lot sooner than that.

L: I'm kidnapping you from your kidnappers.

L: Meet you outside your hotel at 8:30am.

L: Don't worry, I'll bring you coffee. ;)

Tomorrow. Tomorrow morning. Way too early tomorrow morning. She was going to see Landon again. Celia looked up at her friends with a dazed expression. Ava was currently devouring a large mound of fries, but made a *well?!?* gesture with her free hand.

'I think I might get laid tomorrow?' Celia said hesitantly. Fries went flying as her friends piled on to her for a celebratory group hug. Yes, she really did have the best friends ever.

Chapter 7

After dinner, exploring the wharf, and many, many dirty jokes, they were back in their hotel rooms. Celia opened the door that connected her and Fredi's room to Ava's and Bonni's. She banged on their closed door.

'Hey, you, open up in there!' She thumped on the door again and went on thumping until Bonni pulled it open.

'What's got your panties in a twist? I was in the bathroom.'

'Where is Ava?'

'She went down to get ice,' Bonni answered, and came into Fredi and Celia's room. She dropped on to the couch by the window. 'I am pooped.'

Fredi rolled over on the bed. 'Me too. I need a shower. When you said "sunburned and salty" earlier today, Celia, you were bang on. I feel like yuck and, as I predicted, my hair is a complete rats' nest.'

They heard the door open and close in the adjoining room. Ava's voice called out. 'Are you guys in there?

'Yep. We're in here,' Bonni said, swinging her legs up on to the couch.

Ava came in with an armload of beer and glasses, as well as a grocery bag full of potato chips and dips.

Fredi stared at her. 'What happened to getting ice?'

'I think we're set for the night!' Ava said. 'Did you check and see which movies we can get on demand? Or shall we just watch something on Netflix?'

'More food?' Celia moaned and held her stomach.

Ava nodded and unpacked all the junk food and organized it. 'Okay, I'm going to get into my yoga pants.'

'Phew, I want a beer and I'm a bit hungry too.' Bonni took off her boots, tossing them on the floor, and gestured at Celia for a bottle.

'You're almost as bad as Ava, Bonni,' Fredi said. 'I don't know how you stay in shape with all the food you eat.'

'It's called "the gym". I work out hard so I can eat what I want.' Bonni drove her point home by reaching for the bag of chips. She took out a handful and munched.

Celia grabbed a beer too and picked up the remote, scrolling through the hotel's movies. Folding her hands, she turned back to the girls and pleaded, 'Can we pleeeeze watch a horror movie? *Drag Me to Hell* is available and it's scary, and funny too.'

Both Bonni and Ava, now comfy, replied in unison, 'Nope.'

'Booo!' Celia took a swig of her beer before landing on the newest Channing Tatum flick. While she loved horror movies, you could never go wrong with hot guys strutting across the screen.

Celia watched her friends ramble on to each other while the movie played in the background. No one was saying anything of any particular importance; they were just being together, chatting about stuff. It was what she needed. The camaraderie of her best friends was the best medicine to help a girl forget what was going on.

Picking at the label on her beer, her thoughts turned to Landon. Sex with him in Vegas had been exciting, fast and frantic, leaving her with a taste for more. In the beginning, their random texts to each other had always held a teasing, slightly sexual tone to them. If they did have sex tomorrow, it sure would be nice to have an orgasm not given by her battery-operated boyfriend. She'd relied heavily on her B.O.B. when writing her book and reliving their Vegas fling for inspiration.

But over time their texts to each other had deepened. He asked about her kids, sent funny memes he saw online, and they just . . . talked. It wasn't exactly like the texts she exchanged with the girls, but he wasn't a stranger, not anymore. Her musings were interrupted by a pillow slamming into her face, and she startled, trying to keep her beer from spilling.

'What the hell, guys?' she said.

Fredi cackled. 'If you're distracted from Channing, there can only be one thing on your mind. Reliving your passionate tryst in a closet with Landon?'

'It wasn't in the closet!' Celia nearly shouted. She wasn't sure why she was correcting Fredi, because it wasn't like an oversized bathroom stall was much better. Feeling a little anxious and restless, she got up to poke through the junk-food offerings.

'I should call my kids,' she said.

Fredi rolled her eyes at the painfully obvious subject change, but Bonni asked, 'Do they know about him?'

Celia made an effort to shrug carelessly, as if introducing Landon to her kids had been no big deal. 'He's Skyped with

Jilly and Colin. Somehow, he'd heard Jilly needed some new cleats.' She gave Bonni a narrow stare because Celia just knew her friend had been the one to tell Landon. 'And he sent them. We arranged the first Skype chat so she could thank him. Then she wanted to call after her first game with them, and then Colin wanted to tell him about a movie he saw. So they've talked a couple times.'

'Wow! That's really cool. What do they think of him?' Ava asked.

'They like him,' Celia said, deciding that she really needed to focus on opening this package of cookies.

'Are you kidding me? That's amazing,' Ava said, a wistful tone in her voice. 'He knows you have kids, he's not scared away and he's coming to pick you up in the morning. I see a wonderful future for you all.' She flopped back on the pillows with a dreamy look in her eyes.

'There she goes. The romantic one has you all married and with a white picket fence,' Fredi scoffed.

Celia started coughing on the bite of cookie she'd just taken. 'Far from it,' she gasped out. 'A fling, sure. But marriage?' She shook her head furiously. 'I will never, ever put my kids through that again.'

'Put them through what?' Ava rose up on her elbows. 'A divorce? How could you possibly jump to an ending like that when you haven't even begun? Don't you want a man in your life again? A father for your kids—'

'They have a father. He might be a shit to me, but I'll never let my kids know that,' Celia said, dropping the rest of her cookie into the garbage can.

An awkward moment filled the room and Bonni was the first to break the silence.

'Kids adapt. Trust me.' Bonni continued: 'You owe it to

yourself to make sure you take care of yourself. You have to, or you'll be no good for your kids.'

Fredi and Ava nodded in agreement.

'When did you become so wise?' Celia said, then rubbed her hands against her face. 'I'm going, aren't I? But I'm not ready for more. With the looming custody battle and everything, I'm not in a place where I can be someone's girlfriend.'

'We can tell you're not yourself, but we want the best for you. We love you, Celia. And no matter what, we're here for you.' Ava got up and wrapped her arms around Celia, and she had to fight back tears.

'Oh, you guys. You know just what to say,' she sniffled.

'No crying,' Fredi stated, studiously looking at the credits rolling on the TV. She was never comfortable with the big emotions.

'Nope, this is a happy time. For us all.' Bonni sat on the corner of the bed and reached out to touch Celia's knee.

Fredi yawned loudly. 'Well, I don't know about you guys, but stick a fork in me, I'm done.'

'Yep, and you need your beauty sleep, sugar,' Ava told Celia. 'You've got a big day ahead tomorrow.'

'Me too.' Bonni rubbed her eyes and walked to the door that adjoined their rooms. 'Lights out and up with the birds for breakfast, eh?'

Ava gave Celia a last hug and followed Bonni to their room.

Fredi had already cleared off her bed and gotten beneath the covers. 'Turn off the light so I can get to sleep, okay?'

A few minutes later, as she lay staring at the ceiling in the dark of the room, Celia's mind was spinning. Ever since having kids, her sleep patterns had gone all out of whack. She still had baby monitors in her kids' rooms so she could listen and make sure they were breathing during the night. Rolling over, she punched her pillow and started reviewing the clothes she had brought with her to figure out what she was going to wear. There had to be something that said, *I like you and I want to have sex with you but also I'm not ready for more than a fling, okay?* Her train of thought was interrupted by a questioning 'Celia?' from Fredi.

Tilting her head, she looked at the shadowy form of her friend in bed. 'I'm awake.'

'I'm having the strongest sense of déjà vu, Bonni and Ava crashed out in the other room, while you and I stay up. Remember how we used to talk about all the things we'd do once we graduated?' Fredi shifted to face Celia.

'I remember. I was going to be social-media famous and you were going to be the next Betsey Johnson.'

'And now I'm a junior designer for a Vera Wang wannabe.' Fredi's voice was bitter.

'You can always change that, you know. There's nothing stopping you from going out on your own. And, as for me, being famous is overrated. Look at all the crap the Kardashians have to go through. My kids are all I need,' Celia said. It felt good to say, like a reminder that her life may not have gone exactly accordingly to plan but it still ended up how it was meant to be.

Fredi was silent for so long Celia had thought she'd gone to sleep. Her mind settling a bit, she snuggled down into the bed, finally feeling drowsy herself. Then Fredi spoke, her voice barely a whisper. 'I think you and Landon would look good together behind a white picket fence.'

And now she was completely awake.

Chapter 8

Showered and with her bag packed and ready by the door, Celia checked the time on her phone. 8:21 a.m.

'I suppose I could head down now,' she said, nerves edging her voice. Why was she nervous? It was Landon. He already knew she gave awesome sex, and she had giggle-snorted on a Skype chat once. What more did he need to know?

'Only if you want to look eager,' Fredi advised. 'I'd be fashionably late if it were me.'

Ava jumped off the bed and pulled Celia up with her. 'Don't listen to her. You go when you're ready.'

'Holy shit, guys, you're getting awful bossy.' But she didn't argue. Her belly fluttered with a new excitement. She was definitely looking forward to seeing Landon. She'd killed some time this morning by scrolling through their texts, rereading them. Maybe they'd have sex today and maybe they wouldn't, but she was starting to realize that she and Landon had a pretty solid friendship.

However, Celia wasn't too proud to admit she was hoping

for sex. Boy, did he have the right stuff. It was easy to be obsessed with him, with the need to feel him again, to touch and taste him . . . Celia's breath shallowed as her thoughts ran erotic. He was all about raw passion. And God, *what* passion. Her mind was still scorched by it and it made her full of anticipation for another sexcapade.

So even though this was the man who could talk *Minecraft* endlessly with Colin, and helped her pick outfits for interviews she had to conduct, and freely admitted that his favorite Chris was Chris Evans, she would be perfectly happy to spend the day rolling around in bed with him. She'd just keep Text Landon for friendship and Real-life Landon for booty calls, and never would the two Landons meet.

She looked at herself in the mirror. 'Do I look okay?' After having two kids, her body was a far cry from the toned one she had had in college days. Her sex life had started dying after Colin was born. She had tried to resuscitate it, but Frank had always put her off with one excuse or another and it had affected her self-confidence. Now she knew it was because he was a cheating bastard, but her confidence hadn't quite rebounded and it was really hard to pick an appropriate outfit when you didn't have a clue where you were going.

'I just love those embroidered jeans, and the way you rolled them up is cute. And those sandals! The ties around your ankles totally match the color of the flowers on the pants.' Ava pulled the shoulder of Celia's blouse down a bit to expose more skin. 'Only you could pull off such a sexy, chic look. And your hair . . .' Ava gently pulled the long blond strands back and unnecessarily smoothed them down Celia's back. 'It's beautiful.'

'Celia, you would look amazing in a burlap sack. Stop fishing for compliments,' Fredi told her.

'Bitch, you're just jealous because you're not tall enough to ride all the rides,' Celia replied in mock-outrage, absently glancing around for her purse.

Fredi waited until Celia looked her way again and flipped her off. 'Honey, slap a pair of black leather thigh-high boots on me and I get no complaints.'

Ava made a little whip-cracking noise and giggled at herself. Bonni came through the door from the other room, lugging Celia's huge carry-on and purse.

'Here's your purse,' Bonni told her. 'Stop bickering and get going.'

'Wow, Bon-Bon, you are the least fun fairy godmother ever.' Now that it was time, Celia's nerves came roaring back. Maybe she should just stay with her friends. It would be rude to ditch them after they had gone to all the trouble of kidnapping her.

'Forget about Cinderella.' Bonni shoved Celia's purse into the huge satchel and slung the strap over Celia's shoulder, nearly causing her to buckle under the weight. What the hell had she packed? 'Her fairy godmother had a wand to bring the carriage to her. You have to take the elevator down to yours.'

'Yes. Go, have fun. And we won't expect you back until . . . well, we won't expect you back today, anyway.' Ava shrugged and winked at her.

Celia half-turned to look at the door to the hallway but then turned back. 'I don't know, guys, you've done so much for me, and it's only another hour and a half to the vineyard. I should just meet Landon there so we can properly finish our road trip.'

'Oh no you don't. I want the back seat to myself so I can take a nap,' Fredi said. 'Okay, listen, enough of this tongue wagging. You've got to go down to meet your man.' She opened the door to their room and gestured impatiently for Celia to leave.

Ava linked arms with Celia and gently ushered her forward.

'We know you haven't really dated since your divorce,' Ava said, 'but that's why this is perfect. It's Landon. He knows you, he knows your kids, he knows about your life. Time to get back in the saddle. Have fun and enjoy yourself. You deserve it, sweetie.'

Celia dug in her heels at the threshold. 'But—'

'I put everything that you need in your bag,' Bonni said. 'C'mon on now, you're starting to interfere with our schedule.'

'Oh, no, not the schedule!' Celia muttered sarcastically. The sudden realization that she was mere minutes away from seeing Landon had her belly doing all kinds of flip flops. She hadn't been this excited for a date, since . . . God, not even with her ex. Her phone buzzed and she slid it out of her pocket.

'It's him,' she whispered.

Landon: *I'm here, babe. Come on down.*

'Perfect timing. Now get going!' Fredi said, waggling the door at her.

'Atta girl!' Bonni called to her.

'Be good! Well, no, don't be good, that's too boring,' Fredi instructed. 'Don't do anything Bonni would do! Or Ava!'

Ava waved to her. 'Just be you! You're going to have a blast!'

Then Fredi let go of the door and Celia could just make out Bonni lunging for it with a 'Fredi, do you want to wake up the entire floor?' before it shut with a quiet click.

All right, then. Heading to the bank of elevators, Celia waited a minute for one to arrive. Once inside, and away from her friends, doubts started creeping in again. She was on her way to a man who could, maybe, perhaps, change her opinion on the male species. Her heart thumped in her chest and she couldn't believe how much she felt like a teenage girl going on her first date.

But she didn't have anything really nice to wear, hadn't even packed any of her sexy lingerie. Celia gritted her teeth, thinking of the plain cotton panties and bra sets she had brought. They were fine for a girls' weekend away but not when you might be sexing up a wealthy high-society businessman. Maybe she could dash out to a Victoria's Secret.

Celia knew people thought she was highly extroverted and that nothing fazed her. However, right now, she was feeling super-vulnerable. She'd been living in a bubble. A self-induced bubble, to be sure, but how could she not after her divorce and everything that had happened since? She'd hidden away. She was beginning to see what she'd been doing, shunning social contact, becoming a hermit. Focusing exclusively on her children and her failed marriage and forgetting that she was a person with needs of her own. Maybe this weekend would get her set back on the right path. Forcing the thoughts away, Celia drew in a shaky breath as the elevator doors opened.

She squared her shoulders and lifted her chin. She shook her head so her hair would fall down her back in a smooth curtain. One last look at herself in the mirrored walls before she stepped out of the elevator and into the hotel lobby proper, clearing the emotion off her face. Time to go find Landon.

She scanned the area, looking for him. She knew his tall Viking good looks would stand out, but she couldn't see him. Celia found she couldn't remember if he'd said they were meeting in the lobby or if he was waiting for her out in his car.

Maybe he was standing her up. Maybe he was trying to do a nice thing for Bonni since she was dating his brother by taking out the woeful single mother, but he'd realized he couldn't go through with it. Maybe he wasn't attracted to her anymore and was trying to figure out how to tell her he only wanted the friendship, not the benefits.

Or maybe he was standing right over there.

Chapter 9

When Celia had started to slow down her communication Landon had reached out to Bonni. She had no problem keeping his younger brother in line, so he knew she could come up with a fix for this. When she'd gotten back to him with the kidnapping plan, he was determined to make sure he spent time with Celia. He'd moved heaven and earth to shift things around on his schedule to free up the next three days.

She'd been on his mind for months. He'd texted her for the first time a day or two after he left Vegas, and their casual and sexy texts messages had kept him wanting more. If you'd asked him last year, he would have told you that he was in no hurry to settle down and he didn't have any interest in a ready-made family. But getting a chance to virtually 'meet' her kids and having them like him enough to start calling him Uncle Landon? It felt better than when he had pulled off his first merger.

Landon wanted to make sure Celia and the kids had everything they needed, but he wouldn't soon forget how Celia had chastised him after the cleats debacle. She certainly was a mama bear, and he respected her for it. He was so used to being wanted for his money, it was a true novelty to meet a woman who wanted nothing to do with it.

Quinn had been razzing him for months about his addiction to his cell, the way he was constantly checking for new messages. It didn't help that, with Quinn no longer single, their mother had redoubled her efforts to set Landon up with an appropriate society belle. It wasn't like he could tell her that he wasn't interesting in dating anybody but a sassy single mom with a way with words and a fierce loyalty to her loved ones.

He wasn't even sure he could say it to Celia. Hence this weekend.

Landon couldn't help the smile that broke out on his face when he saw her step off the elevator. She looked around, presumably for him, but he stayed leaning against the pillar for a few extra moments so he could take her in. He'd kept the memory of her burned into his brain these past months and now, there she was in person. Looking more intensely at her, he was alarmed at how pale her complexion was, and she'd lost a bit of weight. Nor did he fail to miss the anxious way she scanned the lobby. What had her damned ex put her through?

Landon straightened off the pillar, moving a little to his left, and the movement caught her eye. He swore she breathed a sigh of relief as she started toward him, her movements hampered by the giant, unwieldy bag she was carrying. He met her halfway and relieved her of her burden, swinging it to rest on the hotel floor before hugging her. 'Here's my foxy beauty,' he said.

He heard his voice, heavy with passion, and liked how she

melted into him. But he curbed the passion. He wasn't in this for just a quick fling. He wanted to make sure things were still good between them, so that she'd be comfortable for the day ahead.

'I'm surprised to see you this weekend, even though I know you instigated this whole thing.' Her voice was barely a whisper. 'Landon, I'm so sorry for my silence the last while. It wasn't you, I was just . . . well, things have been sucky.'

'Then I'm glad I was able to surprise you.' He cupped her face, sweeping a thumb across her cheekbones. 'And I figured something was going on – no need to apologize. I'm really happy you're here.'

She flushed a light pink as she lowered her gaze. 'Me too—'

He couldn't resist and bent, covering her mouth with his and dropping his arm to her waist, pulling her tighter to him. Celia wound her arms around his neck and pressed her body even closer. Feeling the soft curves of her body, the press of her breasts against his chest, it was like all his fantasies had suddenly come to life.

Her response to his kiss was electric. He delved his tongue into her mouth, demanding and finding hers. He wanted to steal away any of her concerns with this wild kiss in the middle of the hotel lobby. It had him spinning a bit; he was quickly getting out of control, like a lopsided top. Her fingers tightened on him, as if her world were tilting as well and he was the only solid thing she could hang on to.

This kiss was a stark reminder of their frantic lovemaking in Las Vegas. It had been insta-lust, an intense attraction that had led to them to the nearest private place they could find. It had been a powerful desire that meant just enough clothing disarrayed so he could appreciate her luscious breasts while pounding into her.

They hadn't even seen each other naked yet. The anticipation of that, of seeing her in all her glory, had him almost gasping for breath. He was used to biding his time, thanks to his father's so-called life lessons, but he wanted to gorge on Celia.

But later. Oh, later, it could be so much more.

He lifted his mouth from hers and they stood for a fraction of a moment longer, quiet, breathing in each other. Her scent filled him, familiar and wonderful. Gradually, he felt her trembling settle down and he loosened his grip on her, letting her slide down his body. Landon sucked in a sharp breath, feeling her every curve rub over him until her toes touched the floor.

But he didn't release her. He continued to keep his hands on her, so close that the heat of her body scorched him. Yes, they still had that electric connection, one that made him sizzle with anticipation.

Celia tipped her head back and looked up at him. She barely came to his chest, and he'd forgotten how magnificent her green eyes were.

'So what did you have in mind?' she asked him, rubbing her palms along his shoulders.

'Oh, I have a few surprises up my sleeve. Then perhaps a sequel to our time together in Vegas?' He gave her a crooked smile and liked how her face softened.

'That sounds like fun,' Celia whispered. It felt like another victory, to have her place herself in his hands and follow him on the adventures he had planned. He saw a brief shadow cross her face and wondered what was weighing heavy on her mind. He hoped she'd open up to him, eventually, today.

'My car is just outside. Ready?' He gazed down at her and she nodded.

He picked up her bag and took her hand, leading her through the lobby.

'Are you hungry? Do you want to stop for some breakfast?' Landon asked her as he held the door for her to step through.

Celia laughed, shaking her head, her long hair brushing against his arm.

'What's so funny?' Landon smiled down at her before reaching for her hand. She looked momentarily startled before entwining their fingers.

'It's just that last night we went down to the wharf, ate a bunch, then came back to eat junk food, drink beer and watch a movie. So, hungry? Far from it.'

'Okay, then. I do have a coffee for you in the car.' He closed an eye and said thoughtfully, 'If I remember correctly, you're a three-creamer girl.'

Celia tilted her head to beam up at him. 'You remember correctly.'

He guided her across the hotel driveway to where his car was parked. His plans for the day were intended to distract Celia from her problems and to revive the vivacious, vibrant, spirit he was so attracted to. He also planned to romance the hell out of her.

He gazed down at her sunny blond head as he opened the door to his car.

'Everything okay?' he asked, and rested his hand on the top of the door as she turned to face him.

'Sure. Why do you ask?' She gazed up at him and he swallowed at the clarity in her sea-green eyes. He'd never seen such a compelling color before and, in the sunlight, they were even more vivid.

Landon gave her a slow smile and he could see her catch her breath. Yes, they still had that unique sexual chemistry but, finally, with her by his side, he felt something more. Something deeper.

'It's so good to see you, Landon.' Her voice was breathy; his chest clenched like he'd just been heart punched, and he wanted to drag her into his arms and kiss her again.

So he did.

Chapter 10

Landon's mouth covered hers as he pulled her tighter to him. Celia wound her arms around his neck and arched her body as close to his as possible. The hard planes of his chest against her breasts, the power of his body enveloping her and the slow and steady pulse of her blood through her veins were sensations she'd all but forgotten.

His kiss was electric, his tongue demanding and finding hers. She met his demands and moaned into his mouth. He stole away all her concerns with his wild kiss in the middle of the hotel driveway. Within seconds, he had her spinning out of control. She clung to him, glad he held her tight because no way could her legs support her. This kiss was a stark reminder of their frantic lovemaking in Las Vegas and how desperately she wanted more. Her pulse kicked into overdrive at the thought of their naked bodies sliding sensuously next to each other.

He lifted his mouth from hers and they stood for a fraction of a moment, breathing in each other's breath. His scent filled her, familiar and wonderful. Her nerves gradually settled down and his arms loosened on her, but she kept her hands on his shoulders, gripping them tightly with her fingers as if she never wanted to let him go.

Celia tipped her head back and looked up at him. She barely came to his shoulders – and she hadn't realized just how tall he was until now. Seeing him again, and not on Skype or Face-time, was wonderful. His hair was a bit longer and shaggier, his blue eyes and powerful presence reminded her just how Viking-like he was, and she was breathless.

'So, what are we going to do?'

He gave her a crooked smile and her heart melted for him. 'Depends how game you are for an adventure.'

'That sounds like fun.' His words seemed to promise something. Something thrilling, and she caught her breath with anticipation. 'Now I'm curious.'

'That's good. I aim to keep you on your toes. Now get in so we can be on our way.'

Celia looked at him for a long moment. 'I'm glad you came to get me.'

His slow smile made her belly twist into all sorts of shapes, and heat flared between her legs. Good Lord, if a smile like that was all it took to fill her with desire for him, she could only imagine what he could do to her with a little more time and the touch of his hands . . . his body.

'Oh, Landon, what are you doing to me?' Celia sighed, and rested her cheek on his shoulder.

'Nothing, my lovely. Not yet, anyway.' The seductive tone in his voice caused Celia to become blind to the odd looks they were getting from the bellhops and valets.

She shivered when he slid his hand under her blouse and across the bare skin of her back. She felt her nipples harden and she grew wet for him. 'We might just need to find a quiet place. Otherwise, I'm not going to make it through the day.'

Landon's other hand tangled into her hair and pulled her head back. 'Foxy lady, some things are worth waiting for. You'll be well satisfied tonight, but first is our day of adventure.'

She sucked in a rapid breath at his words. 'You're going to make me wait until the end of the day? After driving me crazy with your kisses and touches?'

He smiled again, and the dimple on his cheek peeked out. 'Oh, yes. I'm going to keep you burning with passion all day. When I finally have you alone, later, you will find out what it's really like when I make proper love to you.' He touched his lips to her cheek. 'All night long.'

Chapter 11

After that extremely sexual moment Landon helped Celia into the car. He could tell she was on a knife edge of desire and he planned to keep her that way for most of the day. The only thing was, he was also turned on, his cock hard and uncomfortable in his pants.

As he rounded the front of his Bugatti and lifted the boot to stash her bags, Landon was looking forward to the next few days. They still had so much to get to know about each other. This weekend would not only be a delicious diversion for him and, he hoped, for her as well, but it could also be an interesting beginning.

Landon slid into the driver's seat and relaxed. 'Now I have you all to myself.' He looked at her and pressed the button to lock all the doors. He waggled his eyebrows at her and Celia laughed. It was a magical sound that reached right inside him and grabbed his heart.

Celia had her head resting on the back of the seat, slightly twisted so that she faced him. She looked delicately small and vulnerable. He wanted to gather her in his arms and make her forget about whatever it was that was bothering her.

'I suppose you do.' Celia waved a hand toward the dashboard. 'Now *this* is a car.'

'Yes, it is. One of my favorites.' Landon patted the steering wheel fondly.

'You mean you have more?'

'Of course.' He laughed, liking her surprise. He started the car. The throaty growl never got old. He expertly wheeled away from the hotel and out on to the road. He knew this car got a lot of attention. It wasn't every day someone drove up in a Bugatti Chiron.

'Wow.' He wasn't sure if her 'wow' was an impressed wow or an over-the-top 'wow'. Strangely, it mattered to him.

'I noticed you had your bag. Your friends didn't want to lug that colossus up to the vineyard for you?' Glancing at her, he took his eyes off the road for only a fraction of a second, but it was enough to see a twinkle of excitement tinged with desire reflected in her eyes.

'Don't get a big head, mister. Bonni basically shoved me out of the hotel room with it.'

'How fortuitous. Now you'll be able to sleep wherever you want tonight.' Flicking on his blinker, he zoomed around a sedan. He couldn't wait to reach their first destination.

She reached out to take his hand, which was sitting on the console between them.

'Aren't you a clever boy?' Her voice was low, sexy and held a promise that made his balls tighten.

Landon laughed but, as much as he wanted to turn and look at her, to see the expression on her face, he concentrated on the road as he maneuvered through traffic. 'I've been called many things, but never a clever boy.'

This was exactly the reason he was enchanted with her. Her quirky, wonderful nature. Her spontaneity. And most definitely her passion. All these traits blended to create a woman who was brilliantly complicated and incredibly beautiful.

He was good at reading people. He'd built his career on it. Yes, he'd been given one of the most powerful companies in the world to run, but he'd had to work for it, starting in the trenches. His father had made sure of it.

When Celia had exited the elevator he'd seen the trouble written on her face. Yet as soon as she saw him, the furrow between her eyebrows and the frown on her gorgeous mouth had disappeared. Her drawn lips plumped up when she smiled, but the fine lines on her forehead were a little more etched. He glanced at her now and saw they were still there. He was going to remove them. Starting today.

'So, where are you taking me?' she asked, her voice light and wonderfully sexy.

'Down the rabbit hole.' He checked his mirrors before giving the Bugatti a touch of gas. The car responded and he steered it, roaring around the traffic and zoomed down the open road in front of them. 'Are you game?'

She didn't answer right away, and he knew she was thinking about her answer. He waited, having learned long ago to be patient. Hurrying a decision along could sometimes result in a conclusion you didn't want. And there was a definite conclusion he *did* want.

It didn't take her long to answer and, when she replied, it was the response he'd hoped for. That he'd anticipated. That he wanted.

'Yes.'

Chapter 12

'I have a day planned that I hope you enjoy,' Landon told her. 'You have your coffee, but still not in the mood for breakfast?'

She held up the coffee. 'This is fine. I usually don't eat much breakfast anyway.' She was silent for a moment before confessing to him. 'That's a complete lie. I love breakfast. Especially a big, hearty breakfast with meat, eggs, toast, tomatoes and pancakes. But I really did eat a lot last night.'

'You do know you should always start your day off with a healthy breakfast?' Landon raised their entwined hands to kiss the back of her hand.

'Please, I'm a mom. You're preaching to the choir.' She tugged her hand free so she could pull her phone from her pocket to check her messages. Nothing from Frank, so she'd try to connect with her kids later.

Landon laughed but kept his eyes on the road. 'It's probably for the best that you don't eat anything yet. What I have in mind for us might be a bit of . . . er, a challenge with a full stomach.'

'What do you mean? I think I need to ask more questions about what you have planned for today.' Celia looked down at her feet, wiggling her toes in her sandals. She had a feeling she'd need to change into sneakers when they reached their destination.

'Something I hope you haven't done before. Something that will exhilarate you. Something that will put your heart in your throat.' His focus was on the road, but she could feel his awareness of her.

'Holy cow! Now I'm not so sure I want to go down that rabbit hole with you.'

'I hope it's a lot more than a holy cow for you.' Landon chuckled and guided the car out on to the highway after going across the Golden Gate Bridge and zipping them north from San Francisco. 'Have you been to San Francisco before?'

She rolled down her window, sticking out her hand to feel the breeze. 'Once, with my ex, for a business thing. Last night was really the first time I had a chance to explore the town a little.'

As they pulled away from the city limits the traffic eased up and Landon reached out to play with the tips of her hair. Celia rolled her head toward him and he curved his palm around her neck, to splay his fingertips into her hair. She closed her eyes as he lightly massaged her head. If the growl of the car combined with the flow of the wind hadn't drowned it out, she was confident he would have been able to hear her moan.

'Then I'm glad to be showing you the city, and the surrounding area.' Over the next half-hour he pointed out sights of interest for her as they drove. She took some video and a few selfies, updating her social-media accounts. Ava 'liked' everything while Fredi made a dirty joke in the comments. Bonni must've been driving again.

'No one is ever going to believe I'm being driven around in such an awesome car.' Landon laughed, and she continued: 'Are we going in the direction of the vineyard?'

He nodded. 'Yes, generally. But we'll be turning off before we get there.'

'Why so mysterious? We're almost there. Why not tell me what to expect?' If she were in a car with anyone else, she'd be worried he was taking her to a remote spot for nefarious reasons.

'I want to surprise you.' Landon had turned off the highway and was on a smaller road going through the countryside.

'What if I don't like surprises?' She didn't really say it as a question, more as a teasing challenge.

'I have a feeling that you do like surprises.' His focus was on the single-lane road they were on but she could see the cat-ate-the-canary expression on his face.

Celia gazed at the trees as they sped past. The rumble of his sportscar engine shattered the quiet air of nature. She let herself be swept up into his world, by his zest for life and decided to accept whatever came. With gusto!

'I've had my share of them, no doubt about that,' she said wryly. 'And not all of them good.'

She was here, and she wouldn't let the thoughts of what awaited her back home ruin her time away. It was so rare that she had time to herself. Her motto had always been to live in the moment, and that's what she would do. Being caught up by everything that had happened in the past and how it would affect her future was not like her. It was stealing away her delight in the present.

'I promise the surprise I have in store for you will rock your world. Just a few more minutes and you'll know.'

Celia didn't answer, just shot him a side-eye look. True to his word, though, they pulled into a clearing very soon. When she got a look at the name of the business, Celia changed her mind. Landon was trying to kill her after all.

Chapter 13

'Skydiving!'

Celia stood in front of the hangar. Her feet, now clad in a beat-up pair of runners, refused to budge. It was like the tarmac had reached up and grabbed her ankles. Unable to move, she stood there and stared at the hustle and bustle inside as the other jumpers were getting their gear ready.

'So what do you think?' Landon asked her. 'Are you brave enough? Wild enough? Ready to live on the edge?'

She looked at Landon, her eyes wide and her heart thumping in her chest like a scared rabbit's. 'I have kids.'

Landon laughed out loud. 'I know you have kids. Have you forgotten that they call me Uncle Landon?'

She shook her head, fear and terror gripping her. 'I know, but if you ever want to meet them in person, I need to be alive.'

'What are you worried about? It's safe. I've jumped many, many times. And you'll be jumping in tandem with an instructor. Not with me.'

Celia swallowed, her mouth dry, and she looked back at the hangar. 'You mean, like, with him?'

She raised her hand and pointed with a shaky finger at a man approaching them wearing a bright red what she figured was a skydiving suit and a harness.

'Yes, him. That's Kash. He's an old friend of mine. We learned to jump together about fifteen years ago. This is his business and he also doubles as the head instructor. You'll be safe with him.'

Celia watched Kash approach. She had to admit he was a pretty hot guy, and she tossed a quick glance at Landon. She smiled at him, since he'd caught her checking Kash out. He had nothing to worry about. Landon was way more her style.

'Hey, man.' Landon walked forward to greet Kash with his hand out, and the two men shook hands and did a bro hug. 'Thanks for fitting us in.'

'No problem. I always have time for friends.'

Landon turned and reached for Celia's shoulder. Wrapping his arm around her, he gently pulled her forward. 'Kash, meet Celia. This is her first time.'

'Wow, then. Time to roll out the red carpet for you.' He smiled down at her and the calm look in his eyes eased her trepidation.

'Hi. I'm not sure about this. I have kids.'

Kash laughed the same way Landon had. 'I'm glad you have kids. That's awesome, because maybe you'll introduce them to skydiving after you jump out of the plane.'

'Oh God. Jump from a plane.' She turned and looked at Landon and shook her head. 'I can't do this. Heights and I are not friends.'

'Sure you are. I seem to remember a story involving you and

a water tower.' Celia made a mental note to kill Bonni if she made it through this. 'But once you're up in the plane, if you decide you don't want to, you don't have to. No one is going to throw you out of the plane.'

'Why would you even say such a thing?' Celia was reconsidering her desire to be friends with Landon.

'I'm just teasing you. You have nothing to worry about. The only thing you should think about is just how much fun you're going to have.' Landon kissed the top of her head.

Kash stepped forward and took her hand. 'Celia, it's really quite safe. I've been jumping for a lot of years and my safety record here at T.D. Zone is prime. And I have many repeat customers. A lot of my jumpers become instructors too.'

He led her toward the hangar and Celia didn't resist. Curiosity started to edge out her fear. She looked up at the sky. 'How high do you go?'

'Usually about fourteen thousand feet.'

'What? Oh my God, that's high!' Celia's belly tightened as the fear came roaring back and a chill slithered down her spine. 'What happens if the chute doesn't open?'

Kash patted her back reassuringly. 'It will open. And we'll be tandem, tethered.'

'Tethered?' She asked. 'What do you mean?'

Kash hooked his thumbs through the harness strapped around his torso and between his thighs. 'You'll have a harness, like me. And you'll be tethered to me, in the front. Your back will be against my chest and, when we jump out, I'm responsible for making sure everything goes right.'

With the confidence of the two men bolstering her, Celia began to settle down. There were a few other first-time jumpers here as well, Kash told her, so she didn't feel like such a newbie.

There was an orientation session that was pretty thorough, and she listened intently. She didn't want to miss a thing. She needed to be alert and informed. However, the excitement of the others began to rub off on her. Her inner adventure girl was trying to sneak out and her responsible-mom persona was doing her damnedest to keep everything in check.

She ran a bunch of things through her mind. What if she died? She remembered that she hadn't updated her will yet. It should've been a top priority after her divorce, but she still hadn't. She sighed. She didn't have much anyway, so it's not like her ex was going to get her vast wealth. Celia made a mental note to fix her will as soon as possible.

Her kids. They would be without a mother. But Dickhead was remarrying, the kids liked his bride well enough, so at least they'd have a stepmother in their lives. Even if she was barely old enough to drink.

'Calm down. I can see a million scenarios running around in your head.' Landon put his arm around her again and whispered in her ear.

'Shhhh. I'm thinking about the fact that I'm going to die and about what will happen to my kids.'

He laughed and clutched her shoulders. 'Celia, you're not gonna die. You're going to have fun. You'll get a new zest for life, and it's going to put the pink back in your cheeks.'

'Live in the present.' It echoed her thoughts from earlier.

'Exactly,' he said.

She felt a little better and realized she was worrying too much. She pressed her lips together and nodded. 'I can be a responsible mom and still have fun.'

Kash came over to them. 'Are you all ready, Celia?'

'I guess so. I'm having to talk myself into this, though.'

'It's common. Don't feel like you're the only one.' He shook out her harness and ran his hands over all the pieces. 'Okay, this is your skydiving rig. Now step into this.' He pointed to the loops for her legs. He pulled the harness up and helped with the positioning. 'With this on, all snugged and tight, you'll get used to the feel of it on your body.'

Celia was surprised at how intimate it felt to have this harness placed on her. A strange man was touching her, taking the straps in his hands as he snugged them over her boobs, then up and around her thighs and almost between her legs. She warmed up, imagining that it was Landon, not Kash, fixing all the straps. She made eye contact with Landon and he smiled at her, nodding his encouragement. Celia watched him as she pictured him strapping her into this rigging. It made her think of some of the erotic research she'd done for her writing. Scenarios involving rigging, ropes and blindfolds floated through her mind. She drew in a soft breath and felt herself flush. He'd made promises for later, and she wasn't about to forget them.

She kept her gaze pinned to his, drawing strength from his calm and steady gaze.

'Okay. You're all set.' Kash clapped her on the shoulder and Landon reached out to take her hand. 'You go with Landon while I get the rest of my crew wrangled.'

'Come on, let's go sit over here and wait.' Landon led Celia to a picnic table with a sun umbrella over the top. There were boxes of donuts and bottles of water sitting on the table. 'Here, have a donut. Since you haven't eaten, you might need the sugar rush.'

Celia reached into the nearest box and selected her favorite. A double chocolate. Landon grabbed a great big honey cruller.

'Are you okay?' he asked.

With a mouthful of donut, she couldn't reply, so she nodded her head. She took a sip of water before she answered him. 'I think so. It was a bit of a surprise to be taken skydiving.'

'Well, what better way to really earn trust on a first date?' Landon wiped his fingers on a napkin as he posed his ever so casual question.

'Oh, is that what this is?' Celia felt her heart start racing for a reason other than fear. He gave her a crooked smile, his dimple winking.

'Well, it is to me.' He nodded and chewed on another big bite of his pastry. 'It's a tough world out there for single people these days, which is why I rarely get involved in the dating scene.'

'Yeah, I have to agree with you there.' She wasn't about to tell him this was her first date since her divorce. Nor would she ever own up to the fact that the idea of going out with a strange man scared the hell out of her.

If her ex hadn't wanted her, how could anyone else possibly want her? But she wanted to be wanted. Of that she was sure. She smiled and dipped her head down so he wouldn't see. *I am on a date.* Could they go from friends to lovers?

Going back into the dating world really had not been on her agenda, because her kids were her first priority and she wasn't going to risk hurting them again. However, Landon was giving her a tiny spark of hope.

Live in the present.

The sound of an engine caught her attention and she followed Landon's gaze to see a rather odd-looking plane approaching.

'Looks like it's time,' he said. He quickly ate the remainder of his cruller and unfolded his long, muscled body from the bench. Standing tall, Landon held his hand out for her.

Celia rose and took a deep breath. She looked at his hand; it was big, strong and steady as a rock. Placing hers in his was the equivalent to her putting her life in his hands.

She looked up at him. 'Okay, then. Off we go into the wild blue yonder.'

Chapter 14

'Normally, I love to fly. I like flying in planes, they take you places.' Celia gripped the railing of the metal staircase she was about to ascend in order to board this very different-looking airplane. 'Only this one doesn't take me places.' She looked at Landon and knew her eyes were nearly popping out of her head. 'What if this is my *Final Destination* plane?'

He tossed his head back and burst out laughing. Celia couldn't help but smile. She realized just how silly her words sounded. She took a couple steps up and turned around so they were at eye level to each other. 'Listen, you, it's not nice to laugh at a girl when she says something dumb.'

Landon put his hands on her hips and drew her toward him. 'It's what I like about you. Your spontaneity. Your silliness. Now, don't take that as an insult. Take it as a compliment.' He pulled her even tighter until they were flush together, so close she could smell his shaving cream. With her on a step, their faces lined up perfectly. He slid his hands up her sides and placed them on her cheeks. His palms were warm and Celia sighed.

'Go ahead if you're going to kiss me,' she whispered.

'After all, it could be your last kiss ever.' He raised his eyebrows and smiled before tilting his head and sealing his lips over hers.

Celia forgot where she was. Forgot that there were people on the plane waiting for take-off and then to jump out of it. Forgot that there were people lined up behind them, waiting to get *on* the plane so they could jump out of it.

She wound her arms around his neck, remembering how deliciously he had kissed her before. He still had the magic, and he cast a spell on her. Celia lost herself in his dreamy kiss until she was jostled from behind and then Kash's deep voice snapped her out of it.

'Guys. This is skydiving. This is not foreplay to the Mile High Club. So I suggest you get a room afterward and quit holding up the line here.'

Celia felt heat rise in her cheeks. She was slightly embarrassed, but she turned to Kash and gave him a wicked look.

'I deserve a last kiss from him, don't I? You know, just in case.'

Kash's mouth lifted on one side in a lopsided smile. He raised his eyebrows in mock-surprise, glancing at the line behind her and then back down at Celia. 'I highly doubt that. I am positive there are going to be many more kisses in your future.'

He turned and ducked into the plane. Celia followed him. 'Now you sit there.' He pointed at the seat then looked at Landon. Jabbing at a seat across the plane, Kash said, 'You're there.'

Kash organized the rest of the people while Celia sat, gripping her thighs. She had been relatively calm after her initial shock at the idea of skydiving, but now she was getting nervous again. Shit was getting real. She was actually *on* the plane and suited up to jump. It wouldn't be that much longer until she dived out of the plane to free-fall at an insane speed, plummeting down to earth.

The most foolhardy thing ever? *Hell*, yeah.

She looked at the other jumpers and wondered if they felt the same way. Kash was finishing up whatever it was he had to do, and the plane started off down the runway. With the jump door open!

Then her gaze fell on Landon. He was calm and gave her a nod of encouragement. It was their first date, the second time she'd spent time with him in person, but she trusted him, bone deep.

She mouthed to him, 'I'm scared.'

He mouthed back, 'Don't be. It's okay,' before winking at her.

The plane began to move quicker and the engine rose in pitch as they went faster down the runway. She turned around to look out the window, but it was too difficult to see anything. Celia decided to just sit and embrace her inner wild child. Who had gone to a country bar to ride a mechanical bull and nearly got arrested for starting a bar brawl? Who had made an ill-fated attempt at trying out for a roller derby team? Who had snuck into Disneyland on Grad Night and flashed the Space Mountain camera? She had this. She knew she was strong. Everything she'd been through the last year proved it.

As the plane lifted into the air at a steep angle she looked around at the other passengers and tried to imagine their stories. That couple was celebrating an anniversary. Those boys just won some kind of sports championship. Her fingers twitched for her keyboard. All these people could be future characters in future books.

It made her think of the work-in-progress she'd left at home.

Her first book, *A Hot Vegas Night*, was about a shy waitress who got swept off her feet by a visiting wealthy businessman, and it had definitely been heavily inspired by her interactions with Landon. She wanted to tell him, just as much as she had wanted to tell her friends, but she couldn't, for the same reasons. Celia glanced at Landon and, of all things, he was texting. You could take the businessman out of the suit, but you couldn't take the suit out of the man.

Finally, they were at the jump altitude.

Kash stood, and she watched as he gave hand signals to his staff. They knew exactly what to do, likely having done this a thousand times. The passengers also stood up, walking in a shuffle, specially those jumping tandem with a staff member, toward the door and simply . . . stepped out.

She gasped as a few just leapt out of the plane on their own. Some went forward, some did back flips and some did a barrel roll. Then it was just her and Landon and Kash left. It had been arranged earlier that she and Landon would jump out within the same time frame so he would be close to her as they fell.

Kash motioned for her to come and stand in front of him. She did, and the plane hit a bit of turbulence. She lost her balance and he reached for her as she stumbled toward the open door.

Celia flailed as she tried to catch her balance. Oh, hell, no, this was not how she was going out! Not today, Death, not today!

Chapter 15

Celia all but launched herself at Kash, since he was the closest. Her arms and legs curled around him like a spider. She clung to him for dear life and squeezed her eyes shut.

'Easy there. It's all good,' Kash assured her.

Celia didn't say anything as he untangled her from him and kept her eyes closed when he turned her around. She felt a tugging on the harness around her waist. Someone touched her cheek and her eyes flew open. Landon. She stared at him as he lowered her goggles to cover her eyes. Then he gave her the thumbs-up.

Her heart beat rapidly in her chest and her stomach was all fluttery. Adrenaline pumped through her, making her feel amazing. Alive. Colors were brighter and her body fairly hummed. Suddenly, she was excited. Now she knew why Landon hadn't wanted her to eat anything substantial earlier. Little did he know that, so long as alcohol wasn't involved, she had a cast-iron stomach. She took a few deep breaths and gripped Landon's hands. He leaned forward and shouted loudly so she could hear. 'I'll be right behind you. You can trust Kash.'

She nodded, her mouth completely dry. She didn't look away from Landon, afraid to look at the door. He leaned forward, gave her a kiss, and she gripped his hands tighter, not wanting to let them go.

In her ear, she heard Kash tell her, 'Let go of him. I've got you. You're mine now. And we just might be fighting for you later.' He laughed, a deep very bass sound that seemed to harmonize with the plane's engine.

Celia looked back and smiled at him, glad for the bit of humor he was interjecting.

'I like it when men fight over me!' she shouted back. 'But it's the first time I've had to jump out of a plane for it.'

Kash smiled and edged her to the door. 'See out there. You're going to have the ride of your life. Are you ready?'

Celia shook her head. 'No!' she yelled back at him.

'Good!' Landon snaked his arm around her waist. 'All righty then, here we go.'

The power of Kash behind her was no match, even if she'd tried to keep herself from jumping. She was glad for his reassuring presence. And the next thing she knew they were sailing out of the plane face first toward the earth below.

Celia screamed with terror and – holy shit! – the sensation of *going over the edge there is no floor I'm going to die I'm sorry, kids.* Then she snapped her mouth shut to stop air from blowing out her cheeks. She remembered to keep her back arched as they had been taught earlier and spread out her arms and legs.

They fell through the air, the wind rushing at her ears, her hair streaming out, making her realize she had forgotten to bundle it up into a ponytail. Her belly got that same tingly feeling she had when she was on a roller coaster.

And she loved it!

This time when she screamed it was with excitement, not

fear. Celia looked down at the ground so far away. She was thousands of feet above Earth, hurtling toward it at one hundred and fifty miles per hour, with a strange man, while her date sailed down next to her. She looked over at Landon. He wasn't too far away and gave her the thumbs-up again. She gave him a thumbs-up back, smiling.

In fact, Celia couldn't *stop* smiling, and then she laughed out loud, a crazy, wonderful, carefree laugh that the wind whipped away. She felt like a dog with his head out the window of a car flying down the highway, lips, ears, cheeks all flapping in the gale.

Still falling toward the Earth face first, Celia reached her hand out for Landon and he did a maneuver that brought him swiftly to her side. He had something on his helmet and she realized it was a Go Pro. She looked down at the ground, which still seemed so far away. The view was spectacular. She glanced back at Landon, making a face, and putting her hands out, splaying her fingers. If he was going to take pictures, she might as well ham it up.

He smiled then rolled off to find his own space.

Kash spoke in her ear. 'Hang on, we're going to do a roll. Pull your legs up.'

'Whaaaat?!'

Then she was somersaulting. The world spun below her before Kash had them back in the right position.

Kash tapped her shoulder, which was the sign that he was going to pull the chute open and for her to be prepared for it. When he did, she looked up, wanting to see how the parachute unfolded itself. And half worried it wouldn't.

But it did. It was glorious.

The parachute snapped open, a burst of red against an impossibly blue sky, and jerked them almost to a halt. Celia felt herself slip in the harness. Terrified she was sliding out of it and would flail helplessly to the ground before going splat, she grabbed hold of the straps. She must have slipped about a foot before she jerked to a stop. Relief flooded through her, on the heels of the terror she'd felt only seconds ago.

While the canopy slowed their descent somewhat, they still fell with incredible speed. Celia looked up to see that Landon had opened his parachute as well, but he was doing some kind of hand maneuvers that made his parachute twist and turn in the sky. Clearly, he'd done this more than once.

'So what do you think? Fantastic, isn't it?' Kash asked her from behind.

'It's overwhelming.'

The ground was rushing up to them faster now. As per the training, she put her feet out in front of her, lifting them a bit. Kash guided them to the ground, and they landed perfectly, sliding along the grass a bit.

When they came to a stop, Kash unsnapped their tether and one of the ground crew helped her to her feet.

She shaded her eyes with her hand and looked up. Landon was approaching fast.

He sailed in, landing on his feet, and had his canopy under control in no time.

Celia ran to him and he caught her in his arms.

'What did you think?' He swung her around.

'Oh my God, there are no words!' She was beaming.

'Would you go again?'

She nodded. 'Yes, I would. And I can't believe I'm saying that.'

'It's the rush.'

She nodded, 'It's certainly something I've never experienced before.'

'I love it.' He wrapped his arm around her and led her back to the hangar so they could get out of their jumpsuits.

Celia stopped and looked up at him. 'Are you an adrenaline junkie?'

He tossed his head back and laughed. 'What makes you ask that?'

She frowned. It didn't fit her image of him as a business-man. He'd never mentioned anything daring or crazy in his text messages. What else didn't she know about him? 'Well, the fast car, jumping out of planes. What else do you do?' She wasn't sure she wanted to know the answer.

Landon dropped a kiss on her lips and then grinned mis-chievously down at her. 'You'll see.'

Chapter 16

Celia started a group chat with Ava, Bonni and Fredi.

Cee: *You'll never guess where Landon took me #craycray*

Bon-Bon: *What? Everything okay?*

Aves: *Did Landon do something awesome? Tell us!*

Fredi: *Give the girl a chance to type, people!*

Cee: *I did something insane & managed to live through it #neardeathexperience*

Aves: *OMG!*

Bon-Bon: *You almost died? WTF!*

Fredi: *How kinky could it have been?*

Cee: *ru ready for it? I went skydiving. I jumped out of a freaking plane #yolo*

Fredi: *On purpose?*

Bon-Bon: *Damn! That is crazy. I didn't know Landon had it in him.*

Aves: *I'm stunned . . . so? Were you scared?*

Cee: *Terrified, but it was incredible.*

Bon-Bon: *Want to hear all about it when you get here.*
Aves: *When are you coming? You should see this place!*
Cee: *Not sure, Landon's talking w/a buddy.*
Aves: *You met a friend? Uhm, that's important.*
Cee: *I was hooked to him.*
Fredi: *Now that sounds interesting.*
Aves: *Talk about kinky . . .*
Cee: *#eyeroll*
Cee: *Later, gators #smooches*

Celia put her phone down on the picnic table, smiling at the responses from her friends. She hoped they were having a great day. She was eager to see them and tell them all about her jump here, but there'd be time for that later.

She had the rest of the day to spend with Landon. Celia looked around. He'd asked her to wait here for him, saying he'd be right back, but he'd been a while now. She'd killed the time texting, but now she was starting to get antsy. Residual adrenaline was no joke.

The hustle and bustle was rather thrilling. All the people were so friendly and seemed to be enjoying every moment. The camaraderie was enviable and reminded her of her relationships with Bonni, Fredi and Ava. Celia wondered if she could ever talk them into jumping. She chuckled and decided she had to figure out a way to get her girls out to skydive. That might take some work, but she would do her best. It would be the ultimate.

It's funny how she felt sort of felt like an old pro now. One jump out of a plane and suddenly she was all that. Celia laughed at herself as a new group came in. Checking the time again, she texted Landon: *Forget something?*

Then she checked the rest of her messages. Nothing new. Checked her voicemail for the hundredth time: nothing from her kids. Still no Landon. Celia sighed and decided the only thing she could do was sit and enjoy the view. It was a glorious day. Blue skies broken only by little bits of puffy clouds, a light breeze, and warm. Perfection.

Even the surrounding area was very lovely, with a flat portion here for the airport with gentle hills ringing the drop zone – as she was told it was called – was very pretty.

'Celia!'

She spun around to see Landon.

'So are you ready for what's next?' he asked as he walked up to her.

'Yup. I think I'm ready for pretty much anything now. What can top that?' She smiled and rose from the bench, moving into his arms.

'Oh, I'm pretty sure I could think of something.' He gave her a playful look and she tipped her head back and narrowed her eyes.

'What do you have up your sleeve now?'

'I can't be giving away any secrets this early.' He leaned down and kissed her. Their lips lingered and she breathed into him.

'Come on. Tell me. Don't keep me in suspense,' she murmured against his lips.

'Shh, relax and trust me.'

Celia molded her body to his. 'Okay. But, remember, I have kids and they prefer their mother alive.'

'I know. But right now you're mine and I want you to *feel*...' His mouth closed over hers, effectively silencing her until he lifted from their kiss, '... everything.'

Celia fully expected they'd be driving to the vineyard. So when Landon took her hand and led her across the apron in front of the hangar she was a little surprised. She was even more surprised when he took her to a fancy little plane.

'Are we going in that?'

'I don't see any other mode of transportation nearby.'

Celia heard the humor in his voice and glanced at him warily. 'What exactly is the plan for the rest of today?'

Landon put his arm around her shoulders and drew her into the warmth of his side. She couldn't help herself and slipped her arm around his waist and hooked her thumb into his belt loop.

'The plan is that I'm spending the day with a beautiful and sexy woman.'

She gazed up at him, trying to read the expression on his face. The sun glinted off his hair and she thought she hadn't seen a more handsome and devilishly sexy man ever before. He took her breath away, and she realized in that moment just how much she enjoyed being with him. This day was turning out to be wonderful and full of surprises.

'Is Kash flying us there?' Celia assumed Kash was a pilot and this was his plane.

'Nope.' Landon handed her up into the seat. She settled down and he reached across to buckle her up. 'You get to sit in the front.'

Celia looked behind her to see another row of seats. While this wasn't a private Learjet or anything, it certainly was posh.

'Are you sitting back there then?' she asked.

'Later.' Landon shut the door and ensured it was secure before walking around to the other side of the plane. He climbed up and sat beside her.

'Hey . . . what? You can't fly this plane.' She swore her voice was pitched super-high like a banshee screech.

'I sure can, yes, ma'am. Captain Landon Bryant at your service.' His face was very serious and he gave her a mock-salute. 'And I'll steal you away to anywhere I please.'

All she could do was stare at him gape-mouthed. It took her a moment to gather her wits.

'Holy shit. What a day of surprises! But you're a pilot? That's pretty damn cool.' She smiled, a little unsettled but also very impressed. What else could this amazing man do? She let herself relax back in the seat.

'Don't get too excited. I'm not flying today. I want to be able to focus all my attention on you.'

'Oh, Landon. You'll make me blush with talk like that.' Flirting with a hot millionaire while sitting in a plush private jet instead of traffic? This was the life! She looked up at him through her lashes and her jaw nearly dropped at the expression on his face. It wasn't seductive, exactly. It was more like . . . tender. It warmed a cold place in her heart, but she also wasn't ready for what it could mean.

'You're in good hands. I assure you,' Landon said, before his attention was caught by a woman walking toward the plane. 'And speaking of which, here's our pilot.'

He slid out of the seat and met the pilot on the tarmac. After exchanging greetings, the pilot began a walk-around of the plane while Landon boarded and sat behind Celia.

Celia undid her seatbelt and turned around.

'What are you doing?' Landon asked, catching her arm to help her balance as she squeezed through the narrow aisle.

'I want to sit back here with you,' she told him.

'Your view will be better up there,' he said, kissing her palm as she settled in the seat next to him.

'Oh, no,' Celia murmured. 'My view from back here will be much, much better.'

Leaning over, she tugged his head down and instigated a deep and passionate kiss, threading her fingers into his hair so he couldn't pull away. He chuckled and kissed her back, and she loved how he let her take the lead.

She vaguely heard the pilot's door open and sat back, licking her lips but not breaking eye contact with Landon.

'See, the view is so much better from back here.'

He smiled, a slow and sexy grin that melted her heart. Good Lord, she couldn't wait until later. But then, that would be wishing the day away, and she didn't want that. She wanted to embrace every minute with him.

Landon took her hand again and she sighed as he rubbed his thumb across her knuckles. Celia couldn't remember the last time she'd been this relaxed. Nothing to worry about, nothing to plan. All she had to do was go with the flow and trust Landon to take care of her.

'So, Mr Mystery, where are we going now? And why can't we drive there? I thought the vineyard wasn't far from San Francisco.'

'It's not. But it would take too long to drive where we're going next, so we're flying instead.'

'Wow,' was all she could say.

Celia turned to watch out the windows as they taxied to a runway. Within moments, they were barreling down it. 'I just can't believe this. I'm flabbergasted. How will we get back to the vineyard tonight?'

'Kash's place is closer to the vineyard than San Francisco, so we'll fly back there and drive to Napa. It'll be a late night. Are you up for it?' Landon relaxed back into his seat, still holding her hand, like he had no desire to be anywhere else.

Was she up for spending hours with the sexiest and sweetest guy she'd ever known? 'Hell, yeah!'

The nose of the plane lifted and they were airborne. For the second time that day Celia was flying high. Literally and emotionally.

Chapter 17

Landon was glad to see the change in Celia. The drawn, pale, features he'd noticed when he picked her up from the hotel this morning seemed to have been chased away by a growing excitement. He loved seeing the sparkle back in her eyes. He saw she'd removed her shoes and was barefoot. This was good. She was beginning to let herself relax.

Kidnapping her from her kidnappers so he could whisk her away for some fun and adventure had been the right idea. Celia had embraced it; at least, she was starting to. It made Landon happy to see the return of the Celia he'd first – yes, he admitted it – fallen for.

The vibrant woman he'd met in Las Vegas was slowly making an appearance. He wanted to see more of this fun and carefree persona and he was bound and determined to have her back by the time their day was done, and then they would be safely ensconced in his room at the vineyard.

Yes, he was going to do everything in his power to make her want to spend the night with him. Keeping his arousal in check certainly wasn't easy. The few kisses they'd had were only a teasing temptation of what was to come later, especially seeing her as she was now. He drew in a quiet, calming breath at the way her white blouse slipped off her tanned shoulder. Her skin was tinged with a bit of pink, like she'd been out in the sun a little too long. Her breasts rose against the fabric and the gentle swell of them above the neckline made his mouth water.

Knowing he'd be seeing her naked for the first time filled him with more anticipation than he'd ever thought possible. It made breathing difficult. Now, more than ever, he was bent on seduction. He couldn't wait to see her white-blond hair spread over his pillow, the green of her eyes clouded with passion, while she lay sprawled across the bed as he made love to her. She was tiny, which normally wasn't his type, but she was so different in every way and he was fiercely drawn to her. A ladyfinger firecracker. Small, but packing a wallop.

And she'd totally blown him away.

She was so goddamn gorgeous it made his eyes ache. The way she looked at him, the curve of her lips into a smile, and then the stomach punch – her even, white teeth denting her bottom lip as she pulled it between them. Did she even know how incredibly sexy, gorgeous and mind-blowing she was? He leaned over and swiped his thumb over her mouth.

Her eyelids fluttered and she met his gaze without hesitation

'I am really glad you're with me.'

'So am I.' Celia reached up with her long and delicate fingers and curled them around his wrist, holding him so he couldn't move his hand away. It was like he'd been poleaxed.

He tried to think of something to say but, when he did, it came out so lame he almost cringed.

'You like to fly?' he asked.

'Yes, I do. Only this is the second time I've flown today. We're not going to be jumping out of this plane, are we?' She grinned, raising her eyebrows. The expression in her eyes held a promise of the wildness he'd seen in her earlier.

'I think you liked jumping. Didn't you?'

She nodded. 'I did, actually. It surprises the hell out of me, though. Wow, the rush! I can still feel it inside.' Celia moved her hands in front of her, as if her nerves were strung so tightly she needed some kind of outlet to let her energy go.

'Will we be flying for long?' She looked out the window and he took the moment to feast his eyes on her before checking his watch.

'Just about another twenty minutes or so.'

'I'm stunned by everything we've done so far,' Celia said.

'We haven't done all that much.'

'How can you say that? We've roared around in a Bugatti, flown in a plane before jumping out of it at fourteen thousand feet. And now ... we're in another plane, flying off into the wide blue yonder, where I have no idea ... no notion of what we're going to do.'

'If you like what we just did you should love what's coming up next,' he said mysteriously.

'Can you give me some kind of hint?' She leaned closer to him and batted her eyelashes. 'Pretty please.'

Landon burst out laughing. 'Well, you can be a little minx, can't you?' He closed the distance between them and took her chin in his palm. 'And, no, I'm not going to give you a hint. Try as you might, tease as much as you like, but it won't work with me.'

As much as he was dying to tell her, he was too excited about keeping it a secret. He wanted to see the expression on her face when they arrived.

He chuckled when she sat back with a pout and crossed her arms over her chest. 'That's no fun.'

He doubted she would back out of this next adventure. It was much tamer than skydiving.

Landon shook his head. 'On the contrary, it makes it even more fun.' He loved how he could tease her and that she played along. He added, 'But if you can jump out of a plane headfirst, this will be a breeze.'

'You're making me crazy with all this,' she said through gritted teeth.

'But you love it, right.' He didn't ask it as a question. Because he wasn't asking a question, he was making a statement. He knew full well she loved it.

'Lord help me but I do.' She raised her eyes to the heavens then swiveled to face him. 'I really do. I wasn't quite sure if I would like skydiving. But once we got up there . . . the thrill. The adrenaline rush. It was like nothing I'd ever experienced before.'

'You have no idea how happy it makes me to hear that. It means we're on the same wavelength. We have the same energy . . . the same thrill-seeking desires.'

She shook her head slowly. 'No, I can't be a thrill-seeker, I'm a mom. I have to be careful about doing things that could potentially kill me. It's not responsible.'

'Haven't you ever heard the expression "You need to love yourself first before you can love anybody else"?' Landon tapped her knee.

She pinned him with a look, her eyes filled with a myriad of expressions, and Landon could see the thoughts racing through her brain.

'When's the last time you put yourself first?' he asked.

Celia was silent, and the sadness now in her eyes chased

away the excitement that had been there only moments before. It made him regret asking her the question. Where had the Celia he'd met in Vegas and started texting gone? The wild and spontaneous woman who seemed ready for just about anything? It was like her spirit was being extinguished by steady drips of stress and unhappiness. This was exactly why he and Bonni had decided that something needed to be done. Landon hoped doing all these fun and daring things would be the answer. He wanted to give her the opportunity to feel alive again. He'd give her anything.

'How long have you been a pilot?' she asked, not answering the question.

'It'll be about ten years. I started flying when I was a teenager, logging hours with an instructor and then taking all the necessary tests, which led to getting my license. I wanted to be a commercial pilot, but that wasn't on the cards.'

'Why? No, wait . . . I think I know the answer to that.'

'You do?' That certainly intrigued him. How the hell would she know what had sent him off course and away from his path?

'It makes sense.' She shifted in her seat and he glanced over at her. 'You're the CEO of one of the most powerful companies in the country. And it's a family company. So anything that you wanted that didn't fit the *plan* would have been discouraged. Am I right?'

'"Discouraged" isn't quite the word.' Landon nodded and pressed his lips together. 'But yeah, pretty much. I often wonder why I was even allowed to get my pilot's license.'

'But are you happy?' She watched him intently and waited for him to answer.

'I am today.' He gave her a big smile then reached over to rest his fingers on the back of her neck. He wanted to kiss her, but they were too far apart and strapped in to their seats, so the next best thing was simply to touch her, feel the warmth of her flesh under her hair. As he lifted the long strands the citrus scent of her drifted on the air. She smelled wonderful, a fantastic mixture of air, soap and wildness. It was intoxicating.

'Is that how you met Kash? Getting your license?'

Landon had to think a moment, because he'd been so distracted by her. So caught up in the way she looked at him, it took a second to connect to what she was asking. It took a bit of turbulence and her yelp of alarm to snap him out of his daydream.

'We're okay. Yes, wow, that seems so long ago now. I actually funded him for his company's start-up, and it's done well.'

'That's really cool. Do you get to see him much?' Celia asked, and she held her hand over her eyes when the plane banked and a shard of bright sunlight came through the window, silhouetting her so that she glowed like an angel.

'Not as much as I'd like, but whenever I get a chance.' The plane shifted course enough now that sun shone on her face, lighting her eyes into the most magnificent color. He could stare into those beautiful eyes all day.

'I'm glad you're happy today. Yet it makes me wonder if you're happy on every other day.' Celia reached out and touched his knee.

She must have had that answer on her mind to bring it up again.

'I make sure I'm happy with myself,' he told her, and was curious to see how she responded.

'But isn't it a bit selfish? Making sure you're happy with yourself first?' she asked softly then turned away to look out the plane window.

'I suppose it could be considered that way.' He shrugged his shoulders then paused when he heard the pilot speak over the radio. 'We'll be landing soon. Anyway, it's not really putting yourself first. Think of it this way. If you don't sleep, get rest, take care of yourself, then you get run-down, possibly sick, and then how can you provide for the needs of others?'

'I think, over the years, I've kind of forgotten who I really am. I've put others before me, and I clearly failed in the marriage department.' Celia fixed her gaze on Landon, and he could see that she was concerned about what she'd said. He nodded at her, trying to indicate that it was okay to talk about her ex and her marriage. He wanted to know everything about her. She went on.

'My kids will always come first. You know, your kids will always be your kids, but your significant other may not always be your significant other. Still, I see what you mean about taking care of yourself.'

'Then aren't you glad today is all about you?'

Her mouth curved into a slow smile as she gazed at him, and a strange but rather nice warmth rushed through his chest. It wasn't all that surprising, since his feelings for her had grown quickly. They had sparked into being when he first met her, they'd blossomed while they exchanged texts . . . and now that they were – finally – together? He liked how he felt with her, and that was a first for him. He had never loved anyone outside his family before. Landon had already admitted to himself that he was falling for her, but the real question was, what would happen when he hit the ground?

Chapter 18

Celia sat quietly as they flew closer and closer to another adventure.

She realized she'd put her life in this man's hands not once but twice now. All within less than six hours. But she acknowledged to herself that he made her feel safe. He'd taken her on a wild ride and the opportunity to step outside of the role of 'Mom' had been liberating. Freeing. It made her see just how much she'd closed herself up. She felt her old exuberance for life and her sense of adventure returning. Her wild heart was blossoming again.

The wildness in her had been buried pretty deeply since she'd gotten married to Dickhead and had little wild children of her own. She drew in a happy sigh, thinking of Jilly and Colin. How they would be shocked when they heard that their mother had jumped out of a plane. She chuckled to herself, imaging the expressions on their faces. Maybe she would Skype them later and tell them all about it. Or maybe it was best left unsaid for the moment. Celia frowned. If her ex ever found out, she was positive he'd find some way to hold it against her. She had to tread very carefully until the custody issues were all settled.

She glanced at Landon, who had relaxed back into his seat, and closed her eyes for a beat. It impressed her that he was a pilot. There was something sexy about a pilot, but then again he was just plain sexy all the way around. She shivered with anticipation about what might come after their day of jaunting all over the place.

'Can you see the airport down there?' he asked her, lifting his chin to indicate below.

'Oh, yes, there it is!' She waved her hand around, indicating the vastness below them. 'Amazing that you found it.'

Landon laughed. 'I know this county like the back of my hand.'

'Thank God for that! Otherwise, I imagine, things wouldn't go too well when you're the one flying.' She kept an eye on the airport below and noticed they were circling it.

'We're in the circuit. She's not flying past the airport.'

'So I guess the circuit means like a line-up of planes to land?' She looked around. 'I don't see any other planes in the area.'

'There aren't any right now, you're correct. But there's still a pattern for landing and taking off.'

Celia fell silent and watched the pilot do the maneuvers she needed to do in order to land the plane safely. She had confidence in Landon and, by extension, the pilot. He'd kept her safe so far, keeping the promise he'd made before skydiving. She was determined to let her guard down as much as possible with Landon. He was exciting, steadfast and made her feel all those wonderful girly feelings that she hadn't felt in such a long time.

Celia pondered that thought. Had she ever really felt girly?

She frowned. Even with her ex-husband, she'd never felt that special feeling. It made her sad. Thinking back, she wondered just when she'd started feeling inadequate where Frank was concerned. A memory flashed through her brain. They'd only been married a few months and Frank had lost his first patient. She had tried to support him, but he had lashed out, saying that she was too immature to understand. And it had hurt. He had apologized later, but that wouldn't end up being the only time he hit out when she tried to help. So she stopped trying. And he went out and found a different way to feel better.

Celia recalled thinking, when she was in her early twenties, that a woman's sexual prime was around thirty-six and she just *had* to have good – no, fantastic – sex before that. Even though she was a few years away from thirty-six, it didn't mean she didn't feel the tick-tock of time. And it wasn't just the sex. It was more. The feeling of being wanted, treasured . . . loved by a man. Celia sighed and realized just how much she *did* want it and how she'd been hiding this desire from herself.

She had her kids. And she didn't want any more. Yet, as she glanced at Landon, she thought he sure would make pretty babies. What special magic did he have to make her feel all these things, things she hadn't thought possible? She chastised herself for going off on that tangent.

'So here we go. Coming in for landing.' Landon broke into her thoughts.

Celia had a good view out the side window as the ground rushed up to them. They landed easy as you please, rolled down to the end of the runway to turn around, and then came back to the hangar.

A few minutes later they were out and walking to the parking lot.

'Now what?' Celia asked him. 'You don't have a car here. Do you have a transporter secreted away somewhere?'

'Ha! Are you a Trekkie?' Landon asked her, surprise edging his voice.

Celia laughed. 'Yup, you too?' She followed as he stepped off the curb.

'That I am, Number One. Anyway, no transporter, and don't worry. I think of everything,' he assured her, and wrapped his arm around her shoulder. A thrill whispered through her and she slid her arm around his waist, liking the feel of him next to her.

He led her over to a dark sedan that was waiting by the curb. The driver got out to open the door for them and Landon helped Celia into the long car.

'A limo? Wow, this day certainly is blowing my mind.' Celia couldn't believe everything that was happening. 'You know, I never expected this kind of treatment. A date in the park, a picnic, a stroll through the forest, wading in the surf on the beach – I would've been happy with any of that. It's just lovely being with you.'

'I somehow suspected that.' Landon reached over and pulled her in to his side. She snuggled into him. 'But I just figured you needed some sweeping away. Somewhere where you could forget about everything. Where you can let someone else take the lead and you just enjoy yourself.'

Celia looked up at him. The smile on his face and the look in his eyes were soft and gentle. She liked that. No one had ever looked at her like that before, so it was something that was rather breathtaking.

He leaned down as he turned her face up with his finger under her chin.

'I'm going to kiss you.'

She nodded. 'I know.' Her breath came in short bursts and her lips parted in anticipation of the kiss he had just told her was going to happen.

'A kiss for now. But so much more later.' The promise in his gaze made her tremble.

'I think I'm okay with that,' she whispered, unable to pull her eyes from his. She searched the blue depths, trying to look deeper, into his soul. Was there something more happening between them? Or was it just a fling? That's what she had originally wanted, she reminded herself.

And now, this wonderful day he had taken her on. Was this something he'd do for just any woman he was out on a date with? Celia didn't like that thought. At. All. She realized in that moment that she didn't want to be *just another girl* to Landon.

He leaned over her, pressed her back into the seat. He hadn't put his seatbelt on like she had. He turned so that he could throw a leg over her thighs, straddling her and effectively pinning her to the leather seat.

The passion in his eyes burned hot and he stared down at her with an intensity that had her breathless and her heart pounding in her chest. But more than that, heat swept through her lower belly and centered between her thighs, heavy, throbbing. His presence, the look in his eyes, the way he leaned over her . . . everything about him was just so wonderful and manly. It was as if he wrapped himself around her. She inhaled and breathed him into every fiber of her being.

She was him. He was her. They were becoming one, as if their passion had sparked from a single flame to swirl with intimate, curling, smoky tendrils, completely blending together to the point where it became impossible to tell one from the other.

'You are the most beautiful woman,' Landon murmured next to her ear, as he scorched a path of kisses at the side of her mouth.

Celia moaned with the desire his words and touch roused. 'Landon, you make me feel . . . ooooh . . .'

Her words trailed away when his lips found hers. His weight pressed her further back into the seat, and she welcomed it. The restriction of being under him, his thighs tight on hers, making her unable to move – she liked it. Landon gathered both her wrists in his hand and raised them over her head, holding them there, while his other hand cupped the side of her neck, his thumb at her chin.

He held her face and Celia's muscles went lax as passion flooded her, melting her into a puddle beneath him. Being pinned and restrained by him was highly erotic. Her mouth opened and that was his invitation in. Celia trembled when she felt his tongue brush across her lips and then inside to find her tongue. She wanted more and was desperate to touch him, to grasp his head, but her hands still weren't free. Using his free hand, he pushed the collar of her blouse off her shoulder. His mouth left hers and followed his hand.

She panted, unable to draw the breath she so desperately needed, to the point that she felt dizzy. A wonderfully powerful, earth-tilting, dizzy.

He let go of her hands and she reached for him but froze mid-movement when he pushed her top down, taking her bra straps with it. His tongue lapped against her skin, a searing heat that she swore made her skin sizzle.

She glanced down at his lowered head as he pushed away the barrier of her bra from her breasts. She gasped when his hot mouth found a hardened nipple and lightning jolts of raw desire raced down her body, sending an aching to between her legs. She wanted this man, more than she had ever wanted a man before.

'L–Landon, you're making me crazy.'

'Ah, Celia. You've come into my life most unexpectedly,' Landon groaned, his words raspy and full of desire, which sent shivers fanning out from her cheek where his lips tasted her. 'You have no idea how glad I am we're together again.'

Overcome with emotion at his words, she squeezed her eyes shut to keep tears of happiness from slipping down her cheeks. She was being silly. She shouldn't be so sensitive, but this man seemed to tap into her deep and hidden soul.

She reached for him, winding her arms around his neck and holding him tight. His hair was soft in her fingers, but this time she turned his face to hers.

'I'm not sure where this is all going. But you've come into my life at a time when I really needed you,' she whispered.

They looked into each other's eyes. No words. They didn't seem to be necessary. A whole lot was being said in silence.

A slow smile lit his face and Celia's heart warmed. It wasn't just arousal she felt for this amazing man, but something more, deeper, intense, which filled her with wonder.

She applied gentle pressure to bring him down to her. Lifting her face, she met his lips with a ferocity that surprised her. The kiss quickly switched from soft and gentle to an urgency that had her grasping at him, never wanting to let him go. Celia needed to be enveloped by him, needed to feel every little nuance of him around her.

They kissed like teenagers in the first blush of love in the back of the car. It was wonderful, thrilling, exciting, just like this whole day had been. All of Celia's troubles faded into nothingness. There was only this moment with Landon.

'I can't get enough of you.' He lifted his head and sat back, her hands dropping to his thighs, still tight on either side of hers. His powerful muscles, solid as granite, bunched under her touch as he kept himself raised slightly above her.

'And me you,' she said, as she gazed up at him, not breaking eye contact, but her hands had a mind of their own. They slid up his thighs to his hips and then around to his front, where she slowly unzipped him. Then she dropped her eyes to see her prize, looking at him for the first time. She sucked in a swift breath, reminded of how he'd felt inside her during their brief coupling in Vegas. He growled as she slid her hand up and down the length of this hard flesh.

He leaned back, giving her more room as she worked her hands on his cock. Celia glanced up and saw one of the most erotic sights ever. Landon's head dropped forward, his eyes closed, and his mouth was drawn into a thin, tense line. His large hands braced on the roof of the limo.

Celia pushed him off her and undid her seatbelt. She wanted to switch places. She licked her lips, craving the taste of him, hoping to bring him pleasure, and the need to do so was over-powering. Landon didn't resist and let himself fall back, and she moved with him until she was on her knees in between his legs.

'I love to look at you.' She moved her hands over his muscu-lar flanks and then back down to tug his undershorts down. He lifted his hips and she sucked in a sharp breath at the sight of him. She lowered her head to his lap, her blond hair swinging around her and brushing against him.

'Now this is a view you don't get every day,' Landon's voice was tight, and she loved how tenderly he caressed her hair. 'A beautiful golden head in my lap. I couldn't ask for anything more.'

Celia gazed up at him and stroked his balls with one hand

and coaxed him to even greater hardness with the other. Even his hair down here was golden and tinged with ginger. Holding the base of his cock, she leaned over and pressed the tip of her tongue to him. Reaching out, Celia flattened it on the underside of him and slowly took him into her mouth. His hips jerked and his hands tangled into her hair, holding her tight to him. She sucked in a breath at the deep and primitive sound he made as she worked her mouth up and down his length.

He was all coiled strength and Celia soaked it up. The pleasure of giving him oral sex went beyond anything she had ever believed possible. It didn't matter that they were in the back of the limo and on their way to another adventure. She had never liked giving blowjobs before, had always viewed it as a necessary chore on the sexual gratification checklist, but for the first time, she enjoyed giving somebody – *this man* – the ultimate pleasure.

'Celia, no, enough.' He tried to lift her away, but she hung on to his hips and shook her head. Landon tried once more and then said, 'If this is what you want, then I am fully on board. Yes, ma'am!'

With her tongue still on the tip of him, she looked up and met his gaze. Pleasure was edged across his features. His brows furrowed, tension corded his neck. She smiled at him and he closed his eyes, resting his head back on the seat. She worked her hands up and down his cock with a passion she'd never felt while doing this ever before.

Celia teased and licked and stroked until she heard him catch his breath and hold her even tighter. She brought him to an orgasm that thrilled her as much as it did him. Slowly, he relaxed back on the seat and he pulled her up into his lap.

'You never cease to amaze me.' His voice was soft and tender.

Celia snuggled back into him and sighed.

Without moving too much, Landon reached into the cabinet beside him. From it, he grabbed a bottle of water, twisted off the top and handed it to her. He got another one for himself and guzzled down half a bottle, his breathing still ragged. Celia took a long drink as well.

'That was the biggest, most wonderful surprise,' he told her.

'Wasn't it about time I returned the favor? Gave you a surprise? Does it make you want to sleep now?' she teased. She slid off his lap and turned around on the seat so she could rest her head on his chest. His heart pounded steadily, powerfully, next to her ear.

'No, it doesn't. It makes me want more.' He looked down at her. 'If we had enough time, I would return the pleasure.'

Celia smiled and licked her lips. 'We have tonight,' she told him.

'Yes, we do.' His voice was deliciously seductive and full of promise as he ran his thumb down her arm and back up to her neck, making her shiver, then lifting her chin. 'All night.'

And he sealed his mouth over hers.

Chapter 19

'I knew you were an extreme-sports enthusiast, willing to risk your life at every moment, but wow!' Celia exclaimed

'No need to be afraid.'

'How can I not be afraid? First you have me hurtling out of a plane—'

'Which you loved, by the way, you told me that yourself,' Landon reminded her.

'Yes, yes, I know.' She sighed. 'But this?'

When the limo had turned into the entrance of Moaning Cavern State Park, Celia's mind filled with possibilities of what to expect. A gourmet picnic lunch. A hike to the infamous geyser. Glamping. Wild and dirty sex against a tree.

But zip-lining hadn't been among those thoughts.

Here she was, about to zoom down a hill – over freaking *trees* – hanging from a cable, and her only protection would be a helmet.

She couldn't fall in love with Landon for many reasons, but the biggest one was that this time *she* was going to kill *him*.

'I don't understand your concern. This time, you're strapped to a very heavy gauge cable.' Landon took her face between his hands, tilting her head up. 'Remember how you felt when you jumped out of the plane? This is so much tamer. Little kids do it.'

'You sure are pushing me outside my comfort zone.' Celia chewed her lip.

He pressed a kiss to her lips. 'I won't force you to do this, but I know you'll love it, just like the skydiving. And it's safe. Look at all the people that are here.'

Celia looked at the line of people waiting to go down the zip line. He was right. If she thought about it logically, he was absolutely right. And she *would* be attached to a cable this time. A cable that had to be very strong and sturdy. She let out a big sigh and looked at him sideways, from behind a fall of hair.

'Okay. I suppose you're right.' She nodded. 'There're more people here than at the drop zone.'

'Excellent. Come on and let's get in the line.'

'What, no special treatment this time?' She lifted her hands palms up, questioningly, a teasing tone in her voice.

'Not here,' he told her with a crooked grin. 'I don't always need special treatment. Just when I know that it will benefit somebody else.' He leaned down and whispered into her ear, 'Like you.'

Celia took his hand. 'I don't need special treatment either. But I do thank you for doing it.'

'Come on, then.' He led her over to the zip-lining building and they got in line. 'It's time to get strapped up.'

Celia dropped her head back in mock-exasperation and rolled her eyes. 'Oh Lord, be with me – us – keep us safe. And during whatever else this man has up his sleeve for later. Don't forget I'm a mom with kids waiting for my safe return.'

'You don't have to keep reminding me you're a mom.' He pulled her toward him and she let her head fall back so she could meet his gaze. 'I like that you're a mom. I want you to stay a mom. I think your kids are lucky to have you.'

Those words made Celia tear up. No one had ever said such wonderful things about being a mom to her before. It always felt like such a thankless thing. She knew her kids loved her but, like any kid, sometimes hers considered Mom a pain in the butt. And her ex – well, there was no point even thinking about that man. She warmed at the expression she saw on Landon's face and reached up, thrusting her fingers through his hair to angle his head downwards.

'You say the most magical words.' She stood up on her tiptoes in order to reach his lips. 'You know, continue to say things like that and you could be rewarded very nicely.'

'I *am* a clever boy.' He grinned, a mischievous glint in his baby blues, and snaked his arms around her waist.

She was powerless to resist him. He captivated her. It didn't matter that they were now in line and waiting their turn to zip down the hill. It was just the two of them. Every moment she spent with him felt more powerful than the one before. He was beginning to show her the Landon behind the texts. Celia was hungry for details about him. Which side of the bed did he like to sleep on? What other cars did he have? PC or Mac? Would he move to California? Her brain stuttered a bit at that one before moving on. Was he a ruthless CEO or did he have concern for his people?

Well, that was an easy one to answer. With how considerate he'd been today, she'd have to say he wasn't ruthless. She liked this Landon.

A lot.

The line shuffled forward and they kept their fingers linked together. Heat from his body did more than warm her, it polarized her.

She watched the crowds ahead as they prepared for their turn. When it was time for them to step up to the platform, she was ready. Ready to zoom down a massively steep hill on a deceptively thin-looking wire. It was official. Landon made her batshit crazy.

In her helmet, goggles and harness, she looked at Landon and struck a pose. Fake it until you make it, right?

He chuckled. 'Now that's a poster-girl look if I've ever seen one. Hang on, picture time.' He got his phone out and she waited while he grabbed a shot.

'Do you have Instagram? Send it and tag me.' She paused for a beat. Should she be worried about being pictured with Landon? What if her ex saw it? No. Why should it be a problem? It would be fine. The kids weren't around and, if Frank could get married, then she could have fun with another guy.

'No, I don't.'

She made a face. 'Okay, we'll do it later,' she said. The staff directed her to the edge and she glanced at Landon.

'Here we go.' She looked at him and chewed her lower lip. Strangely, the closer she got to the edge, the calmer she became. Fear of the unknown was easier to overcome when the unknown became inevitable.

It was a dual cabling system so Landon was able to ride down the same time as her. She saw he was hooked in and then he raised his fingers, counting down. One, two, three and then she was speeding down the hill.

With her arms out and her legs stretched, she flew over the treetops. She was Wonder Woman! First, she had jumped out of a plane and now she was skimming over the trees, looking down at the world. 'Look out, Gal Gadot! I'm after your job!' she shouted.

'Celia!' She heard Landon yell from her left. Glancing over at him, she saw he was videoing her.

'My kids will never believe this.' She waved at him, knowing it would be recorded by the camera. 'Hi, Jilly. Hi, Colin. I wish you could be here with me!' She blew them a kiss before focusing back on her descent.

The end of the cable rushed at her and she put her legs out as she'd been told. Celia glanced over at Landon but he was already in the landing zone.

A flash of a second later she was right there beside him, laughing and unable to control her joy.

'There you are!' Landon walked over and stood back as the team unhooked her before the next rider came screaming down the hill. He took her hand and they ran down the path, heading for the main building.

'Oh my God, that was amazing! I've never done such daredevil stuff before . . . well, I guess that's not really true.' She winked at him and was so excited she could barely catch her breath.

'I love your wild side. I'd like to hear about some of the wild things you've done.'

'Maybe one day I'll tell you.' Celia twirled around, feeling so good after her daring ride down the cable.

'I'll hold you to that. I'm dying for a coffee. How about you?' He took her hand, leading them away from the landing area.

'I'd like something.' Celia skipped beside him, then spun around to face him and walked backward, barely able to control herself. 'Just, wow.'

'Let's see what they've got.' He pulled them into a line, behind a family with a pack of kids screaming for ice cream.

A few minutes later they were in an outdoor seating area, having picked up something to eat in the small food court. A ginormous basket of French fries sat between them, gravy and ketchup on the side, while Landon had a coffee and Celia a large Diet Pepsi. Now, if only she had some rum!

'I don't understand why you won't let me have a beer. Or rum,' She held up her cup then put it down and poked the fries, looking for a crunchy one to dunk in the gravy. Her kids knew she liked crunchy fries and curly chips, and always made sure she got them. *My babies.*

'Because, the next thing, I want you sober for. We can start drinking later.' He grabbed a few fries and swirled them in a puddle of ketchup. Celia made a face. She just couldn't do ketchup.

'I'm not sure if I'm up for anything else. I'm all adrenalized out.' She took the lid off her cup and took a drink.

'I suppose there can be a point when you've reached your limit. Like a container filling up to the brim and unable to hold anymore. But you're not there yet. I can tell.' He checked his watch and sat up in the seat.

'We should get going. Hurry up and finish your drink.'

'What's next?'

'Spelunking,' he said with a happy grin.

'Spelunking! Isn't that going into caves?'

'Yeah, doesn't it sound great?'

Landon watched the expression on her face. He nearly burst out laughing, because he could read her thoughts.

I'm a mom.

I can't die.

Why are we doing this?

I can't do this.

He waited for her to respond. Because he knew, in the end, she'd be all for it. He had learned today that she enjoyed excitement. She might complain about it at first, be unsure about her capabilities, but she got it.

'I have claustrophobia.'

He tipped his head sideways and he looked at her, narrowing his eyes slightly. 'No, you don't. I don't believe that for a minute. You're just thinking of every excuse under the sun to not do it.'

'I've watched those movies. I've been freaked out by those movies. People go into caves. People get lost in caves. People find weird creatures in caves. People get stuck in caves, in the dark, when their flashlights go out. And what about that guy who got buried in the box?'

'What box?'

'The box. In the desert in the Middle East. The movie, you know, he was left with a phone, remember?'

Landon furrowed his brows, trying to remember. 'Oh, *that* movie.'

'It freaked me out,' Celia said.

'Do you watch horror movies or something?' Landon stood up, taking their trash over to a nearby garbage can.

She nodded, taking one final swig of her drink before chucking the cup. 'Yes, I love anything that will scare the shit out of me. Do you?'

He shook his head. Landon didn't mind risking life and limb to drag-race or hang-glide or heli-ski, but sitting through a horror movie designed to give him nightmares? That would be a negative. 'No, they're too scary.'

Celia laughed. 'That's what makes them so great.'

'Then why are you afraid of stuff like caves?' He put his arm around her shoulder and she scooted closer.

'Listen, I've seen the movies! I know how they all end.' Celia matched her step to his, even though she had way shorter legs.

He laughed. 'Calm down, this isn't a movie. The only person allowed to kidnap you is me. And Bonni.'

'But, still, can you imagine! I was dying the whole time I watched that movie.'

'Well, you're not gonna be stuck in a box. And I'll know where you are. This is a professional company. And we don't have to go any further than the entrance if you don't want to go.'

He saw her shiver and pulled her into his arms.

'It's all good. I'm ready for it. And you can bet, if I don't like, I'll be out of there like a cat with its tail on fire.' Celia pressed her cheek to his chest and he heard her draw in a deep breath.

'Are you really that scared?'

'A little bit. But hell, if I can jump out of a plane into the sky, why can't I go underground, right?'

'Excellent point.'

She tipped her head back, her long hair tickling against his arm, and he stroked the strands with his fingers while gazing into her vivid green eyes. He saw excitement in them, as well as a bit of fear.

'So, shall we go and spelunk then?' she asked bravely, pulling out of his arms to start walking again. He thought she looked like a conquering elven queen, until she stumbled over a rock and nearly took a header.

Arms flailing, she did some fancy footwork to recapture her balance and then lifted her arms like a gymnast who had just stuck a successful landing. Landon made a mental note to send his brother a bottle of Scotch for bringing Celia into his life.

'I think I see the wild Celia starting to emerge.'

'I think you do. She has been unleashed! But look at all the kids here.' There was a combination of mama bear and curiosity in her tone as she surveyed some rowdy camp groups being herded around by relentlessly cheery counselors.

'Yes, there are. There's a little bit of everything in the Moaning Cavern Adventure Park. I bet Jilly and Colin will be excited to hear all about your adventure going into the caves.' He hoped the reference to her kids would work in a positive regard. 'They'll probably think you're a cool mom.'

She pursed her lips and glared at him in mock-outrage.

'Cool*er*. I meant a cool*er* mom. You know, we could even bring them here for a visit.'

She tilted her head, observing the camp kids again, and he knew she was thinking about it. He was glad he'd mentioned the idea and realized he'd just planted a seed that he would nurture until it sprouted. It would be the first family vacation he had ever actually wanted to go on.

'We should check back at the visitor center, grab some brochures and stuff so I can take them home,' Celia suggested.

Landon was agreeing, when she burst out laughing.

'What's so funny?' Landon chuckled at the way she laughed. It was infectious.

'Oh, God, look. You have to be four feet five inches to spelunk. I just noticed the sign. Ha! Fredi would barely be able to ride that ride – well, not ride, but you know what I mean. Come on. I gotta Insta that and tag her.' Celia handed her phone to Landon and struck a pose pointing at the sign while he snapped a pic for her.

Landon's heart was full watching her, the way her hair fell over her shoulder, her tongue touching her top lip as she typed and captioned the photo. When she looked up at him his whole body ached for her and the strong sensation made him catch his breath. This woman was exactly what he'd been looking for all along.

She shoved her phone into her back pocket.

'Come on, big boy, time to go caving.' Celia grabbed his hand and he followed her.

He'd follow her just about anywhere.

Chapter 20

Celia's phone buzzed and she fished it out of her pocket. Looking at the screen, she glanced up at Landon with a big smile on her face, 'It's my kids.'

'Put them on video,' he encouraged, and led her to a picnic table under a tree.

'Don't say anything about us going skydiving,' she said sternly.

'Yes, ma'am,' he drawled, winking at her when she gave him side-eye, brushing the small of her back as he helped her sit.

Landon sat beside her so he could see the kids too. Celia answered and held her cell so she could see her children.

'Hello, my babies. What a wonderful surprise for you to be phoning me.'

'Hi, Mom!' Jilly called, and stuck her head in the side of the frame. since Colin had positioned their iPad mainly for him.

'Mom, Jilly is being a pain. She won't let me play my video games and keeps making me practice walking around with that stupid pillow. I'm nearly seven! I know how to hold a pillow!' He made a face and it melted Celia's heart.

Jilly elbowed her brother to the side so she could get a better look at the screen. 'Who's that with you?' she asked.

'Jillybean, we go a little while without talking and you don't recognize me anymore? I'm hurt, kid.' Landon leaned closer to the phone.

'Uncle Landon! I didn't know you were going to be with Mom!' Jilly yelled.

'I just happen to be in the same place as your mom this weekend. What a great coincidence.' Landon moved his hand to Celia's leg, his fingers brushing her knee, but his focus was on the screen.

Celia glanced at him and loved the expression she saw on his face as he spoke to her children. She sat back a little so he had the full frame to see her kids . . . and she watched him.

'What are you guys doing? I bet Mom's not making you hold a pillow,' Colin asked.

Landon winked at Celia, his fingers tapping playfully on her knee. 'Well, we're doing some fun things.'

'Like what?' Jilly asked.

Celia squeezed his thigh, reminding him.

'Guess what we just finished doing? Zip-lining!' Celia took over the conversation to make sure he didn't let the cat out of the bag. Plus, she was excited to tell her kids about one activity, at least. Surely Frank wouldn't be able to find anything problematic with zip-lining.

'Zip-lining!' Jilly's mouth made an 'O'. 'That's so cool. I really want to do that too.'

'Me too,' Colin said as well. Celia hid her amusement. Colin never wanted to be left out of things.

'If your mom says it's okay – and only if your mom says it's okay – maybe one day I can bring you guys here and we can all do it,' Landon told them.

'Oh, Mom, can we?' Jilly dramatically threw herself on the surface holding up the iPad, causing it to jostle.

'I want to! I want to!' Colin yelled, bouncing up and down next to his sister.

'If we can get the time set aside, and Uncle Landon is available, then maybe we can.'

They both squealed in delight, only to stop abruptly when a male voice rumbled in the distance. They looked offscreen in the direction of the voice.

'Dad's calling us.' Jilly's expression fell. 'You're coming home soon, right?'

It was all Celia could do to keep her expression neutral and not show her frustration that her children were being torn away from their conversation and showing signs they didn't want to be there with their father and their stepmother-to-be right now. 'Listen, tomorrow is a big day for your dad. You be well-behaved. And have fun. Put zip-lining out of your mind and be good at the wedding. We'll talk about it next week when we're back together.'

'Okay, Mom. This hotel really is pretty. You should see all the flowers everywhere. I know you love roses, and they're all over the place. Everywhere,' Jilly said.

'Yeah, it really smells.' Colin wrinkled his nose.

Landon laughed. 'Well, my little man, women love flowers. That's important information for when you become a big man.'

Colin opened his mouth to respond, but then suddenly turned to yell, 'Hold on, we're talking to Mommy. We're coming.' Facing the iPad again, he said, 'Imma go, Mom. Dad wants us. Love you. Have fun with Uncle Landon.'

Colin disappeared offscreen, but Jilly hung back just a little bit longer. She waved her fingers. 'Don't worry about us, Mom. Grandma's keeping us company when Dad's busy. Talk to you soon!'

Celia reached a hand toward her phone. 'Bye, Jilly, have fun. I love—'

The screen went dark before she could finish. Celia was quiet for a moment and drew in a deep breath, determined not to be sad at how short the conversation was, or to think about why they were with their father in the first place. Silver lining, she got to be here having fun with Landon. She looked over at him and smiled. 'That was such a lovely surprise.'

'Yes, it was. I'm glad they called you.'

'Me too.' She stuffed her phone back in her pocket.

'Don't worry, it's all going to be fine. You raised two great kids.'

'Yes, they are great.' She sniffed back her emotion. Celia squared her shoulders and took hold of Landon's hand, clutching his fingers fiercely. 'Let's go then. I have to be able to tell them what spelunking is like.' She looked up at him, then away, and muttered under her breath, 'But after the custody case is over.'

'What's that?' Landon asked.

'Oh, nothing, just talking to myself. I tend to do that. It looks like we have to go over there.' Celia pulled Landon down the path and was relieved when he didn't ask her any more questions.

'So, what did you think?' Landon slipped his arm around her shoulder and gave her a little shake.

Celia grasped his hand. His touch and closeness had been what got her through the caves. If he hadn't been her rock, she would have turned around and bolted a couple times. Yet, in the end, she was glad she'd experienced it. Seeing the wonder of the world from beneath – it had really been something. 'I think I prefer jumping out of planes.'

Landon threw back his head and laughed. 'I did not expect that.'

She gave him a smile.

'Aw, come on, that's not a real smile. It wasn't that bad, and you did great.'

She nodded. 'I do feel the adrenaline rush, but I didn't like the other parts of it. The tightness, the feeling of no escape.' She shivered.

'But there was an escape. Just back the way you came in. Besides, I'd never let anything happen to you.'

'I know that, but try telling my overactive brain.'

Celia stopped and pulled Landon next to a tree out of the path of everybody else. She reached up and put her arms around his neck, slid her fingers up the back of his neck and pulled his head down. 'I can think of something that would help me calm down.'

Landon pulled her roughly against him as he pressed her into the tree.

'I will always give you whatever you need.'

His mouth closed over hers and Celia moaned into him as his tongue delved deep into hers. A trickle of fire heat settled between her legs and her knees turned to noodles. Landon held her in his powerful arms and she felt safe. Treasured.

She'd been on a fine edge of arousal most of the day. Being kissed by him so soundly right now, it was almost more than her overstimulated body and emotions could handle.

This kiss was quick, promising and ended much too soon.

When they separated both were short of breath and high on passion. She couldn't open her eyes and her head remained tilted slightly upward as she savored the memory of his lips on hers.

'Let's get back on the road.' His voice was gruff, low, and she knew he was just as aroused as she was.

'Where next?'

'To Kash's place, to pick up my car, and then we'll drive to the vineyard from there.'

She nodded and forced her eyes open. When she did, she caught an expression on his face that made her heart beat double time. Was he falling for her? Had this day together catapulted her into a whole new sphere for him? She knew damn well it had for her. Landon was a very special and unique man. He seemed to *get* her. And that alone was worth its weight in gold. He had a knack for quietly understanding her. He had encouraged her, subtly pushed her to find herself again. Not to mention he was a man who had her heart thumping and her lady parts aching. She had no idea a man could be so . . . in tune with her, emotionally and, of course, physically.

He led her to the limo and they were quiet. Lost in her thoughts, Celia watched him and wondered what he was thinking.

She lifted his arm and placed it over her shoulder, and slid next to him.

'What plans do we have for the rest of the weekend?' Then she sat up with a jolt and turned to look at him wide-eyed. 'I almost forgot about Ava, Fredi and Bonni back at the vineyard! How could I?'

She slumped back against him. Celia had been all set to spend the entire weekend with Landon, completely forgetting about her best friends. He had her tied up in knots.

'What? I'm not good enough company?

She gave him a playful swat.

'Of course you are. But I still want to spend some time with them. It's not often we get together.'

'Was the last time you saw them in Vegas? Where we met?' He winked at her and a tremor of desire tumbled around in her abdomen.

'That's the last time we were all physically together, but we talk to each other all the time. I'm hoping we can manage more weekends away. It's so much better to see each other in person. It's just hard with Bonni and Fredi on the east coast and Ava stuck up in the middle of nowhere in Indiana at the head office of some company that I can't remember the name of right now.'

'I think it's great the way you guys have kept in touch all these years since college. Too many people don't get that relationships have to be worked at.'

'Me too.' Celia rested her head on his shoulder, and she must've dozed a little bit because when he told her they were at the airport she bolted upright.

'Come on, baby,' he said as he reached for her hand. 'Time to head home.'

Home. His home at the vineyard? She liked the sound of that. Only, her home was in the opposite direction. If you'd asked her forty-eight hours ago, she would have said she couldn't ever imagine being in another relationship. But now Celia caught herself wondering if there would come a point soon where she and Landon would discuss going home . . . together.

Chapter 21

The drive from the little airport wasn't nearly as long as she thought it would be. Driving down a dark road with Landon at the wheel was almost cozy.

'We're almost there.' He reached over and put his hand on her thigh, massaging her softly.

'I like it when you touch me.' She turned her head to look at him. The Bugatti's cockpit dash lights reflected across his features.

'I like touching you.' He slipped his hand a little further between her thighs. Celia opened them a bit more.

'It's too bad you're wearing jeans.'

'It is, but then it only builds the anticipation,' she murmured in a low voice.

'Yes, it does.' Landon slid his hand higher and she drew in a breath as his fingers pressed into her. Even through the fabric of her jeans, his touch was fire. She closed her eyes and lost herself in the smooth swirl of his finger. Celia moaned and let her imagination carry her away.

'I can't wait to get you in a bedroom.' She heard the gravelly pitch in his voice, and a totally new inflection as well. One that was far more intimate and full of emotion.

'What you're doing feels so good.' The sensations running through her body were achingly sweet. She couldn't wait until they could finally be together. Naked, loving, warm and on fire in each other's arms. He moved his hand away, having to shift gear, and Celia let out a long and slow breath.

'Here we are,' he said after a while.

Celia looked out the window. It was dark, so very dark that she nearly couldn't see a thing, but the impressive gate, made of stone and wrought iron, told her that there was something fantastic down the driveway. Landon turned and she kept her eyes focused on what was coming. She couldn't see what was on either side of the driveway but there were pretty lights every few hundred feet to illuminate the way. They cast enough brightness that she caught a glimpse of neatly trimmed vineyards and rows of grape vines disappearing into the dark of the night.

'It's hard to see anything.' Celia peered through the darkness, trying hard to make sense of the shadows beyond.

'Just wait until tomorrow morning. The sun rises above the hills of vines and it's spectacular.'

'Well, I'm usually up with the birds, since I'm used to getting up early with my kids.' Then Celia gasped as they rounded the last curve. 'Oh my God, how beautiful. Stunning.'

The sprawling buildings before her were beautiful under the starlit night, and the gardens took her breath away. She rolled down the window of the car as Landon drew closer, the diffused lighting in the flowerbeds creating such a beautiful ambiance that Celia was speechless.

It was like everything sparkled. The softness of the flowers, the twinkling lights on the buildings and the glow amongst the colorful blooms created a such beautiful composition of nature under the night sky, surely Monet would have painted it.

'This building here is the bed and breakfast. There's a breakfast bar and a five-star restaurant. Your friends have rooms there. You do too, if you'd like me to drop you off here . . .' Celia spun her gaze over to Landon.

'The decision is mine?' She smiled at him in the dim lighting of the car. She couldn't make out the expression in his eyes but he did have a playful smirk on his face.

'The decision is always yours. But you know what I'd like it to be.'

Celia didn't have to think hard about that decision.

'And what about the other building?'

'It's the family quarters. It's just down there past those trees. Obviously, it's a prime location. Has the best views. And it's the ultimate in privacy.'

'I see. Well, I'm rather intrigued by this lovely other building. I think I'd like to see it.'

Landon chuckled and drove past the bed and breakfast.

'Your room will be waiting there for you, should you want it. But I'm glad you decided to come with me.'

Following Landon into the magnificent home was surreal. She knew the Bryants were wealthy, and it was clear just how rich they were by the enormity of the house and the quality of everything inside. Still, it wasn't a showpiece; there was also a humbleness to it. It looked lived in, with little trinkets and other signs of family life.

She liked it.

A sense of family and hope permeated the walls and there was even the smell of a recent meal. She smiled as he led her through the grand entry hall and into a spectacular kitchen.

'Holy crap! I've never seen anything like this before. Gosh, my kitchen would fit into the pantry.' Celia stood in the middle of the room and slowly turned, taking it all in.

Landon laughed. 'My mom likes good cooking. She's dabbled in her own creations and made sure us boys knew how to cook.'

'She did? That's awesome. So, will you cook for me sometime?' she asked him.

'Absolutely.'

Celia wandered over to the windows that ran along the whole back wall of the kitchen and looked out on to the vast stone patio, again lit with strategically placed lights.

'Simply beautiful,' she whispered, as she stared out across the terrace into the darkness.

'Yes, it is. I like coming here when I'm on this side of the continent. I find it very soothing.'

'Yes, I can totally understand that. I'm looking forward to seeing it in the morning. And the bed and breakfast over there doesn't bother you?'

Landon stood behind her, his hands on her hips, and she leaned back into him. 'No, it doesn't. As I said, it's the ultimate in privacy. We're just far enough away that you don't hear the people. The B and B has its own pool and there's a tree line with a hidden fence that keeps the properties separated. Now, listen, we haven't had much to eat today and I'm starved. What about you?'

Celia realized she *was* pretty hungry. The snacks they'd had through the day had been enough to carry her along at the time, but now she wanted something substantial. 'I am actually quite hungry,' she said.

'This kitchen is stocked with pretty much anything you want. I can cook you steak, salad, any kind of seafood. Whatever your heart desires.'

'Well, for starters, I would love a glass of wine. You did promise that if I stayed sober during the day, there'd be alcohol later.'

Landon grinned. 'Of course. Where are my manners? And what kind of wine would Madame like?'

'You choose. Something that you like.'

'Okay, then.'

Celia watched Landon walk over to a heavy wooden door with huge iron hinges on it. The top was arched and it looked ancient.

'Do you want to come with me?' he asked her, pointing at the door.

'Okay.' She nodded. 'What's behind door number one?'

'A treasure trove that'll make your mouth water.'

She followed him through the door and down stone stairs that seemed to have been carved right out of the rock around them. The temperature dropped as they descended.

'What a mysterious place. Are there no lights?' Celia felt along the stone wall, just the light from the kitchen guiding their way.

'Yes, give me a second. I want to surprise you.'

'I think I've figured out you're a man who likes surprises. But you've already given me so many today, I don't know if my poor soul can withstand another.'

'We're almost there, and I like to see the look of happiness on your face. Surprising you gives me pleasure.'

The light from the doorway vanished behind them as the stairway curved and they were plunged into darkness.

'Landon?' She was reminded of the caves earlier today. She tentatively took another step down then saw Landon, a darker shadow in the dimness, with his hand outstretched, and she reached for it.

'Here we are.'

Then the room was illuminated with subdued lighting.

Celia drew in a quick breath, delighted at the sight before her. It was absolutely stunning. She gazed around in wonder. 'Oh, wow. What a place.'

'It certainly is special. We can only guess what it was originally used for. Probably some kind of contraband, keeping valuables out of sight from the law, but it's the perfect wine cellar.'

Celia moved forward, deeper into the stone room. The ceilings were fairly high, but they were rough, raw, as if chiseled out of the surrounding rock. Pillars supported the rounded ceiling.

'Is it safe down here? It's not going to suddenly collapse or anything, is it?'

Landon came up behind her and chuckled. 'I certainly hope not. But we've shored it up in places to make sure, and there is a secondary exit out. It's certainly stood the test of time.'

Celia saw the racks of wine lining the walls.

'Oh,' she gasped. 'You were right, it *is* like a treasure trove.'

'There are some of the rarest wines in the world down here.' He walked forward and ran his hands over the bottles, gently tipped so the corks were facing down.

'Are these barrels also filled with wine?'

'No, these barrels are mementos of what started the vineyard so long ago. We also had many oak wine barrels shipped over from France and Italy to use in the early days of the vineyard. You know, for ageing the wine, as well to keep them for posterity's sake and to add to the decor, like you see here. Tables and such for events.'

'You have parties here?' She looked around and realized that the space did lend itself to entertaining. Not elaborate affairs, but smaller, more intimate gatherings.

'You'll have to show this room to Fredi. She would love it. I bet she'd love to do a photo shoot down here. But you might have to bribe her with a big bottle of Jack Daniels if you want to keep her from raiding your wine collection.'

'We could talk about it, if she's interested. Now, let's find a bottle of wine.'

Celia watched Landon as he bent his head to read the labels on some of the bottles. His hair fell forward and she thought how amazingly sexy he looked as he peeked through the strands. She'd been waiting for the time when they would be alone, and here it was.

Over the last hours she'd begun to see a more passionate, thoughtful side to him. She wondered if he took that with him into the business world.

'Here we go, a nice little bottle of wine from France.' He pulled a bottle out that didn't have a speck of dust on it.

'I half expected these bottles to be all dusty,' Celia said as she inspected the label on the bottle he held out for her. 'I really don't know anything about wine. Other than I like it.'

'We make sure that this room is maintained and the bottles are dusted regularly. This wine is one of my favorites.'

'How do you know the differences between countries, and how the wines taste?' Celia thought the label was quite artistic.

'Well, it's all about the grapes, the region they're grown in, the soil, the temperature, the amount of rain and the crush.' Landon set the bottle down on the table.

'Crush?' Celia inquired.

'Harvest,' he said, expertly uncorking the bottle. He sniffed the cork then held it out for her. 'Tell me what you smell.'

She leaned forward and sniffed. 'I don't know – grapes.'

'No,' he said in a soft voice. 'Come here.'

She stepped closer to him.

'Now close your eyes.' He put his arm around her waist and drew her closer.

She looked up at him briefly, skeptical.

'Do it. Close your eyes,' he repeated.

She did.

'Now inhale.'

'Through my nose or my mouth?' Celia felt the sexual tension building between them. With her eyes closed and his body so close to hers, the sensual touch of his hands and the mystery of being in the darkness, built a powerful sensation within her.

'Through your nose,' he said quietly.

Celia inhaled slowly and focused on the scent.

'Now tell me what you smell.' His voice was so close to her ear it ruffled her hair. She squeezed her eyes shut, not wanting to lose the sensation of intimacy between them.

'I – I smell . . . fruit.'

'That's a start. Sink deeper and inhale again. There's more complexity than just fruit.'

She sniffed, and now it was like the scent from the cork spread through her body in a luxurious warmth. Much like she'd actually tasted the wine. Explosions of smell had her seeing a variety of images in her brain.

'Blackberries, vanilla, earth, cherries?'

His lips pressed on her cheekbone and Celia startled.

'Don't open your eyes. That's very good. Now I want you to tell me what you taste.' His voice was erotically seductive and she was swept away.

With her eyes closed, her other senses took over. She heard him pouring wine into a glass. Setting the bottle down. The soft steps as he came back to her. The rustle of his clothes.

'I'm going to bring the glass to your lips. Take a small sip and swirl it around in your mouth.'

She nodded. He had one hand supporting the back of her head and she waited with her lips parted, trembling, to feel the cool of the glass next to them. When she did she allowed him to tip her head back, trusting that he would make sure she didn't choke and the wine flooded into her mouth.

She swallowed and held her breath. What was he going to do to her next? The anticipation was killing her. And if he was going to kill her with desire, what an awesome way to go.

Chapter 22

Celia was floored, overrun by a multitude of sensations in her mouth. Her senses, especially taste, were heightened by her lack of sight. She could hear Landon's ragged breathing as he seduced her oh so sweetly. The earthy, stone smell of the wine cave hung in the air and it wasn't altogether unpleasant. The cool air was almost like a soft balm over her heated flesh.

Wine flooded her mouth and it was delicious. Giving up her control to Landon, with her eyes closed, had to be one of the most erotic moments of her life.

'You're trembling,' he said, in low, gravelly voice that told her he was just as turned on as she was.

She nodded and whispered, 'Yes.'

'I like that.'

'Oooh,' was all Celia could manage. His words spoke to a deep and mysterious place inside her, lighting her up like a sparkler.

She heard a clink, probably him setting down the glass.

'Don't open your eyes,' he instructed.

'I won't.' Her voice was quiet as she waited to see if he would give her any further instructions.

Celia drew in a ragged breath while doing what she was told, and with no idea what to expect next. She stood like a statue with the stone wall at her back, Landon in front of her, mysteriously there, somewhere. She could sense him. Feel him so close to her and yet still not touching. It was like she had sonar and could see him behind her closed eyes.

His hand gently grasped her upper arm and she drew in a swift breath. Lifting her hands, she held them out and paused when he instructed her to stay still.

She jumped when his fingers circled her neck, warm, strong, and as they slipped down, they took the neckline of her top with them. Celia was unable to keep her breath even and her chest heaved as her heartbeat fell out of time, with a rapid and crazy beat.

Her top had delicate little buttons and she imagined his fingers working on them, opening each one up until he finished with the last.

The silence in the wine cellar was deafening. She could hear her blood roaring, the sound of her breathing, his sharp intake of breath when he touched her chest.

Slowly, his fingers slid down her torso, between her breasts, skillfully keeping away from them as they cried out for attention. Celia lifted her chest, her back arching, hoping he would take her invitation and give her nipples the attention they craved. But he didn't. All he gave her was the satisfaction of a low rumble in his throat, as if he were having the hardest time resisting her.

Then his fingertips touched her belly and he spread the edges of her top. The fire coming from his flesh against hers and the cool air whispering across her heated skin was polarizing. Celia's knees began to wobble and she pressed her palms back into the wall for support.

'Can I open my eyes now?'

'No.' His hands rested on her sides. 'Keep your eyes closed, it will enhance the sensations.'

Celia nodded. She licked her lips, wanting to reply to him, but she couldn't form words as his hands slid higher on her ribcage.

'Tell me what you smell.'

Landon's voice was close to her ear, teasing, sensual, and his hands were the only physical connection to her. Yet she felt his presence as powerfully as if his body were flush to hers. It was like the air between them had an energized, magnetized pull on them. She leaned into it.

'I – I . . . smell . . .' Celia inhaled. '. . . Water, but not damp-ness, like rain. Sw–sweetness, fruit. Stone.'

'That's very good.' Behind her eyelids Celia could almost imagine Landon in front of her, the glow of his hair under the lights in the room, and his eyes, those wonderful expres-sive bedroom eyes that made her want to melt. It was like his essence was shifted into a fiery presence, and her lips curved in pleasure. Never had she felt so in tune with her own existence, emotions, feelings, than she did with Landon.

'What do you hear?' This time she felt the butterfly touch of his lips against her cheek, and it was wickedly arousing. She nearly jolted out of her skin and reached for him. 'No, no. No touching yet.'

Celia dropped her hands and pinched the seam on her jeans. She had to do something with her hands if he wouldn't allow her to touch him. This was a first for her, being told what to do and not to do. Was she being dominated? It didn't matter. She was loving every second of it.

'I hear . . .' She paused and turned her head slightly, trying to distinguish sounds to work out what she was hearing. 'You. I hear you, your breathing. The rustle of your clothes as you move. And . . . dripping? A soft fan, I think, or air conditioning. Humming.'

'See how attuned you become to your surroundings when you turn off one of your senses?'

Landon slid his hands higher, trailing so lightly over her skin that goosebumps rose in the wake of his touch. He found the hooks to her bra and, quite expertly, had them undone.

Celia drew in a sharp breath, holding it, waiting to see what he would do next.

He chuckled, his voice low and oh so wonderful. A sound that she wanted to hear more.

'Talk to me,' she said in a barely-there voice, wondering if he would hear her.

'What do you want me to say to you?' His lips pressed her cheekbone and she sighed, tipping her head into him. The voltage coming from that tender kiss was off the chart and almost more than she could stand. Her legs trembled and, this time when she reached out to grab him, he didn't deny her. She had his hips, gripping until she twisted her fingers into the belt loops of his jeans.

'I will always be here to support you and give you anything you need.'

Celia's heart swelled with emotion at his words, spoken with such tenderness and meaning. She tilted her head back, keeping her eyes closed, absolutely loving this exchange between them. 'I know.'

'Good. That's important.'

His hands pushed off her top, setting off a quake of tremors through her body. His fingers ran up her arms and pulled the straps of her bra over her shoulders, tugging them down, taking the bra with them.

'This is the first time I've seen you.'

Celia almost opened her eyes when Landon said that, but she didn't, squeezing them shut, wanting to keep the tension. 'You've seen me before.' Her words were hesitant as she anticipated what he might do next. Even though she was dying to look at him, to watch what he was doing, she didn't.

'I meant naked. Completely bare to my eyes.'

She shivered delicately.

He kissed her, his lips pressing into the soft space under the curve of her jaw. His tongue, warm and wet, touched her neck, where her vein throbbed with the heavy pulsing of her blood. 'You taste wonderful. Like the fresh air, sky and you.'

He lapped at her, following her collarbone, and she arched her back, pressing her head against the stone wall. Her breasts felt full and heavy and her nipples tightened into excited and sensitive points. She could no longer control her breath as it quickened when he moved lower, and then his mouth disappeared.

Celia finally opened her eyes, wondering where he was. He hadn't gone far. He had stepped back just enough so that he could gaze at her. Then his eyes trailed up her body to meet hers. He smiled. A warm, loving smile that showed in his eyes.

'You are beautiful. No words can describe how you look in this light.' Then he stepped forward, his eyes darkened and his brows furrowed. Tension etched into his face and Celia's belly tightened at the look she saw, knowing she was the reason he was looking so intensely passionate. No one else but her.

'The words you say . . .' she breathed.

'. . . are truth.' He pulled her to him roughly, and she was a ragdoll in his hands, not resisting, wanting his power to be unleashed. He lowered his head to the tops of her breasts, kissing, nipping, and his breathing was ragged as he inhaled her. His gentle movements of earlier disappeared. This was a new Landon. A fierce Landon. Her lover Landon.

He was insistent. His mouth demanded. His hands cupped her breasts and he pushed them together, his thumbs rubbing against her nipples.

She cried out and dropped her head back, her body becoming fluid and weak. She gripped his shoulders and held him tight. It was like he couldn't get enough of her, and the ache in her belly flared throughout her body, making her desperate for him and oh so ready.

'Suck me.' Celia murmured the words. Part of her felt shy at saying them, but the rest of her felt so emboldened by her lust. And he listened. Landon turned his head and pulled an aching nipple between his lips, suckling and flicking it with his tongue. She was dying. Truly and wonderfully dying.

This time she really did collapse in his arms.

'Hey now.' Landon swept her up and carried her to the table in the center of the wine cellar. The scars and gouges in the wood table spoke of a long and mysterious life. He gently lowered her on to it until she lay flat, her knees at the edge of the wood and her legs dangling over. She spread her arms out and her fingers found scars in the table, digging into them as if to create a new memory for the table to hold.

Celia watched him as he looked at her. He pulled his shirt over his head and tossed it aside. She sucked in a quick breath, absolutely mesmerized by him. Seeing him naked for the first time was intoxicating. How could someone like her be with a man as magnificent as him? His desire for her thrilled Celia. It washed her clean of all her insecurities and memories of rejection.

This man wanted *her*!

'Oh, Landon. I could look at you all day.' She rose up on to her elbows, causing her breasts to jut out, and she loved seeing Landon's gaze drawn to them.

'I could feed off you for a week.' He quickly undid the button and zipper of her jeans. Lifting her hips, he slid them off and discarded them on to the floor.

Sitting up, she reached for him. 'Your turn. I want to see you.'

Celia hooked her fingers into the waistband of his pants and pulled him toward her. He didn't resist and placed his hands on her shoulders, gently massaging up to her neck and down her back. 'I'm an open book to you. But you should hurry up. I got yours off much quicker.'

'Oh, is this a competition? Which of us is the prize, I wonder.' She gave him a coy look but the passion clouding his face was all she needed to see to hurry her up. Yet her fingers wouldn't work she was so excited. She took a steadying breath.

Calm the hell down, Celia.

She finally had his zipper open and pushed his pants down to his ankles. Celia was about to slide off the table so she could be closer to him, but Landon stopped her.

'Oh no, darling, you stay exactly where you are. Lay back,' he instructed. He guided her back and the palms of his hands slid along her arms as she reclined until he held her fingertips. He pushed her arms out to her sides and she watched Landon as he leaned over her. The muscles in his shoulders and arms bunched. His long, reddish-blond hair swung over her skin, tickling her. She giggled at the sensation.

'Your laughter is like magic.' He buried his face between her breasts and ran his lips up to a hardened peak, teasing it with his tongue. She was mesmerized, watching him reach his tongue out to touch the tip of her nipple and play with it before sealing his lips around it.

Heat exploded between her legs and swept through her body like a flash fire, scorching her until she was sure her body would melt.

Celia groaned and dropped her head back to the table when Landon moved to the other nipple, making her mindless with desire. She grasped at his shoulders, trying to pull him up, needing his mouth on hers. Wanting him closer, in her, around her, on her, but he held her down on the table with his large hand, fingers splayed between her breasts. He shifted his hand enough so that his thumb continued to sweetly torment her nipple, inching his way down her body with his mouth.

'L–Landon . . . what if someone comes?'

His voice was muffled against her belly. 'No one will come, so relax and enjoy.'

Celia did as he said. She relaxed back into the table. All the tension in her ebbed away and she focused entirely on his mouth. His caresses. His tongue licking, hot and wet, to her belly button. He swirled it around and then moved lower, bringing a hand down her side and behind her to cup her ass, squeezing her as he lifted her up and continued lower.

She gasped.

He groaned.

With her legs dangling over the edge, she felt totally exposed to him, even if she still had on her white cotton panties. He didn't say a word and the heat from his breath through the fabric raised her body temperature even higher.

She was frustrated that the fabric was between them. Yet he used it to his advantage, butterfly-touching her, making her nerves sing. She grew wet for him when he ran his fingers along the edges, gently brushing her folds to higher sensitivity.

He inched deeper and Celia let out a cry when he found her entrance and teased around her opening. She whimpered and reached out for something to grasp. But there was nothing except the wood beneath her fingers. She pushed them into the surface, trying to keep herself rooted in place.

With his lips, he pushed aside her panties and she was exposed to him.

'Now if that isn't the prettiest sight I've ever seen.' Landon's voice, a heavy growl and thick with his desire, only ramped hers up even more.

One hand held her bottom tightly while his other hand slowly pressed into her as his lips swept through her folds and found her clitoris.

Celia bucked on the table, unable to lay still as he worked her with his hands and mouth ... and, oh such a talented mouth. He let go of her ass and hooked her knees over his shoulders, never missing a lap, a beat, a stroke, with his tongue.

'I – Land— oh!' Celia sucked in and held her breath when he drove his fingers deep into her, finding her G-spot with ease. He was the first to ever find and bring to life that mysterious, nerve-charged place of wonder.

She rocketed toward her orgasm as he plunged with his fingers and lapped with his tongue until she let out a keening that echoed off the stone walls and ceiling. Her body tensed and he held her until she slowly came back down and lay inert in front of him.

Landon kissed up along her torso and planted a loving kiss on each highly sensitive nipple before working up to her mouth.

She took his face in her palms and stared into his eyes. 'Oh ... my.' She licked her lips to moisten them and drew in a very shaky breath. 'Now you.' She murmured against his mouth. 'My purse, upstairs . . . condoms.'

He chuckled and stood to reach for his pants, which were lying in a heap. He held up a package. 'Just in case, you know? Boy Scout and all.'

Celia smiled. 'Yes, just in case. Now put it on.'

She already knew what he felt like inside her but she couldn't help writhing at the idea of having him above her, caging her with his arms, being able to hold him while he moved. In Vegas, there hadn't been time for thought, just a passionate, lust-filled coupling, slightly awkward due to the confined space. Here, there was no worry about being caught, about accidentally falling. It was the two of them, after a day that had revitalized her spirit, in a cool and shadowed cavern.

As she watched him fish out the condom from his pants, Celia thought that this wouldn't be fodder for another erotica. No. This was a *romance*.

Chapter 23

Landon ripped open the package and slipped the condom over his cock. He stroked himself to keep himself hard, which there was really no need to do. He was like a rock, just from looking at her lying before him on the table, flushed from her orgasm. Her breasts, firm and high, more than a handful, rose, and her nipples were a dream. She was so sensitive, he wondered if she'd ever come from nipple-play alone. He added it to the list of things that he was determined to try with her.

She hadn't lowered her legs when he stood. Her heels rested on the edge of the table and her knees were spread, allowing him full view of her gorgeous pussy. He stepped forward and placed his hand on her mound, his thumb pressed into her slightly.

'No need to warm you up again.' He smiled at her slick wetness.

'No, no need,' Celia agreed. He loved how wild she was. A vision with her hair fanned out over the honey-colored table.

He couldn't resist and leaned over, pressing a kiss to her

belly, a few stretch marks were reminders that she had birthed two children. A small flash of jealousy surprised the hell out of him. Jilly and Colin were fantastic children, but he almost hated that another man had put babies in her. It almost, but not quite, made him want to rip off the condom. Suddenly imagining her pregnant with his child created an unfamiliar ache inside him. He knew how he felt about her, but this was next-level stuff.

'What are you waiting for, big guy?' Celia reached out to him and he came to her.

Her gaze dropped to his cock and she licked her lips, reminding him of the incredible blowjob she'd given him earlier.

'Nothing.' He grabbed her ankles and pulled her closer, the table a perfect height for him to fuck her.

No, wait a minute. That word grated. He shoved it from his head. No, he'd not *fuck* her. He'd make love to her.

Holding his cock to her opening, he slowly pushed into her tight heat. She was wet and slick and he gave little thrusts until he was buried deep, unable to control a deep groan once he was fully seated inside her.

It was all he could do to keep from coming like a virgin teenager. Landon paused and caught his breath. He gazed down at her and was full of wonder at her beauty. His heart beat harder as her hips rose to meet him. He glanced down to where they joined and was moved to the core. She was his, right now, and he realized that a single weekend would never be enough. He wanted more. He wanted everything.

Landon gritted his teeth and nearly lost it when her hand reached between them and she swirled her fingers over her clit, sighing with delight.

This woman was one of a kind. And one he didn't plan to let

out of his sight. Grasping her hips, he drove into her, and she accepted him with a small gasp of pleasure, meeting him stroke for stroke until he was unable to bear it any longer.

His balls tightened and his fingertips dug into her, he didn't want to leave little bruise marks on her and tried to lighten his hold. Yet, if he marked her, it would mark her as his.

'Take me, Landon. Come for me.' Celia's voice was the last straw. Their gazes met and then she arched her back, her mouth open, and he felt her pussy pulse around him. She orgasmed and he let himself go.

Roaring his release so loudly it bounced off the walls like thunder. He braced his knees and leaned on the heavy wooden table; otherwise, he'd collapse on top of her. It was all he could do to keep standing.

'Holy shit,' was all he was able to say, moments later.

'Ditto,' Celia's voice was soft, like an angel's, and her eyes caught the light with an ethereal glow.

He was drowning in her, and he didn't want to be saved.

Chapter 24

Celia's eyes snapped open and her heart pounded in her chest. She had no idea what caused her to wake up so suddenly. For a moment, she didn't know where she was. She blinked and looked around, not recognizing the darkened room. She had a bad feeling something had happened to her kids and she grabbed her phone, but there were no texts or calls from her babies or from Frank. Slowly, she began to relax and her galloping heart found its rhythm again as she breathed deep and slow.

She heard soft snores next to her and glanced at the sleeping form under the sheet. Celia smiled. It was the first time she'd woken up next to a man she actually *wanted* to wake up to in far too many years.

She crossed her legs and leaned back into the pillows, looking at the man who had given her the most amazing day yesterday, and let her gaze roam over him. In the dim lighting she was able to see the carved planes of the muscles across his shoulders, his arms and down his back, rising to a rounded and very firm ass, unfortunately covered by the sheet, which had a lovely high thread count which Celia loved the feel of, almost as much as she did his touch.

When she'd first seen him all those months ago, he'd reminded her of a wild and untamed Viking.

They'd flirted casually at first, but Landon had worked his way under her skin until they'd been lost to lust. It hadn't seemed real, merely a fever dream. Now, in this bed, his body seemed like perfection, as if carved from marble, but Celia realized he was so much more. He certainly had a knack for invading her brain and making her think lusty thoughts, and yet over the months she'd grown to *know* him a little more.

He wanted a dog, but he didn't think it would be fair because of how much he traveled. He liked starch on his collared shirts and a precise crease on his suit trousers. He loved his brother and mother but tolerated his father. And there was still more to learn. This was the absolute worst time, thanks to Frank and his custody demands, to start a new relationship, but the connection she felt couldn't be denied. She wanted to continue down this path and see where it might lead.

She couldn't be more thrilled with how things had turned out. Watching him sleep peacefully, contented, all male and naked, with just the sheet draped over his hips, she couldn't be happier. Celia sighed and shook her head in wonderment. She reached out, needing to touch him again, but stayed her hand above his back. He was lying on his belly with his arms up over the pillow and his face turned away. His long hair tumbled around his head.

Her hand hovered. She didn't want to wake him. She'd learned a long time ago to let sleeping babies lie.

Although he wasn't a baby. Clearly. He was all man. And right now, he was her man.

As much as she'd like to stay with him, the tenderness between her thighs told her she needed a little bit of a break. After their romp in the wine cellar they'd raided the kitchen on wobbly legs and devoured the food while sitting on stools at the massive island before sneaking off to bed. They fell together again, but it had been slower, more intimate. Celia shivered, remembering how they'd stared into each other's eyes as he moved in her. It had felt almost like a promise.

She didn't really want to leave him. It felt too soon, which didn't make any sense.

But she should also check in with her friends. See if they had kidnapped anyone else while she'd been gone. She wouldn't put it past Ava to have stumbled across a particularly dreamy guy.

Celia slipped quietly from the bed and grabbed her clothes. She thought about leaving him a note but didn't want to spend time looking for paper and a pen. She knew he would text her when he was up and about. Celia blew him a kiss with her fingertips and left.

The walk from the house to the bed and breakfast was a moment of quiet solitude which Celia absolutely reveled in. It wasn't often she had no demands on her time, no urgent deadlines, no expectations, so the leisurely walk thrilled her. It was still very early, with just a tiny hint of a sunrise staining the far horizon. She stopped on the path and looked out over the rolling hills that were beginning to share their beauty with the world. She could see darkened lines, which she assumed were endless rows of grapevines. Drawing in a deep breath, she was filled with such a sense of contentment.

She thought of her children and wondered what they would think of it here. The pool she had seen last night through the windows had looked amazing. She could almost hear Jilly's and

Colin's laughter as they jumped and splashed around in it. But was that all a pipe dream? She shouldn't get ahead of herself. It was way too early in this fragile relationship she was building with Landon to think like that.

Celia knew Landon liked her kids – really, who wouldn't? – but he hadn't really said anything about wanting to be a dad, and it wasn't a subject she was ready to bring up. She was afraid she might not like the answer. Love me, love my kids, that was the way it worked. Wandering down the path toward the other building, she reflected on how she'd sworn off men. After Frank, she'd been in no hurry to tie herself down to another man, especially now that she was a package deal. And if she did, the next man she chose would have to prove he deserved her.

Much like Landon already has? her inner voice whispered.

She found her way inside the B and B and stood before the room Landon had said was hers. Taking the key he gave her last night, she slid it into the lock and pushed the door open. Once inside, she nearly died. It was gorgeous, like a princess room, luxurious, decadent, breathtaking and with a view from a balcony on the other side of leaded French doors. She stood in awe, gazing around and not quite believing it.

Her friends' rooms were all connected by the same balcony and Celia saw the sun was starting to rise up a little more above the hills. She didn't want them to miss the sunrise. Going out on to the balcony, she banged on the next set of doors and then decided to try the handle. The door wasn't locked.

She barged in and yelled, 'Get up, you crazy bitches! It's sunrise in Napa. And you're not staying in bed.'

Ava sat up and blinked her eyes. It was always easy to get her up. Then she rolled out of bed with her hair all fluffed up.

'What are you doing, honey? Why are you up so early? We

have a long night of wine coming on. Too early,' she muttered, and sat back down on the bed.

'Ava, you're supposed to be a morning person. What's wrong with you?' Celia flipped on the lights and pulled the drapes open.

'What? Why?'

'It's our first day – we need to get this party started. Can I get to the next room through there?' Celia asked, pointing at what looked like an adjoining door.

Ava nodded, rubbing her eyes, then walked into the bathroom and shut the door.

The next room was Bonni's. You'd think a cop would be easy to get up too. But when Bonni slept, it was always rough and ragged. She had the worst sleeping patterns. So when Celia saw her cuddled up under the blankets snoring softly and absolutely dead to the world, she was almost sorry to wake her. She thought for a moment and then decided. Yup. Still doing it.

She walked over and touched Bonni on the shoulder. Nothing.

'Bon-Bon,' Celia whispered.

Still nothing.

'Bonni!' Celia said more loudly, and gave her a firmer shake.

Bonni bolted straight up in bed, her eyes all confused, and muttered sleepily, 'What, what's happening? I'm awake. I'm ready.' She glanced around like she was still in a dream. Celia giggled.

'Rise and shine, honey. Time to get up!'

Bonni turned and looked at Celia, bewilderment on her face. 'What's happening? Is something wrong? What do you need me to do? I'm here. Are the kids okay?' Bonni babbled and then swung her legs over the edge of the bed before pulling out the bedside-table drawer to search inside it.

'It's not here!' She bolted to her feet. 'My gun, it's not here.'

'Bonni, stop. It's me, Celia. It's okay. Shhh.' Celia took Bonni's hand and recognition finally came into Bonni's eyes.

'Is something wrong?'

'Nope, everything's okay. But up and at 'em. As she had in Ava's room, Celia went to open the drapes. 'It's going to be a glorious morning and we're not missing this sunrise.

She turned around and saw that Bonni was flat back down into the pillows. 'Girl, get up. Ava is up and I'm going to get Fredi.'

'You're such a pain in the ass, Celia. I was in one of the best sleeps.'

'I'm sorry, Bon-Bon. It's the country air, and the wine, so you'll sleep good again tonight. I promise.'

'You know nothing, missy,' Bonni muttered.

'I'm a mom. Don't you know moms know everything?' Celia went to the other door, which she assumed led to Fredi's room. Girding her loins to repeat the process, she entered, only to find Fredi wasn't in bed.

Hearing the sound of running water, Celia stood beside the window and waited quietly for her to come out of the bathroom. Even with a few moments of downtime, her thoughts were carried away by everything that happened, remembering all that was Landon. When the bathroom door opened and Fredi came out of the dark room into the even darker bedroom, it startled Celia out of her thoughts.

'Hey, I'm glad you're up,' Celia said.

Fredi let out a scream that made Celia's blood run cold. Her heart nearly faltered. It had scared the shit out of her.

Celia's voice got stuck in her throat, then she blurted out. 'What the fuck! Fredi, it's just me!'

Within moments, Bonni had barreled into the room.

'What's happening? I'm here.' She had her arms out and Fredi jumped, letting out another screech, which had the three of them clutching their chests.

Ava rushed and turned on the light. 'What's going on? Quit screaming or you'll have the whole place awake.'

'Guys, relax. No need for the theatrics.' Celia finally calmed down enough to get a good look at her friends. Then she burst out laughing.

'What's so funny?' Fredi demanded, her hands on her hips.

'You lot.' Celia nearly doubled over. 'Look at you. What on earth did you do last night? Your hair – ha! Mascara, lipstick. Jeez, enough to scare Frankenstein.'

'We were asleep!' Bonni retorted. 'What do you expect?

'Yeah, but looks like you partied hard.'

'Have you looked at *yourself* in the mirror this morning?' Bonni asked.

Celia shook her head. 'Nope, I'm good. But listen, the sun's coming up and I want us to watch the sunrise together.'

'Are you kidding me? For that, you woke me out of one of my rare deep sleeps? I could brain you.' Bonni gave her a cop stare.

'Oh, Bonni, come on. It's a glorious morning. The sunrise is going to be gorgeous and I don't want you all to miss it.'

'Oh, I get it.' Fredi nodded.

'Get what?' Celia asked.

'It's just like when you did the walk of shame back in college. Other girls would be dragging their asses after a night of being rode hard, but not you. And since you're all bright-eyed and bushy-tailed this morning, that tells me your tail got yanked last night.' Fredi gave her a sassy smile.

Yeah, Celia definitely needed to get new friends, ones who didn't remember every damn thing.

Chapter 25

'So, enough of that.' Celia shook her head, then said, 'It's almost sunrise time. So get your clothes on and come down to the patio.'

'Oh, no, no, you don't get away that easy,' Fredi said, and wagged her finger at Celia.

Celia looked at Bonni and Ava.

'Yeah, I'm with her.' Bonni hitched her thumb in Fredi's direction.

Celia eyed Ava, fully expecting she would give her some kind of support.

Ava raised her hands, palms out. 'You're on your own, girl.'

'Are you guys really doing this?' Celia asked, feeling suddenly put upon at having to talk about her and Landon's night together.

'Well, that's pretty easy to answer.' Bonni raised her eyebrows and put her hand on her hip. 'Yup.'

'Ohhh, I get it.' Celia nodded and pressed her lips together.

'You're referring to *your* morning after in Vegas.' Celia looked pointedly at Bonni.

Bonni nodded. 'Mm-hm.'

'You guys looked pretty cozy in your pics on Instagram,' Ava said, combing her fingers through her hair.

'Clearly, you got much more than cozy,' Fredi said, suddenly invading Celia's personal space. 'Is that stubble burn on your neck I see?'

Celia sighed and knew they wouldn't let her get off that easy.

'I'll make you a deal. You want to know more, you get your asses dressed.' She smiled sweetly at them and then walked to the door leading to the hallway. 'You've got less than five minutes to get downstairs on that patio I saw below our balcony. Or mum's the word.' She opened the door and stepped through, closing it behind her.

Pausing, she rolled her eyes when she heard a bunch of excited female voices inside the room and the sounds of them rushing around. If she knew her friends, they would be downstairs in a heartbeat, wanting her to spill her guts. Celia beat it down the hall so she could give herself time to figure out just how much she was going to tell them.

Luckily for her, the chef had been up for a while, and the smell of baked treats and coffee was divine. The spread was laid out on a wonderful old buffet by the doors leading to the terrace beyond. The windows were all pushed aside so there was no door, like the inside and outside had become one, and the view overlooking the vineyard was beautiful.

Celia fixed herself a big mug of coffee and put a few pastries on a plate. She carried it out to a table and chairs with colorful cushions near the edge of the terrace by a stone wall topped with an intricate ironworking that ringed the outside patio. She sat and gazed around, barely able to comprehend the beauty of the land. Sipping her coffee, she closed her eyes and enjoyed the caffeine rush.

'Oh, I so need this,' Celia murmured, hiding her surprise when Bonni appeared next to her. Geez, her friends were determined.

'Talking to yourself again?' Bonni asked her.

'Just enjoying my first morning sip of java. You know how good that is.' Celia cupped the mug in her hands.

Bonni sat beside her with her own mug and a chocolate croissant.

'Isn't it gorgeous out here?' Ava pulled out a chair and sat down with her back to the building. 'Just look at that view. I'm glad you woke us up, Celia. This is going to be a magnificent sunrise.'

'Yeah,' Bonni grudgingly agreed, taking another swig of her coffee.

'My bed was so much better.' Fredi dropped into a chair with a grumpy look on her face and chugged back her first cup of coffee. As always, Celia noticed, Fredi already had another full cup sitting in front of her.

'You double-fisting already?' Celia asked innocently.

Fredi made a face and held her second cup high. 'You betcha. You get me out of bed at the ass crack of dawn and I'm gonna need some fortification.'

For the time being, their coffee was more important than grilling her about Landon. The hush of the vineyard seemed to capture everybody and they sat in easy silence.

It really is beautiful. Celia could imagine living here. It would be something special, that's for sure.

'Wow.' Ava was staring off over the hills as the sun began to rise on the horizon. 'This.' She waved her hand, indicating the scenery in front of them.

'Stunning,' Bonni agreed. 'But don't think that this stops you from telling us what happened yesterday. Time for that once this beautiful sunrise is complete.'

'That's right.' Fredi had finished her second coffee and was finally waking up.

'Let's just be quiet and enjoy the glory of this morning,' Celia said.

The women lapsed back into silence, watching the sky in front of them gradually shift from indigo to lighter blues with streaks of rose and yellow and, eventually, a beautiful, glorious azure. Along with the waking of the sun came the rising of the birds. Their song filled the air. A slight breeze picked up and blew gently across the terrace. It held the promise of a warm day. There were no clouds in the beautiful sky, only ribbons of fading shades of pink and orange. It was a magical color that cast a spectral glow over the fields, their table and the grounds.

'You think this means there'll be a storm? You know, red sky in the morning and all,' Ava asked.

'No,' Bonni said. 'It's just an amazing morning.'

'Certainly is,' Fredi agreed, as she snapped a few photos on her phone.

Celia turned to look at her. 'I can't believe you said that. Is the infamous night owl actually enjoying the sunlight?' She pursed her lips in mock-shock.

Fredi huffed. 'Well, so what if I am?' She gestured at the view before them. 'You don't get this color green in Florida.'

'And if I hadn't woken you up, you would've missed it,' Celia pointed out smugly.

'Are you saying, "I told you so"?' Fredi asked.

Celia finished her last pastry with a nonchalant air. '*Moi?* Never.'

'I need another cup. Anyone else?' Bonni asked, starting to get up.

'Oh, don't go yet! The show isn't over,' Ava said, and sighed, resting her elbow on the table and dropping her chin in her palm.

Bonni settled back down, and Celia was happy. Her friends were all together, they'd forgiven her for rousing their asses out of bed, and everybody was enjoying the morning so far.

The sun burned in the sky and the long shadows across the vineyards rapidly diminished as it rose higher.

'Well, that certainly was something.' Bonni stood. 'Give me your orders, girls. Because, when I get back, it's interrogation time.' Celia knew her reprieve had just ended.

'I know, I know. I promised. I'll have another coffee, and if you could bring me back one of those delicious little pastries with the caramel chunks on top, that would be awesome. And thank you.'

Ava and Fredi also gave their orders for more caffeine. Celia took a moment to check her phone: nothing from Landon yet. Checking the time, she decided to wait a little longer before she reached out herself.

'Are you waiting for him to text?' Ava asked, stretching her arms over her head.

Celia nodded, placing her phone on the table. 'I left him asleep in bed. Didn't have the heart to wake him.'

'Hey, not until I get there!' Bonni called from inside.

Seconds later, she carried over a tray laden with all manner of goodies and slid it on to the table. Grabbing her coffee, Bonni put it down in front of her and then sat, wriggling a little to get comfortable. Lacing her fingers, she rested her hands on the table. She turned to Celia. 'Okay, Ms Fox, you know why you're here. Now spill.'

'I don't know where to start.' Celia shrugged, avoiding her friends' gazes. She really wasn't sure where the beginning was. Was it when he remembered that Colin had auditioned for his elementary play and asked to come? Was it when he admitted that he'd been worried about her and reached out to Bonni to make sure she was okay? Or was it when he said hello in Vegas?

'Don't give us that. Don't be spinning any yarn here, we want straight goods,' Fredi told her.

'Whoa, Fredi, back off. It's not like I'm not going to tell you guys anything, it's just that things with Landon are . . . different.' She felt like she was facing the Spanish Inquisition. Between Bonni's interrogation skills and Fredi's ability to argue anyone into submission, her secrets didn't stand a chance.

'How so?' Ava asked.

Celia took a sip of coffee and attempted to gather her thoughts. 'You know things with Frank were difficult before our marriage ended, and they only got worse after it did. I really thought I was completely and utterly done with men, but Landon's making me re-evaluate.'

Fredi was taken aback. 'I thought this was another fling, but you sound serious about him. Like take-him-home-to-Mama Fox serious.'

There was a bird singing nearby and Celia listened to its song for a moment, trying to put her feelings into words. 'You know I love my kids – they are my life, my heart, my everything. But . . . Landon, he took me skydiving. Then zip-lining. Then we explored caves. Underground caves, no less. Never in a million years did I think I would jump out of a plane. Yet Landon somehow knew, knew that I needed to reconnect with the woman I was before Frank, before the kids.'

Ava reached out to clasp Celia's hand. 'You've always had a

wild heart, and I'm glad you've found someone who recognizes that and cherishes you for it.'

Next to Celia, Bonni was sliding her mug between her hands, the ceramic scraping against the metal table. Abruptly, she stopped and pinned down Celia with a cop stare. 'So is it serious? Could Jilly and Colin be my niece and nephew someday?'

It hadn't occurred to Celia that, with Bonni and Quinn so hot and heavy and marriage likely on the horizon, and if things went in that direction with Landon, they would be sisters-in-law in addition to being sisters of the heart. She tried, for a heartbeat, to picture being married to Landon, but her mind shied away. She wasn't ready yet to go there. 'If you think about it, Landon and I have just gone on one date. It's a little too early to be talking about in-laws. Besides, with Frank and the custody battle, I don't want to drag Landon into all that.'

Her friends exchanged a look and Celia could practically hear their thoughts. #denial

Taking pity on her, Bonni said, 'Well, I'm glad things went well yesterday. And that you had fun. I can't believe he got you into a cave!'

'I know! For the first and last time. But it was a fantastic day.' Celia sighed. She pressed the home button on her phone to check the time. When the interrogation stopped, she'd text Landon to see what his plans for the day were.

'Right then, now that we've established you had a great day, it's time to hear about the night,' Fredi said, making *gimme* motions with her hands.

'Okay, well, did you know there's another house over there?' Celia raised her hand and pointed to the other side of the trees.

'Is that the family's compound? Quinn was telling me about it. The boys used to come out here with their mother during the summers sometimes.' Bonni glanced in the direction Celia indicated.

Celia leaned in, folding her arms on the table and dropping her voice. 'I didn't get to see much of it, but it's huge and incredible. Ava, you would love the architecture.'

'And why didn't you get the grand tour?' Fredi asked. 'I would imagine some hijinks and shenanigans between you two occurred.'

Celia nodded and tried to keep a silly smile from curving her lips. She pressed her lips together and looked up to the sky. 'Ya, well, yeah, sorta. Um . . . It turns out there is a really cool wine cellar. With a very large antique table in the center of it.'

Ava gasped. 'Nooooo, you didn't!'

Bonni tilted her head back, likely trying to erase the knowledge that her best friend had had sex in her boyfriend's family wine cellar. 'I can never go down there now. If I go into that cellar, that's all I'm going to see. You and Landon banging on the antique table.'

Fredi raised her hand for a high-five and Celia happily obliged. Then she said, 'The bathroom sex was incredibly heated, but the table sex was the most fantastic, unbelievably erotic sex I've ever had.'

'How many times?' Bonni asked, in a tone that suggested she wasn't entirely sure she wanted to know.

'How many times did we have sex? On the table, one. Then we made out in the kitchen for a bit before he carried me up to his bedroom.' Celia could feel her cheeks flushing as she relived pieces of last night.

Bonni shook her head. 'No, that's not what I want to know. How many times—'

'—did you orgasm?' Ava said in a squeaky voice. Celia could tell she was on romantic overload.

'Shush,' Celia said, and looked around to see if anybody had heard her. 'Nothing like shouting it out loud.'

'Whatev, answer Bonni's question,' Fredi said sternly.

'Well, let me see,' Celia replied teasingly, pretending to talk to herself and counting off on her fingers. 'There were the two on the table. Then the kitchen – well, I don't know if that counts. We were dry-humping. But then in the bedroom, it was another two because the man really knows his way around a g-spot.' Looking back up, she said, 'Four. And a half. I'm counting the kitchen.'

'What is it with these Bryant men?' Fredi demanded, but she looked impressed.

Ava suddenly slapped her hand down on the table and they all jumped.

'What the fuck, Aves?' Bonni said, 'You scared the crap out of us.'

'Come on, there has to be another Bryant brother. These guys are like sexual dynamos. I want a brother.' Ava folded her hands in silent prayer.

'Sorry, not as far as I know,' Celia said. 'Bonni, are there any more brothers floating around out there?'

Bonni gave Ava a sad look. 'Sorry, honey, just the two.'

Ava sagged in her chair. 'That really blows.'

Fredi pushed her chair back from the table and stood. 'Well, now that we've established that all existing Bryant brothers are hot, wealthy dynamos in the sack, and taken, I'm going back to bed for a while.'

Celia pulled her phone over and checked the time. 'It's just after 7 a.m. You can't go back to bed now.'

'Babe, I know you miss your rugrats, but you are not the boss of me. I can go back to bed anytime I want. And I want.' She raised her eyebrows and looked sideways at Celia. 'I am all caught up on the drama in your life, especially since you kept sending me Snow White dwarf jokes yesterday after you went cave-walking, and I saw your sunrise. Since Landon has kidnapped you from us, you are his problem now, which means I can go back to bed.'

'But we were going to do stuff today. If you sleep for a few more hours, then you're sleeping the day away,' Celia said petulantly.

'She's right. We have plans.' Bonni nodded at Fredi. 'There's a wine-tasting festival at some nearby vineyards. Quinn is providing a car for us, and it's leaving at ten. So have your ass down in the lobby by then,' Bonni instructed.

Celia was glad that Bonni had taken over. She didn't want to waste the day. There was so much to see and, while she wanted to spend time with her friends, she also wanted to be with Landon. So she had to make every minute count.

'It's awesome you got that organized, Bonni. So what should we do until then?' She turned to look at Bonni. 'Should we give ourselves manis? Or walk around to burn off those divine pastries? What about after the festival? Did you have something in mind or—'

Ava interrupted. 'It's okay, Celia, don't worry about all this. Let's just go with the flow and see where it takes us.'

'Yes,' Fredi agreed. 'We want you to relax and enjoy being here. But honestly, I do need as much more sleep as I can get.' She came over and gave Celia a hug. 'Love you, babe. Now just chill.'

Celia sat back in the chair and broke off a piece of a pastry, popping it into her mouth. She watched Fredi head back into the B and B. Her friend was the only person she knew who could down three cups of coffee in a row and still be tired. Celia knew Fredi would be dead to the world the minute her head hit the pillow.

Across the table, Bonni asked Ava about a concert she and her boss had attended. Ava responded while Celia let her thoughts drift off. Maybe she should go back to bed too. Sneak back under the covers and give Landon a wake-up call he'd never forget. Yet she knew if she did that she'd have a hard time meeting her friends for the festival.

It had never bothered her when Frank spent long hours at the hospital. She had her writing and then the kids. She'd missed him, of course, but it was in the vague sense of something being off. With Landon, though, she found herself wondering if he was awake, if maybe he'd want to come to the festival, if they could make plans for after. She had a *longing*.

Celia glanced at her phone, hoping to see a text from him. But there wasn't. Once again, she found herself thinking of texting him. *Good morning. With my girls, you still naked? Last night was amazing and you make me think happily ever after isn't just a fairy tale.* Shaken, she shoved her phone into her pocket.

She gazed out over the rolling hills. This was a beautiful place. Landon was a wonderful man. Then why did she feel so unsettled? Why did she have the urge to find her kids and run away with them where Frank, Landon, no man, could find them?

And why did her heart break when she pictured leaving Landon behind?

Chapter 26

'It's a damn good thing we're only stomping white grapes,' Fredi said, as she did a fancy two-step inside the vat. 'I don't even want to think about what our feet and legs would look like if they were red grapes.'

'No kidding! Can you imagine the stains we'd have? Likely they'd take forever to fade,' Ava agreed.

'This is actually quite fun. There is something very satisfying about squishing these grapes into oblivion,' Bonni said, as she marched around the tub.

'They can't seriously be using these grapes for wine, though. What if somebody has athlete's foot, or fungus in their toes?' Fredi shivered.

Ava immediately halted and stared down at the squishy mess around her ankles. 'There must be a sterilization process. Or they don't use them. Right?' she said uncertainly.

Celia hopped in place, sending little splashes of grape goo toward her friends. 'Don't worry, Aves, alcohol kills germs, remember? That's why they pour good booze over wounds in the movies.'

Fredi immediately whipped out her phone and Celia rolled her eyes, knowing she was googling it. A young woman wearing a polo shirt with the vineyard's logo embroidered on the chest approached them.

'Excuse me, ladies, but we have a wine-tasting session set up if you would like to join us,' she said. 'Right over there. Here are some towels, and you can rinse off your feet with the warmwater tap by that bench.'

Fredi shoved her phone into her cleavage and climbed out of the tub. 'I'll be right there!'

'Fredi, don't put your phone next to your boobs. It's not good for them.' Celia watched Fredi to make sure she removed it. When Fredi gave her the stink eye, Celia pointed at her. 'Do it. Now.'

Fredi stuck her tongue out but took the cell and shoved it into her back pocket. 'Is this okay, Dr Celia?'

'Yes.' She pursed her lips in a kiss.

'Now, wine,' Fredi announced.

'What happened to "I'm quite happy with Jack"?' Bonni asked, as she swung a long leg over the side of the tub.

It was a little more awkward for Celia and she lost her balance for a bit when she got out, but avoided falling.

'I'm just impressed Fredi was able to get out of the tub without a boost,' Bonni snickered.

Fredi flipped her off as she began to wash off her feet. Ava gracefully exited the tub, doing a little plié using the rim as a barre, before heading toward the cleaning station. Celia took a towel and slung it over her shoulders as she waited for her turn with the water. She said, 'They do have this well thought out. When we left the B and B, it didn't occur to me that we'd need to wash off.'

Her feet free of grape residue, Celia sat down on the bench before realizing her shoes were back by the tub. 'Wait, Bon-Bon, before you rinse off, can you grab our shoes?'

'You owe me. If I attract ants, I get to buy Jilly and Colin whatever I want. Even if it's the noisiest toy in existence.' Bonni walked back to the tub area and collected their shoes, dropping them at her friends' feet with a thud before going to rinse off.

'Anyway,' Fredi continued. 'Free booze is free booze. We must get our money's worth, and who can pass up free booze?' Drying off her feet, she regarded them thoughtfully. 'Geez, these paws need a pedi.'

'We could do that later,' Ava suggested, inspecting her own toes and frowning.

'I'm done. Wine is calling my name.' Fredi stood, slipping into her sandals, before following the path and disappearing behind a lovely flowering bush that served as a wall.

'Hang on, wait for me!' Ava jumped up and followed her, leaving Bonni and Celia to finish up. Celia retied her sneakers and stood, bopping a little. While this didn't make her heart race like yesterday had, it was still really nice to do something new with her friends.

Bonni got up and rested a hand on Celia's shoulder as she pulled on her boots. 'Are you having fun, Cee?'

She nodded. 'Yes, this is the best. I really do appreciate you and Landon masterminding this weekend.'

'We knew you needed it.' Bonni squeezed her shoulder before they set out on the path.

Celia let her fingers trail along the bush, feeling the softness of the flower petals against her skin. 'So, how are you and Quinn doing?'

'Great. To go from a fling to something more, it does take work. There was a little bit of an adjustment period when he first moved in, but my lucky streak continues! I seriously can't imagine my life without him. Who knew things would work out so well?' Bonni raised her gaze to the sky, smiling at some secret memory. It warmed Celia to know that things were working out for her friend.

Bonni continued, 'I would feel even luckier if we became sisters for real . . .'

Her friend had unwittingly echoed Celia's earlier thought, and it freaked her out. 'Oh, wow. I do really like Landon, but marriage?' She plucked a leaf off the bush and twirled it between her fingers. 'How can I even think of anything more? I have kids. He's a CEO with a million demands on his time. I'm divorced and in the middle of a nasty custody battle. He's never been married. I won't say that this is just a casual fling, but I don't think we're meant to be.'

'Don't say that! You don't know what the future holds. I'm a prime example of life having other ideas about what's best for me.' Bonni reached out and picked a flower from the bush, tucking it into Celia's hair.

It was a sweet gesture and it reaffirmed why Celia worked so hard to keep her friendships solid, despite the demands on her time. Ava's laughter rippled through the air from the other side of the bushes and Celia and Bonni smiled.

'Sounds like we're missing out,' Celia said, as they rounded the corner to join their friends.

Ava and Fredi were mingling with other guests, and soon they were all sampling a variety of Napa Valley wines from whites to rosés to reds. Celia felt wonderful and her contentment from this morning came back with a vengeance. Being with her friends and having fun like this was just what she needed.

Celia hung back and watched Ava, Bonni and Fredi. She

loved her friends so much. At the barest hint that she was struggling, they had dropped everything in their lives, taken vacation time and flown to her rescue. Putting up with their elephant-like memories was worth it for this. She walked over to them and shimmied her way into their little group, loving the sense of family and friendship that enveloped her here, under the beautifully set up arbor, heavy with fragrant flowers.

'This looks like an Italian back garden where you see families having meals al fresco. You know, with a big long table groaning with delicious Italian foods.' Ava sighed. 'This is all just so romantic. I think I could get married here.'

'Ava, you would get married anywhere. All we'd have to do is throw a white dress on you, give a posy of dandelions and stick a willing man at the end of an aisle and you'd be good to go,' Fredi laughingly teased.

'You'd better just be nice to me. Otherwise, I won't let you design my wedding dress. I'll buy something off the rack,' Ava threatened, planting her hands on her hips and wearing her serious face.

'First of all, the way you've been hounding me over the past couple years, you'd better not think of buying a fricking rack dress!' Fredi said, acting outraged, before she went over and slipped her arm around Ava's waist. 'Second, if you think I won't design you the wedding dress of your dreams, one that princesses around the world will be jealous of, you are even crazier than I thought.'

Tears swelled in Ava's eyes and Celia had to fight back tears too. She had always been a sympathetic crier and getting married had always been one of Ava's dreams. In college, she had taken a culinary class, just so she could learn how to fold napkins into the shapes of swans.

'Oh, Fredi, you're gonna make me cry. You are the best. And

I love you.' Ava wrapped Fredi in a fierce bear hug. Fredi made a show of protesting the touchy-feely moment, but Celia could see her hug Ava back equally fiercely.

Celia glanced at Bonni, who was busy inspecting her wine glass, but Celia could see that her chin was quivering a little bit. She walked over and put her arms around her.

'What's wrong with us all today?' Celia asked Bonni.

Bonni sniffed and raised her head, blinking her eyes. 'I have no idea. I have to guess it's lack of sleep. We're all overtired because *someone* had to drag our asses to see a sunrise.' She bumped Celia with her hip. Celia released her and waved a hand dismissively in her direction.

'Whatever. You know you loved it.'

'I love that we're all here together,' Bonni told her.

Celia tucked her hands into the back pockets of her jeans as she watched Fredi finally attempt to break free from Ava's monster hug. 'Me too. If you guys hadn't kidnapped me, we wouldn't be here doing this, having so much fun. Plus, wine!'

Fredi finally resorted to stepping on Ava's foot and twisted free at her pained yelp. She immediately reached for another glass of wine so as to soothe her discomfort at having shown *feelings*. Ava started yelling at her and Bonni went to referee. Celia stood back, taking a beat to enjoy the moment before she redirected them to tasting wines and sampling the magnificent display of charcuterie that was set on the table beneath the heated sunlight that poked its way through the arbor of wood, leaves and flowers.

It was magical. Her friends were magical. And slowly Celia began to feel even better. This weekend was exactly what the doctor ordered.

Chapter 27

One vineyard later, Celia's phone buzzed in her back pocket and she pulled it out. Wandering off to lean against a pillar surrounded by an abundance of beautiful climbing roses, she took a second to appreciate the magnificent smell. She balanced her wine glass in one hand and her phone in the other, as she was eager to see who the message was from.

Her heart leapt when she saw it was from Landon. Quickly, she read it and then held her phone to her chest with her eyes closed as if it would somehow allow her to send him a cyber-hug. She looked at the message again.

Landon: *How's your day going, babe? Didn't hear you leave this morning. Missed you beside me.*

Celia thought for a minute about how to reply. Her first reaction was to tell him how much she missed him, all the fun things they had done today, and how much she wished he was there, but she held back slightly and chewed her bottom lip while she thought about it.

Celia: *You were sleeping like a baby :*) didn't want to wake you. Woke my girls up early instead. cu later? XO*

Landon: *Definitely. Have fun and I'll be counting down the time until you're back.*

Celia felt a nudge on her shoulder and turned.

'Was that your man?' Ava asked. You wouldn't think it from how sweet Ava was, but she could really hold her liquor. Still, she was rapidly approaching tipsy.

'He's not my man. Exactly.' What would it be like if he really were her man? 'But yes, it was Landon.'

'I'm really happy for you, Celia. I hope he fills you with joy and brings back the sparkle to your life. I know you've been off. We could all tell.'

'I didn't realize it was so evident. I was doing my best to hide it. And I didn't want to bring you guys down.' Celia dropped her gaze and scuffed a toe against the patio.

'Never. What else are friends for? If you can't complain about your dickhead of an ex to us, who can you talk to? For what it's worth, I'd be sorry for not kidnapping you before your wedding, if it didn't mean there would be no Jilly and Colin.' Ava gave her a hug and Celia returned it hard as she could. 'Wow, you must be going to the gym. You squeezed the breath out of me.'

Celia jokingly struck a bodybuilder pose, attempting to flex her biceps. 'Nah, it's just all the heavy lifting a mom has to do. Laundry baskets, kids, grocery bags, vacuum—'

'Okay, okay.' Ava chuckled. 'I get it.' She took Celia's hand and led her back to the crowd of people milling around the sampling table.

The next hour flew by as they left the second winery to go to a third. Now well past tipsy and sliding toward drunk, they were heading to a local market.

'Having a driver is pretty damn fantastic,' Fredi said.

'I have to agree with you there.' Celia nodded solemnly. Then she had a thought. 'I wonder if there'll be anything at the market I can buy for my kids.'

Ava shrugged her shoulders. 'Who knows? I think it features artisan vendors. So maybe not.'

'Glasses, girls. Let's finish off this bottle and then I think it'll be time for an alcohol break.' Bonni leaned forward and poured wine into their glasses.

'Yum, wine.' Fredi said with a big smile, and took a big sip.

'What's the deal with Mr Jack? Are you cheating on him?' Bonni asked her, clinking their glasses together.

Fredi shook her head, her curls tangling around her face. 'Nope. We have an open relationship. I'm very vulnerable to Mr Cabernet-Sauvignon's seduction. How on earth shall I resist?'

'I can see the attraction.' Ava nodded, her cheeks flushed from the alcohol.

'Me too.' Celia smiled and lifted her glass in the air. 'We haven't done a toast yet.'

She wished like hell they could toast her book. Hitting a bestseller list was something to celebrate, not to bury deep and hide. It just made her hate her ex-husband even more. She could only toast herself secretly for now. Hopefully, once the custody issues were settled, she'd be able to share the news with her friends really soon.

'Yes, a toast. But what to?' Bonni said, as she corked the empty bottle and rested it on the floor.

'How about to a great day? And great friendships. And great lives,' Ava suggested.

'I like that toast.' Fredi raised her glass up.

They all clinked their classes together and called, 'Cheers!'

Celia rested against the plush seat, as her friends chatted with each other and checked their phones, just comfortable being in each other's presence. They all seemed good with Bonni cutting them off. Perhaps they'd had a bit of a bender last night and that's why they had been so cranky about getting up early.

Her phone buzzed and she yanked it out. She had spoken to her kids before they had left for the tour and they'd been a weird combination of excited and miserable about the wedding. She had wished she could swoop in and make it better for them, but this was a new reality for all of them and they had to adjust. Her heart dropped when she saw the notification on her lock screen. It was an email from her lawyer. She debated whether to open it or ignore it. She really didn't want to drag her day down, and an email from the lawyer, on a Saturday, for crying out loud, could only herald some kind of disaster.

Celia decided she was going to forget it for now. If it had been urgent, she was sure the lawyer would have called. But the storm cloud that just materialized over her head was ominous, sending lightning bolts every which way. She had to shake it.

She snapped a few candid shots of her friends while they weren't paying attention and then called them. 'Hey, girls, look up and smile.' Celia took a few more photos.

'I wasn't ready!' Ava whined. 'Take another.'

'No problem. We're not taking enough pictures. We need more to document our trip. And I'm totally sharing these on Instagram. I think I'll create a new story for us.'

'Ugh, you clog up my Insta with all this stuff,' Fredi huffed.

'You and your social media, Celia.' Bonni shook her head. 'I just don't understand the attraction.'

'Well, if you're going to go out on your own, Fredi, then

you're going to need to understand social media. It's a valuable promotional tool, especially for fashion,' Celia said.

'Who said I'm going out on my own?' Fredi looked around. 'Is something happening I'm not aware of?'

Ava looked at the others and shrugged her shoulders, holding her palms out and up as if to say it's a no-brainer. 'Not unless you've got something cooking. We just think you need to. We've talked about it a few times and we don't understand why you're so resistant to the idea. You have an amazing talent and create fantastic designs. And you're wasting it on that, that . . .' Fredi held up her hand and Ava stopped in her tracks. 'Fine. I won't call her a cow.'

'She's right, you know, Fredi. You really do need to consider it,' Celia told her.

'I'm happy to help you. Any business information you want – spreadsheets, Google documents, anything you need to get set up – I'm your girl,' Ava said.

'I appreciate it, guys, I really do. And trust me, it's not like this is something I haven't thought about.' She looked down at her hands and twisted her thumbs together. 'But I think I'm scared.'

'That's not surprising. Starting a new venture can be scary. But it can also be fun, exciting and very freeing,' Ava told her.

'Sometimes you just get comfortable. And you're afraid to make a move. And then sometimes things happen and decisions get made that you never expected. Like this weekend for me,' Celia said, pointing at herself with a big smile.

'Do you have any designs that you haven't shared with the boutique?' Ava asked Fredi.

'I've got a ton of drawings. You should know that. You're the worst offender about asking me to "just whip up a sketch".' Fredi made air quotes and spoke with a wry tone.

'I do not!' Ava said, aghast.

'Uh, yes, you do. But it's okay. It puts more in my portfolio.' Fredi gave her a wink.

'Then that means you have a whole line of wedding dresses ready for a collection!' Ava was excited.

'And you know you're going to have us as customers,' Bonni reminded Fredi.

Everyone swiveled their heads and looked at her in shock.

'Is there something you want to tell us?' Ava asked.

Bonni shook her head. 'I'm just saying. That you have three confirmed clients sitting in this limousine right now.'

'Three clients does not a company make,' Fredi advised.

'Regardless, we're not pressuring you,' Ava said innocently.

'Oh, yes, you are, Ava,' Fredi said, her eyes wide.

'Maybe a little. We'll stop talking about it. But just know we support you,' Celia said. She meant her words, but she didn't want to talk anymore about the possibility of her purchasing another wedding dress one day.

'Thanks, guys. I know you do. When I'm ready – if I am ever ready – you'll be the first to know.' Ava tried to hug Fredi again, and Fredi fended her off with years of experience.

Celia knew she related to how Fredi felt. It was like her writing. People didn't get it, didn't understand how it all worked, how creative people were so exposed. And it *is* terrifying. Once again, she wished like hell that she could share her career news with them.

'Look, we're here,' Ava said, gazing out the window of the limo. 'Doesn't it look cute.'

'Oh, I like the look of this place. I think these might be my people,' Fredi said.

'I thought *we* were your people.' Ava's voice held a slight hurt tone to it.

'You are. Of course, but arteests ... you know.' Fredi shrugged.

The women piled out of the limo and Celia was determined to take some pictures. This place was such book fodder! Already a plot was forming in her mind for a new setting and an artistic heroine. Maybe a vegetarian painter meet-cutes a guy like this, and it turned out he was a rancher, selling organic beef. Opposites attract was always a popular trope.

Just like her and Landon.

Chapter 28

'We have some of the best adventures,' Ava said, as she flopped on to her bed, shopping bags in a mountain surrounding her.

'We certainly do.' Celia didn't have nearly the number of bags the rest did.

'Oh my God, we have the wild-women adventures down to a fine art! I thought that guy was going to have a heart attack when you offered him five bucks for that sculpture, Celia,' Bonni said, as she went through the door into her adjoining room.

'How was I supposed to know he was a world-renowned something or other and his work went for thousands of dollars? It looked like something Colin would do in kindergarten,' Celia protested.

Her friends proceeded to tease her about her lack of class until Bonni shouted from her room, 'I don't know about you guys, but I could use a soak in the hot tub.'

'Oh, yes! Hot tub. I think that's a great idea! And you know what, now that we're back safe and sound, I'd really love some wine with my soak!' Ava rolled off the bed and put her bags against the wall.

'I'm going to go with my main squeeze, Mr Jack Daniels. I'll leave the wine for you ladies,' Fredi said, shouldering her bedroom door open to go through.

'Okay, that sounds like a plan. Let me just go change into my bathing suit,' Celia said, as she walked out on to the balcony. 'Downstairs in fifteen minutes?'

A chorus of 'yup's followed her from her friends' rooms. She stopped before her balcony door. Despite not having as many purchases as the other girls, being thrifty and all, she had managed to find some cute little things her kids might enjoy. Like a wall hanging with birds for Jilly and this weird little penguin game for Colin. He was so wrapped up in gaming now, she had to limit his screen time.

She also got something for Landon. Celia placed her treasures on the dressing table and took out what she had got for him. It wasn't anything big or expensive, but it had caught her eye. It was a paperweight and looked like it was carved out of an opaque rock. It had reminded her of the stone she'd found on the beach, and she just had to have it for Landon. He could put it on his office desk, if he wished, and maybe it would make him think of her.

Then she spun around to find her bathing suit. She had texted Landon during the day to ask him to drop her satchel off in her room. It appeared not only had he done so but that someone had unpacked and put away her clothes. Her bathing suit was tucked neatly into a drawer. Having her clothes hung up and folded was a surprise, since she hadn't had anyone take care of her like this since she'd said a mournful goodbye to the housekeeper. On the con side, having everything properly sorted showed just how poorly she'd packed in her haste to be kidnapped.

Celia pulled her bathing suit on and grabbed a fluffy robe from the bathroom. She remembered seeing a circular staircase that led down from their balcony to the terrace below. Dashing down the wood and wrought-iron stairs, she found the hot tub tucked behind a wall of beautiful flowering bushes, a fair distance away from the pool. She was the first to arrive and claimed a lounge chair in the sun.

Moments later, a waiter came to ask if she wanted anything, and Celia ordered a nice bottle of Pinot Grigio and a bottle of Jack for Fredi.

'Could we also have a jug of water with a lemon in it as well? And four glasses.' She smiled at the waiter,

'Of course, ma'am,' he said, as he walked away.

Well, wasn't that interesting? When Landon said, 'Yes, ma'am,' all she wanted to do was order him to pleasure her in bed, but hearing it from that young kid made her feel old. It was all about context, she supposed. Well, that, and the oh-so-seductive tone in Landon's voice as he said it. She shivered deliciously, despite the warmth of the day.

Celia stretched out on the lounge chair, waiting for her girls. The sun was going to go behind the trees shortly, so she decided to get in a bit of tanning. It was easy to drift off into a snooze, being serenaded by birds and enjoying the soft feel of the breeze over her skin. She drew in a breath and the scent of flowers filled her nostrils. This place was heavenly.

She grinned to herself when she heard her friends approaching. When they arrived, it was like they filled the little area with their energy. She could feel her old self bouncing back, emerging and rising up from the depths of despair she hadn't even really realized she'd sunk to. It was rather alarming to realize just how low she'd become, emotionally.

'So we need to get some wine,' Ava announced.

'No need.' Celia waved her hand, pushing herself up on the lounge chair, and fixed the back so it was upright. 'I've already taken care of that. Wine, water and Jack all on the way.'

'I cannot wait to get in that hot tub,' Bonni said, taking off the extra-large T-shirt she was using as a cover-up, folding it neatly and dropping it on to another lounger.

Ava gave a wolf-whistle at Bonni's reveal of a burnt-orange bikini that perfectly complemented her skin tone. 'Wow, since when do you wear bikinis?' Ava asked her.

'Why, don't you think I should?' Bonni lifted her arms, craning her neck to check herself out.

'No, of course not. You look great in a bikini. You just never wore one when we were younger. It was always a one-piece for you,' Ava replied, taking off her own cover-up to reveal a royal-blue tankini.

'I guess I changed then. Exercise has always been a priority for me, but I was never that comfortable with my body until I met Quinn. He makes me feel beautiful no matter what I wear.' Bonni smiled secretively to herself, her gaze lifting to the sky, before lifting one shoulder in a slightly sheepish manner. 'So feel free to check me out as I get into the tub.'

Bonni sauntered over to the stairs into the tub, giving her hips an extra swing or two, and Celia yelled, 'Work it, girl!' Bonni's words had stirred something up within Celia, as her sex life with Frank had begun to deteriorate after Jilly was born and had died completely after Colin's birth. She had been able to lose most of the baby weight by pushing Jilly around in her stroller every afternoon under the hot Californian sun, but her breasts, her belly – they weren't the same. And when Colin came along, it was even harder to find time to exercise, or to eat healthy when it was easier to eat what the kids ate.

Landon, though, he didn't seem to mind the stretch marks

or what *she* felt were no-longer-perky boobs. They still weren't bad, and she resisted the urge to cup and push them up a bit. His passion for her made her feel sexy and desirable. She knew, logically, that her self-worth should never be based on what a man thought, but after what Frank put her through, it felt really good to know she could still make a cock crow.

'I'm coming in too.' Celia pushed herself out of the low lounger with a grunt and walked over to the tub. Holding the railing, she reached out with her toe to test the water. 'Holy shit, it's hot. What's the temperature?'

'A hundred and four degrees, and absolutely divine,' Fredi, who'd already got in, informed her.

Celia made hissing sounds as she slowly lowered herself into the tub, her arms curled up and hands fisted. 'Geez, who are you, Khaleesi or something?' Finally, she was in shoulder deep. 'Oh yeah, this is nice.'

'Khaleesi? Who's that?' Fredi asked, languidly moving her arms through the water.

'I'm dumbfounded. You don't know who she is? Mother of Dragons, the Unburnt, who can walk through fire and bathe in scalding water. Khaleesi, widow of Khal Drogo, Breaker of Chains, Daenerys Stormborn of the House Targaryen?' When Fredi gave her a blank look, Celia continued, 'You know, the Iron Throne, "Winter is Coming". Fredi! *Game of Thrones!*'

Fredi shook her head. 'Nope, never watched it.'

Celia was aghast and stared at Ava and Bonni. Ava, who was sitting on the edge and dangling her legs into the water, just shrugged, and Bonni mirrored the action. Celia looked back at Fredi, who was now resting her head against the tub's rim, her long, curly hair piled on her head and her eyes closed. 'No words, I—'

Fredi held up her hand. 'Not important.'

Celia snapped her mouth shut. There was a lot she could say about *GoT*, but there was no point. Instead, she duck-walked her way over to an underwater seat that had a multitude of jets pulsing out water. She maneuvered into the seat and groaned when the pounding water massaged her back and shoulders.

'Who in their right mind has never seen *Game of Thrones*? I mean, Jason Momoa and Jon Snow, for crying out loud,' Celia muttered under her breath. 'She knows nothing.' Tilting her head, she rested it against the edge and closed her eyes. Her body was somewhat battered after skydiving, zip-lining and having extremely passionate sex, all in one day. A slow smile curved her lips as she remembered the time she spent with Landon. They had texted a couple times during the day, and she was expecting to see him tonight. 'Ahh, this is the life.'

'Now, that's for sure. No cranky clients, hanging with my girls, all the wine I can drink. I could so get used to this,' Ava commented, as she slipped into the tub and found her own spot by some jets.

Celia opened one eye to check out where all her friends were. Each had a corner in the big tub. She smiled at the contented look on their faces. Once again, she thanked her lucky stars for that professor and the crazy seating arrangement that had allowed them to meet. She shuddered to think what her life would be like without her friends.

The waiter returned with their drinks. Sliding the tray on to a nearby table, he offered to bring them something. Bonni opted for a glass of water while Celia requested wine. Curling her fingers around the delicate stem of the plastic – which could totally pass for crystal – wine glass the waiter offered, Celia thanked him and then relaxed back in the tub. Honestly, this is not how she expected to feel on the day her ex-husband was getting remarried.

'Oh, my!' she said, pressing her toes against the floor jets. 'Heaven.'

'Mm-hm.' Bonni agreed with her. Celia didn't think she'd ever seen her friend this relaxed. After spending years as a cop in Canada, Bonni was preparing to move down to Virginia to be closer to her dad in the next while. Normally, a huge move like that would render her completely uptight and unable to rein in her control-freak tendencies. Yet here she was, just going with the flow. Celia absolutely credited Quinn for that.

As if thinking his name invoked him, Celia heard masculine laughter and easily picked out Landon's rich tones, and then someone said, 'Would you look at these bathing beauties?'

Celia sat upright, blinking away the moisture in her eyes, to see Landon and Quinn standing over them with appreciative expressions on their faces. Fredi jerked with a jolt, splashing a little, and Celia realized she'd fallen asleep. Fredi would be nocturnal if she could.

'Quinn!' Bonni rose from the water and stepped out of the tub.

Quinn handed her a towel, which she wrapped around herself, and he pulled her into the circle of his arms, paying no attention to Bonni's hair dripping on to his shirt. 'You made it,' Bonni said.

He nodded. 'That I did. My favorite cop breaking the law by aiding and abetting the kidnapping of her best friend? Wouldn't miss this for the world,' he said, winking at Celia. She toasted him with her wine glass.

Fredi twisted so she could fold her arms on the colorful tiles surrounding the hot tub and look up at the boys. 'Hi, Landon. Don't you look mighty fine today,' she said, batting her eyelashes at him and deepening her southern drawl.

Landon laughed good-naturedly, well aware of Fredi's master-flirt status. 'Well, hello, Miss Fredi, aren't you the prettiest picture I ever did see?' He tried hard to mimic Fredi's accent but failed miserably. His New England voice couldn't quite manage it. Fredi shook her head and half-heartedly splashed at him, catching Ava in the crossfire.

'I think you mean "pretty as a peach", my fine gentleman.' She gave him a coy look.

'Fredi, you got my hair wet!' Ava wailed, shaking her head, like she could shake off the water somehow.

Fredi quickly pushed herself up and out of the hot tub, heading for the table with the drinks. Pouring herself a measure of Jack, she replied, 'Don't look at me. Blame Landon's Yankee-ness.'

'I do apologize, Ava, for not being able to imitate Miss Fredi's oh-so-dulcet tones,' Landon said teasingly, 'but despite her very unladylike action, I can assure you that you are still a vision from heaven.'

Ava shielded her eyes from the sun when she looked up at him. 'Do you practice that charm, or does it just come naturally? And do you happen to have any attractive single male cousins? Perhaps a youngish uncle?'

Fredi had arranged herself on another lounger, her assets displayed to perfection in her emerald-green bikini. 'Celia, come get your man before Ava turns him into her pimp.'

Celia rolled her eyes but stood and began moving toward the stairs. Landon leaned down to grab a towel and met her by the bottom step. He offered her a hand to hold as she climbed up them, and she liked how gentlemanly he could be. He wrapped the towel around her shoulders and pulled her into his embrace when she shivered at the temperature difference.

'I'm going to get you all wet,' she protested half-heartedly, not wanting to leave his arms. It felt so good to be there.

'I don't mind.' He rubbed his hand over the towel, creating a lovely friction that warmed her up.

Turning slightly so they were facing her friends, Landon said, 'I'm sorry to report that, while we do have cousins, they are assholes and quite unworthy of Ava, and all our uncles are doddering old men.'

Quinn and Bonni had been whispering to themselves but, at Landon's words, Quinn interjected, 'I'm going to tell Uncle Randall you said that.'

Landon gave his brother an irritated look before focusing on Celia. 'I'm actually here to steal you away again.'

'You are rekidnapping me? What now? Off-roading in an ATV? Hang-gliding? Swimming with sharks?' Celia was being flippant but was half afraid one of her guesses would be correct.

He smirked. 'Well, those are interesting future date ideas, but I was thinking we could take a drive down to San Francisco for the night.'

'For the night? Like a sleepover?' She bit her lower lip and looked up at him through her lashes.

He tightened his arms around her and her belly did a little tumble. He said, 'Well, first, I thought I'd romance the hell out of you over a nice dinner, but then I'd be very, very open to a sleepover. Can we play games?' His tone was heavy with innuendo and his eyes held a mischievous glint.

'But my friends? I've barely spent any time with them,' she said in a lower voice, hoping they wouldn't hear.

'Are you out of your mind? We spent all day together. Go, silly!' Ava burst out. She had reclaimed her seat in the hot tub, stretching out her long legs, now that she had it to herself.

'If you don't go, I will,' Fredi said, her eyes hidden behind her large sunglasses. 'Besides, I'm sure Bonni will ditch us too.'

Bonni flipped Fredi off without looking and said, 'Quinn and I have some things to do tonight so we're tied up. Go have fun.'

'I don't know, Bonni,' Quinn replied, 'Perhaps we should spend time with Ava and Fredi after all, and that way we could get our money back for that deluxe spa package you arranged for them.'

Ava's arms shot up in the air triumphantly. 'Yes, free spa day! Imma gonna get a pedicure.'

Fredi said regally, 'That is an acceptable offering. You may abscond with our friends.'

'On that note . . .' Landon said, and Celia reluctantly stepped back so she could collect her things. She bent to the lounger to pick up her robe and, when she turned back to Landon, she caught him checking out her ass. He grinned unapologetically before taking the robe to hold it open so she could slip in. Once she had her room key and her phone, he took her hand, kissing the back, before entwining their fingers.

Celia turned and waved goodbye to her friends. 'Have a great night, guys. Talk to you later.'

Ava said, 'Details, please, when you get back.'

Landon tipped his head toward Celia. 'It's all up to her. She'll have to tell you the details, because I never will.'

'Don't be good! Play "Never Have I Ever"!' Fredi called after them.

Celia tossed her a look over her shoulder and saw Ava waving goodbye and laughing.

'I think kidnapping her was the best plan we ever had,' Celia heard Bonni tell her friends as Landon whisked her away.

Oh, girls, you have no idea.

Chapter 29

The drive to San Francisco passed quickly as they chatted about life events, the latest movies they had seen and got into an argument about whether or not peanut butter should be smooth or crunchy. When they arrived at the hotel Landon had booked for the evening, he parked in a spot that was tucked between a couple pillars. The valet didn't say a word except for 'Evening, Mr Bryant' as he held open Celia's door.

Taking Celia's hand as she got out of the car, Landon stopped before the man. 'How are you tonight, Robert? And your daughter, is she doing better?'

'Yes, she's doing much better, thank you for asking, Mr Bryant.' Robert looked pleased and Celia couldn't say she blamed him. She glanced at Landon, seeing another side to him. He couldn't stay at this hotel that frequently, and yet he still remembered the valet's name and his family. She smiled to herself as Landon grabbed her overnight bag and discreetly slipped Robert a large tip.

They walked across the driveway toward the hotel, and she

looked up at the glass-and-chrome structure. It had a very modern element to it, but it was clear to see how the architecture of an older and more classic San Francisco building was incorporated into the building's design.

'Do you stay here often?' she asked. 'It's a gorgeous building.'

'Thanks. We own it,' he replied, nodding at the doorman and opening the door for her himself. 'I don't spend too much time here, though, because I usually prefer to stay up at the vineyard if I'm in the area. This is like my lay-over stop, if I have business in the San Francisco office.'

'Wow.' Celia was blown away. She'd known Landon was rich, of course, but it had never sunk in that he was *rich*. Standing inside a luxury hotel that he owned, it hit her like a ton of bricks. She was a single mother struggling to support her kids, fighting with her ex for desperately needed alimony and child support, and she was involved with a man who could probably afford to send both her kids to Ivy League universities with the spare change in his pocket.

'There's a store I want to take you to,' Landon said, leading her through the lobby of the hotel and down a wing to a row of stores. He escorted her into a very posh store called Feminine Wiles, and she saw a sales associate take one look at Landon before racing to the back of the store.

'Why are we in here?' Celia walked over to a rack and held up a lovely sundress by the hanger. The fabric was so soft and the pattern was very appealing. She checked the price and froze in shock.

'I want to buy you a few things.' Landon took the dress from her hands, holding it below her chin. 'Do you like this one?'

Numbly, she pointed at her bag, which he'd set on the floor. 'I brought clothes. You don't have to buy me anything.' What was happening right now?

'Yes, I realize that. But I do want to buy you something. A gift.' He gave her a cocky grin.

'Landon . . .' Her voice trailed off as she tried to find the words. 'You've indulged me way too much already. I can't accept anything else.'

'Of course you can.' She wasn't sure what was written on her face, because she barely understood how she felt herself, but he sobered and raised his hands to cup her cheeks. 'Darling, I wanted to get you a present and I thought you would enjoy picking it out yourself. If you don't want a new dress, there's a jeweler I like two doors down, and a great chocolatier on the third level. It doesn't matter to me what it is, Celia, I just want to do something to make you happy.'

She lifted her hands to grab his wrists, searching his eyes. He could have bought her a candy bar and she would've been happy, but the only gestures he knew how to make were grand ones, by normal standards. She could turn down the gift, but she knew it would hurt him. And that was something she couldn't bear to do.

'You make me happy by just being you,' she said.

His gaze softened, and he replied, 'Celia . . .'

She released his wrists, pressing a finger against his lips and leaning a cheek into his hand. 'But if you insist on showering me with expensive gifts, I will accept out of the kindness of my heart. Because I too am a giver.'

Landon beamed at her – there was really no other way to describe it – and smacked a kiss against her lips. Letting go of her face, he dragged her over to a nearby wall. 'Take a look. Anything you like?'

Celia's clothes these days leaned toward durable and washable, but she'd been friends long enough with Fredi to recognize talent when she saw it. 'These look like couture.'

'Not yet, but they will be one day,' Landon said, waving off the store manager, who was hovering at a discreet distance.

She looked again at the display. 'What do you mean by that?'

He grabbed a slinky olive-green dress that she knew would wash her out and held it up against her. Shaking his head, he put it back, saying, 'The designer's name is Samantha Wiles. She worked in the hotel here for a long time, starting out in housekeeping, before going to college on a Bryant Enterprise scholarship. She got her degree in fashion and is slowly making a name for herself. I like to support her as much as I can, so this store carries her designs.'

Celia smiled, liking what she heard. 'You don't realize what a nice guy you are, do you?'

He frowned and furrowed his eyebrows to make a mean face. 'Who, me? I'm supposed to be a ruthless CEO without a heart, if my dad has anything to say about it.'

Celia laughed. 'Okay, okay. To help Samantha along on her journey to couture, let's see if anything will flatter me.'

During the next few minutes they chose a few dresses for Celia to try on. They really were quite beautiful, and she was eager to tell Fredi all about the store and how Landon had helped this designer along. She bet that Bryant Enterprises had a hotel somewhere that was a popular wedding destination and would be the perfect location for a wedding-dress boutique. She wasn't comfortable asking Landon for things for herself but, for Fredi, she'd sex him up until he saw reason.

The store manager opened a changing room for her and Celia tried on two dresses, which Landon quickly rejected. Pulling the last dress on, she fell in love with it immediately. It was vibrant, a deep blue-toned red with yellow polka dots. It hugged her waist and flared out over her hips, ending just above her knee. The collar was low and wide with narrow straps that sat at the edge of her shoulders. She had to take her bra off due to the positioning of the neckline.

When she exited the changing room, Landon stood immediately when he saw her. He stared at her silently, taking her in from head to toe. His gaze scorched her as if he were touching her with his hands. She began to breathe quicker, as she stood under his gaze. Her desire was rising and she could see it was equally matched by his.

'It's perfect,' he told her, and stepped forward. Taking her fingers in his, he held them up so she could spin around slowly. 'Yes, absolutely perfect.' With his free hand, he gestured to the store manager and she handed Celia a pair of yellow shoes. They were high heels but still wouldn't make her tall enough to look at him eye-level. 'And these,' Landon said.

Celia lifted the shoes to look at the size and saw their red soles. With a surprised look, she met Landon's gaze. 'Loubies?'

He nodded and grinned at her, looking utterly delighted with himself. Her earlier reluctance at accepting such an expensive gift from him completely disappeared because of the way he made her feel like a princess. Rising on to her toes, she leaned up and kissed his cheek. Softly, she said, 'Thank you for my present.'

Bringing her hand to his lips, he kissed it again, and then asked, 'You're happy?'

There was only one response she could make. 'Yes, sir.'

His nostrils flared and his hand clenched on hers. Winking at him saucily, she went into the changing room to redress in her street clothes. Once out of the dress and after hanging it up, she was about to pull her clothes back on when she heard her phone buzzing in her bag. Fishing it out, she saw it was a call from Frank.

'Why is he calling?' She fumbled to open the phone, suddenly panicked that something was wrong with Jilly or Colin. 'Frank? What's wrong?'

From outside, she could hear Landon say her name, and the door handle rattled. On the other end of the phone, Frank said, 'Have you read the email yet?'

'What email?' Just hearing his voice made her grit her teeth. Then she remembered the email from her lawyer that she had received earlier today.

'Try not to be a ditzy blonde, Celia. Your lawyer would've sent you one earlier today.'

Her hand clenched on the phone. It was moments like this when she wanted to go back in time and shake some sense into her younger self. 'Frank, your wedding is today. Why are you calling and bugging me? You should be with your bride.'

'Katarina is in full support of this. She's equally worried about the element you're exposing our children too.'

Celia froze. He knew about her writing career. That had to be why he was calling. She was desperate to look at the email right now, but she didn't want to put Frank on speaker, because people would be able to hear him. Namely, Landon.

'What *element*? What are you talking about?' she demanded, as she struggled to put on her clothes. She'd be damned if she continued this conversation while naked.

'This Uncle Landon the kids keep referring to. I can't believe you've actually brought some likely a leech of gambling addict that you met in Vegas around our children.'

Celia's mouth went dry. Had he seen the Instagram photos? Had she been wrong about posting them? Oh God, had she just shot herself in the foot? Or . . . maybe the kids had talked about him. Yes, that was probably it, since Frank didn't really do social media all that well. 'Landon's a friend, and he's certainly not a leech or an addict. Most importantly, he's no concern of yours.'

'That's where you're wrong, Celia. It is my concern. Anyone who chooses to vacation in Vegas most definitely has question-able morals. I hope you don't bring him into your bed with the children asleep in the next room,' Frank said.

The truth of why Frank had agreed to watch the kids when she went to Vegas with Bonni and the girls had suddenly been revealed. She should have known he would never do anything out of the kindness of his heart. 'Don't be a dick, Frank. You're just doing all this to make me miserable. May I remind you that you're the one who left? You're the one who fucked around and now you want to drag Landon into this? I never stooped to attacking Katarina. You have some nerve. You do realize that the longer you drag this out and the more acrimonious it gets, the more it's going to affect the children. Think of them.'

'I am thinking of them, and that's why I'm going for full custody,' Frank said smugly. She wanted to reach through the phone and strangle him.

'What?' she shrieked, and her vision began to go dark.

A knocking on the changing-room door snapped her out of a red haze.

'I have to go, Celia. It's almost time for the reception. Read the email.'

'Frank, wait—'

The phone went dead and Celia grabbed it in both hands with a fury that burned like a solar flare, and she tried to twist the phone, to destroy the instrument of her anger, before throwing it into her purse as she flopped down on the chair.

'Celia, are you okay?' Landon called.

She drew in a shaky breath and rested her head on the wall, staring up at the ceiling.

'Yeah, I'm fine. Be out in a minute.' She did her best to compose herself, but how she hated that man. She had to bank her anger, to put it aside. Landon was waiting. So she stood, gathered up her purse, the polka-dot dress and the shoes and opened the door.

Seeing Landon on the other side, his face etched with concern, made her feel miserable. What a difference a few minutes and an encounter with her ex could cause.

'What happened? Who were you talking to? I heard you yell.' He took the dress and the shoes and handed them to the store manager.

'Nothing.' She had no energy to say anything other than that.

'Don't tell me it's nothing. I can see it on your face. Hear it in your voice. Something happened.' He backed her into the changing room so they could have some privacy.

'Landon, I don't want to talk about it.' She heard the pissiness edge her voice. Damn Frank for ruining things. She looked at Landon, and his face shuttered closed. It broke her heart to know that her failed marriage was causing this new tension between them.

'Celia, don't shut me out.'

She shook her head, unsure what to say. She couldn't burden him with her problems.

'Celia, you have to understand that, if we are going to grow together, we have to be honest. Let me in. Let me help you.'

She couldn't meet his gaze. It was too painful to see the hurt in his eyes. 'I can't. It's not your fight.'

He grabbed her arms, giving her a little shake. 'Don't you know by now that I would fight windmills for you? I'd bend over backward to give you and the kids anything you needed. I am not your ex-husband, why can't you see that?'

Now she looked at him and the anger she felt for Frank came rushing out. 'Don't tell me what to do. Why is everyone always so ready to control me?'

Landon released her and took a step back. He looked like she'd just tried to slap him. 'I'm not trying to control you. I only want to help you.'

'Well, you can't. Just let me figure it out,' she snapped.

He didn't respond. He met her eyes for a moment and then walked out of the room. Pivoting on his heel, he walked back, framing himself inside the doorway. 'I have spent my entire life under my father's thumb. He's told me, practically since I was born, who to be friends with, what sports I can play, what subjects to study – everything. And he and my mother, their marriage, it's more like a business partnership. She brought in family money and he used it to grow Bryant Enterprises into what it is today. He would love nothing more than for me to find some wealthy society debutante and lock her down in some iron-clad prenup that lets me do whatever I want while giving her nothing. I don't want that. I've never wanted that.'

Celia caught her breath at Landon's intensity. Frank's behavior paled in comparison to that of Landon's father. How could anyone want that kind of life for their child? 'Landon, I'm sorry—'

He shook his head, interrupting her. 'There's a part of me that doesn't remember my life without you in it. And there's a part of me that *can't* see my life without you in it. So I forget that, really, we haven't known each other long. I can wait for you to catch up. I'm here for you whenever you're ready to tell me. Whenever you're ready to let me be there for you.'

There was a pause as he seemed to wait for a response from her, but Celia was trying to remember how to breathe. Straightening, he glanced over his shoulder and then reached out a hand to her. 'Come on, darling, we have reservations for a sunset dinner. Let's go buy your presents and collect your bag. Then we'll go up to the room so you can change.'

She nodded and took his hand with trembling fingers, still silent. Landon guided her over to the register, and she avoided the speculative gaze of the store manager as she tried to process what had just happened.

All Celia knew – the only thing she was absolutely certain of – was that Landon was different to her ex. She couldn't paint him with the same brush. The only similarity they shared was that they were both men. One man shattered her heart and the other was putting it back together.

One piece at a time.

Chapter 30

The tension between them hadn't entirely gone away, but it settled to a low hum after he brought her up to the owner's apartment on the top floor of the hotel. After gawking at the incredible view and luxurious furnishings, she had spent entirely too long getting ready for dinner. She didn't feel her new dress was appropriate for a fancy dinner, so she wore the sexy pale green dress she had packed and paired it with her new shoes. They didn't quite match, but she wanted to show Landon she really did appreciate his gift. Judging by his reaction when he saw her, it worked.

Now, Celia was stunned by the opulence of the restaurant as the maître d' led them to a table set with white linen, silver and fine bone china at the windows overlooking the bay. 'This is so spectacular.' She gazed out the windows and couldn't believe the view.

'Reservations for this restaurant can be as far off as six months,' Landon said in a low voice as the maître d' held out her chair for her. She was slightly taken aback when he helped her closer to the table. He took the napkin from in front of Celia and draped it over her knee, then rounded the table and repeated the process with Landon.

Celia made eye contact with Landon, and she saw he was trying to hold back a grin at her discomfort. She stuck her tongue at him and was grateful that the maître d' pretended not to notice.

Once the man left, Celia settled into the chair and put her purse on the little stool the maître d' had placed beside her. She looked at Landon under her eyebrows. 'Seriously? They have a chair for purses?'

Landon laughed. 'Yes, they do.'

'Wow, I'm impressed.' Celia subtly fished out her phone and took a picture of the purse chair to post later to her author Instagram account. Her followers would get a kick out of this.

A waiter, dressed in a very subdued black suit and tie, approached their table. The man bowed his head slightly and handed Landon the leather-clad menu. 'Mr Bryant, the wine list.'

Landon glanced at the wine list before replying, 'We'll have a bottle of 2009 Two Sons with dinner. Celia, would you like a cocktail beforehand?'

She thought frantically. She had no idea what to say. She couldn't exactly order a rum and Coke at a place like this.

'Hendricks with Fever Tree tonic and a slice of cucumber, please.' She was so relieved that the idea for that drink had popped into her head. The only other thing she could think of was a martini, shaken, not stirred, and this didn't seem like a place that appreciated pop-culture humor.

'Of course, madam.' The waiter looked at Landon. 'Your usual bourbon, Mr Bryant?'

'Yes, thank you, Michael.'

Moments later, Celia reached for the glass Michael had just placed on the snowy white tablecloth. She hadn't been much of a gin drinker until a friend bought a Hendricks for her in a bar a few years ago. 'You come here frequently when you're in town too?'

'It is a bit of a snobbish place, but the food is excellent,' Landon said, and took a sip of his drink.

'So do you come here alone, or on business or, with . . .' Her voice trailed off because she was suddenly not sure she really wanted to know.

He gave her a tight smile. 'Do you really want to talk about that right now?'

He was right, but something had made her ask and it was bugging her that he could have brought other women here. But he'd had a life before her. She had to remember that and not let the little green monster creep in and disturb their peace.

'No, you're right.' She shook her head. 'I was just being nosy and I should mind my own business.'

Landon opened his mouth to reply when a different waiter brought a basket of breadsticks and flatbreads, placing it on the table with a small bowl of whipped butter.

'You really have to try this.' Landon picked up a triangle of flatbread and broke the tip off. 'I have no idea how they prepare it, but it's addictive, and this butter is as well. It's got a sweet flavoring that I can't place.' He pointed to the pot of butter with his knife and then scooped a bit out, spread it carefully on the corner he'd broken off, and handed it to her.

Celia popped it in her mouth. 'Oh God. This is so good, I could probably have just this bread for dinner.' Landon buttered another piece and offered it to her before buttering one for himself.

They munched in silence for a bit, and then she felt compelled to speak. 'I have to thank you.'

She sat forward in her chair and rested her forearms on the table, lacing her fingers together. He dabbed at his mouth with his napkin and then asked, 'Why is that?'

'Well, you've treated me like a princess, right down to my fabulous new "slippers".' She made the air quotes with her fingers and was encouraged by a corner of his mouth quirking up. 'I'm so spoiled. How on earth will I ever re-enter my normal life? Ah, it's been so magical, and I'll carry the memories with me for ever.'

Landon mimicked her pose, folding his hands together as if to keep from reaching for her. 'I told you. I'll always do whatever it takes to make you happy.'

His quiet and serious words dropped on the table like an unexploded bomb and the simmering tension ramped up again. Twisting her fingers together, she looked down at her hands. This felt like one of those moments, the ones where the world was holding its breath for a decision to be made. Raising her gaze, she found Landon watching her, waiting for her.

'You know I'm divorced.' An expression of relief crossed his face and she knew she had made the right choice. 'I thought it was settled and we could all start moving on. But Frank, my ex-husband, also known as Dickhead, decided to take me back to court, to try and reduce his payments to me and the kids and change our custody agreement. And he's pulled the trigger on all this on the same weekend that he's getting married to the woman he cheated on me with.'

Landon was silent, and she waited for him to say something. But he didn't. She realized then that he was giving her space to tell him everything she wanted to without interrupting.

'That's where the kids are, with their dad, being a flower girl and the ring bearer. It's why the girls chose this weekend for the kidnapping. I only answered his call because I thought something might have happened with the kids.' Her mouth felt dry and she took a sip of her drink. 'Earlier today, I received an email from my lawyer, while I was out with the girls. I chose to ignore it. Because, seriously, who in their right mind does legal transactions on their wedding day? He used it as a pretext for the call.'

She sighed and drooped in the chair. 'He's going for full custody. The kids have talked about you, called you Uncle Landon. I think that's what set him off.'

Landon straightened, as if his spine had been replaced with a steel rod, and his hands tightened into fists. 'Seriously? He's angry about me and he's the one who is getting remarried? To someone he cheated on you with? And he's trying to take Jilly and Colin away from their mother – from *you* – so he can save *money*?' If tone could kill, Frank would be dropping dead at his reception right about now.

Taking another swig of her drink, Celia waved the glass in the air as she said, 'That's the gist of it. Now you see what poor decision-making skills I have.'

'In no way should you see this as a reflection on you.' His voice was icy, and Celia knew the ruthless CEO had made an appearance. 'Since I now seem to be part of this equation, you will let me help.'

'Oh, *will* I? No, Landon, it's not fair to you. And I have to do this on my own. I need to. I have to know that I can take care of my kids myself.' She hated the pleading tone in her voice, but she needed to make him understand. Celia could see the frustration on his face and, while she didn't want to offend him by not accepting his help, this was bigger than a dress and shoes. This was her life. This was her kids' lives.

He stared piercingly into her eyes for a moment. Then he dropped his gaze and reached for his bourbon. 'How are Jilly and Colin taking this?' he asked.

'I've been protecting them from it as much as possible. I don't want to put them through any more. The divorce was hard enough on them, what with being ripped away from the home they were born and raised in. We had to move to a smaller place so that I can manage the payments on it and put food on the table. The other house got sold and the proceeds were put into a trust for their education. Frank insisted.' She paused and looked at him. 'I'm not having a pity party here, it's just reality.'

She shook her head and took another big gulp of her drink. 'It's just so hard, trying to keep them in the sports and the activities that they love . . . no, I would never let them know what's going on. It's not fair to them, and he is their father, after all.'

Celia saw Landon's jaw clench, but before he could respond the waiter brought over their menus. Landon took a moment to order them starters and requested that the wine arrive with those dishes instead of their entrees. The waiter discreetly faded away. Before she could open her menu, Landon said, 'I can make it all go away. You do know that, right? I can bury him in lawyers, dig out every skeleton he has and make him apologize for every iota of hurt he's ever caused you.'

Celia wasn't going to lie: it was just as tempting as when Bonni had suggested it. Yet she knew she needed to be able to stand on her own two feet. It was impossible to predict what could happen in life and she needed to know that, no matter what, she could take care of her kids alone.

She slid her hand across the table to capture his fingers with hers. She said, 'I'll make you a deal. Let me handle this, my way, and not only will I keep you in the loop, if I feel things are getting out of hand, if I feel there's a possibility I might actually lose my kids, I will let you unleash the dogs of war. Deal?'

He brushed a thumb against the back of her hand before saying, 'It would be a lot easier, and faster, if you would just let me—'

'Deal or no deal?' she interrupted. She wasn't going to budge on this, and he had to prove that he respected her stance.

The struggle was clear on Landon's face as he battled his internal impulses but, finally, he lifted their hands and gave a little shake. 'Deal.'

The wave of happiness she felt was indescribable. Forty-eight hours ago the possibility of entering into another relationship seemed as unlikely as Pluto being recategorized as a planet, and here she was establishing a solid foundation with Landon. If he wasn't careful, pretty soon she was going to start thinking of him as the 'B' word. Squeezing his hand, she let go and opened up her menu.

Chapter 31

'There are no prices,' Celia whispered, leaning over the table.

'I know. It's fine. Don't worry about it. Please, just order what you think you will enjoy,' he said, as he opened his. She studied the list of dishes, chewing her lower lip.

'I always try to have something I would never have at home. So I think I will have the venison.' Most people thought of Bambi when they thought of the dish, but she'd had it once a long time ago and had found it tasty.

'What would be your next choice?' Landon asked, as he put his menu down on top of hers.

'I think I would probably get the lamb. That's something else I wouldn't normally have at home.' She eyed the bread basket again, questioning if she wanted another piece or if she could hold on until the starters arrived.

'I tell you what, since you're getting the venison, I'll get the lamb. That way you can have a taste,' Landon said.

'That's really thoughtful of you. And, of course, I'll share my venison with you.' He really was the perfect guy. Not everybody could share food. Ava, for example, would give you the shirt off her back if you needed it, but try to steal a fry from her plate and you could expect a fork being stabbed into your hand.

'I think it's going to be an amazing sunset.' Celia rested her elbow on the table and propped her chin on the back of her hand.

'It certainly appears to be that way,' he replied, but his gaze was fixed on her.

Seconds later their starters were brought to the table and the sommelier presented the bottle of wine to Landon. After the process of uncorking and tasting, she filled their glasses and left. The waiter then magically appeared, and they ordered their entrees. After he left, she picked up the goblet, swirled the wine and sniffed at the bouquet that rose up.

'You do that like a pro,' Landon told her.

'Well, I had a good teacher, did I not?' Celia gave the glass another swirl and then raised it to her lips for a sip. 'Mmm, this is delicious.'

She reached for the bottle and turned it so the label faced her. 'Two Sons? Napa Valley. Oh my God! This is from your vineyard.' She looked at him, stunned.

'Why is that such a surprise?' Landon asked her, and took the bottle to pour more into their glasses.

'I don't know really.' She raised her hands in wonderment. 'I mean, you have a vineyard. Vineyards make wine. But, for some reason, I never put two and two together. I guess I just thought you'd have wine at your vineyard and the B and B and it wouldn't be available out in the wild.'

'It's one of our top sellers, actually. Our mother decided to call this brand of wine after Quinn and me. She always says that, despite its immature start, it has a lot of potential.' He laughed.

'That's not very nice thing to say.' She couldn't help but giggle. She knew he was much fonder of his mother than he was of his father. She wanted to talk about what he'd said in the store about his father, but this didn't feel like the right time. They'd already addressed one heavy topic tonight.

Twisting in her seat, she took a picture through the window of the sun setting behind the Golden Gate Bridge. Turning back, she caught a look of disapproval from a snooty-looking woman two tables over, and she flushed in embarrassment. Slipping her phone into her purse, she picked up her salad fork and stabbed a tomato.

'Why are you so fond of social media?' Landon asked, clearly having not missed the small interaction.

She swallowed before replying. 'Well, I've always been big about documenting events through photos. My father died when I was very young, and my mom had these big photo albums full of pictures. It made me feel connected to him, even though he was gone.

'So when Facebook came around, I started posting pictures there, to share with all my family, and things just kind of snowballed from there. I like connecting with people. Plus, you know what they say, when you put things up on the Internet, they're there to stay.'

Landon didn't respond at first, and Celia was afraid he thought she was childish, but then he stopped a passing waiter. 'Would you take a picture of us, please?'

She was beginning to think she was falling in love. Quickly unlocking her phone, she passed it to the waiter and scurried to sit in Landon's lap. He was a little startled, but adapted fast, ignoring the scandalized gasp that came from two tables down. Beaming at the camera, she looked at the lens as the waiter took a couple shots.

Happily taking the phone back as she returned to her seat, she scrolled through the photos. Picking the best one, she texted it to Landon and the girls, choosing to wait until later to post it to her Instagram. He pulled out his phone to look at the photo and then said, 'I told you. I'm here to support you.'

Simple words from an incredibly complex man. He went on calmly eating his salad as if he hadn't just rocked her world. Was it too soon to tell what her feelings truly were? She had far too much drama going on, and the baggage she carried was ridiculous. It wasn't fair to embroil him in her life until it was more settled, but it was too late now. He was hers, and she was keeping him.

Chapter 32

Landon watched her look around, quietly taking in her surroundings, and the expression on her face told him how much she appreciated what she saw. The other women he'd been with had been so full of expectations and a sense of entitlement, simply because they were with him and he had money.

This was why he'd become so jaded with women. But Celia was different.

She had started reawakening him to the world around him. When had he become immune to its beauty? Why didn't he notice the glorious sunsets and sunrises and the wonders of nature like he used to? Somewhere along the way he'd started taking it all for granted. He huffed out a breath. He'd been taking a lot for granted lately. It wasn't until meeting Celia in Vegas and being bowled over by her exuberance for life that he realized just how much he'd been missing. It was like he was seeing the world through a new set of eyes.

Part of him was surprised at how easy it was to forget that he had to go back to the office and the ever-growing number of emails waiting for him. Being with Celia was so much more important right now. He loved being with her. He loved seeing her delight in things around her. He loved getting to know her better.

And right now he knew, with all his being, that he loved her.

Of course, he had plans for a delicious seduction of Celia, but it was so much more than that. He wanted to whisk her away to other places, show her things she'd never seen before. And he was definitely going to figure out how to get her kids up to the adventure park, her ex-husband be damned.

Listening to Celia talk about her divorce and her ex-husband brought forth emotions that he'd never felt before. Instantaneously, he hated the man. It took every ounce of control he possessed to keep that feeling from showing on his face when she was telling him what happened. He couldn't tell her how he felt because it would have been for him and not for her. All he could do was be here for her, a safe place for her to share her feelings, and not have her worry about visiting him in the slammer after he killed the man.

Besides, he was rich. He could hire someone to do it.

Suddenly, Landon felt calm. Like a huge weight had been lifted from him and he was filled with light. The odd poetic turn of phrase made him think of something.

'How is your writing coming along?' Before Celia, he had never known anyone who earned money by writing poetry to sell to greeting-card companies.

Her head snapped around and he saw alarm reflected in her eyes. Landon furrowed his brow, wondering why.

'Writing? Well, it's going good. I've sold a couple greeting-card things. And I'm waiting to hear back from a few magazines.' Celia reached for her glass of wine and he noticed her fingers trembled a little bit.

'That sounds interesting. What kind of magazine articles?' he asked.

'Ah, I pitched another music article, one about gun control versus gun banning, and a series on pairing teas with romance novels. I'm hoping I get to do that one. After looking at this view, I think I'd like to pitch something for a travel magazine. Oh, and a parent magazine contracted me for a column about being a single mom. If I get lucky, they might make it into a regular feature.'

'I'm impressed.' Landon thought that to write such disparate articles took a lot of skill. 'Tell me more about the column.'

'It was a single-mom story, actually. I hadn't realized I could write funny and, apparently, I can.'

He laughed. 'You do have a sense of humor, there's no doubt about that. I'm not surprised that someone recognized how talented you are. Congratulations.'

Landon finished off his bourbon and put the glass down at the edge of the table, where it was quickly removed by the very attentive staff. 'Do you think you'll ever write a novel?'

That odd look crossed her face again and she picked up her gin to finish it off. 'Oh, maybe. I've kind of been working on one.' She put her glass down with a *thunk* and Landon was about to pursue the topic further when their entrees were brought out.

There was quiet for a few minutes as they dug into their meals. 'How's your venison?' Landon asked as he cut off a piece of rack of lamb and put it on the edge of her plate.

'It's very good. And this sauce is life-changing.' She rolled her eyes upwards in an overly dramatic expression of delight, and he laughed at her.

'That's part of what I love about you – how deeply you feel things, your emotions. How you find pleasure in pretty much anything,' Landon said, forking up another bite of his lamb.

Had he just said the 'L' word? Celia didn't know what to think of it and tried to be nonchalant and not react, but it was the hardest thing she'd ever tried to do. How could you not freak out when a man like Landon used the 'L' word?

'Oh, I hadn't really thought about it.' She pushed around the tip of an asparagus on her plate. 'People go through a lot worse than what I've gone through, so I can't really complain. I just have a bump in the road right now and that road will even out eventually.' She jabbed the asparagus with her fork and chomped it between her white teeth.

'An excellent way to look at life. You force me to see the world through new perspectives all the time.' Landon put his knife and fork down and reached for the crystal salt-and-pepper shakers.

'I do?' She looked surprised by that.

He nodded, answering her while he shook a bit of pepper over his potatoes. 'Yes, you do. It's no secret that I grew up privileged. I was raised to want – and expect – the best of everything. The world opens up when you have money; there are no barriers and very few limitations. However, paradoxically, it also narrows your world. Since you exist in this wealthy bubble, you lose touch with how things work for everyone else. It's easy to become arrogant, ruthless, controlling.'

'You, arrogant or ruthless?' Celia pressed her lips together and shook her head. 'Nope, I don't think I can see it. But controlling?' She shrugged playfully. 'There is that.'

He laughed, but her words did give him a pang.

'Well, two out of three isn't bad, but trust me—' He took a forkful of his very peppery potato. 'I have a bit of a reputation.'

'Well, if you don't want that reputation, you can always change.' She cut another piece of venison and before putting it in her mouth she caught his gaze with hers. 'But you've never shown me that side of you, so I have a hard time imagining it.'

'I think you have a pretty good imagination. You are a writer, after all.'

'Yes, but I can't see you as an alpha a-hole hero,' Celia said, and a startled look crossed her face before she clamped her mouth shut.

He laughed. 'What the hell is an alpha a-hole hero?'

'Oh nothing, just writer talk.' Celia focused on her dinner and Landon smiled.

He suddenly had a burning desire to never let her go. To keep her close to him, so he could ease whatever ailed her. She had children. Would she want him to be involved in their lives? Children had never been on his radar before. But he wanted to give her and her kids a life where they'd never have to worry about anything again. However, he knew it would have to be something they discussed. Celia had made it abundantly clear that she wasn't with him for his money and that she wasn't comfortable with him sharing it with her. Despite being able to have everything he wanted with a snap of his fingers, Landon began to feel like something was missing in his life.

What if it was Celia and her kids?

Chapter 33

After dinner and a scrumptious dessert, they returned to the hotel apartment and stood on the terrace outside his bedroom. Celia leaned back into him and sighed when he wrapped his arms around her waist. 'Thank you for the wonderful evening.'

He stood behind her and pressed her up to the balcony railing. She still couldn't believe he occasionally lived at the top of this posh hotel. Landon slid his hand over her torso and up along her shoulders to caress the side of her neck. She tilted her head toward his hand, loving the feel of him. He ducked his head and pressed a gentle kiss against the corner of her mouth. 'I'm glad you enjoyed it.'

She nodded. 'I did, and I'm glad we talked.'

'Me too. I'm happy you felt comfortable to share everything with me,' he said, dropping another kiss on the curve of her neck.

She hadn't shared everything. Firmly pushing her book out of her mind, Celia turned in his embrace and draped her arms over his shoulders.

'Thank you.' She loved being close to him like this and was so glad that her confession over dinner hadn't made him run screaming. Instead, he'd offered help.

'You're very welcome, and now here we are,' he murmured against her lips, igniting a longing in Celia.

'Yes, together. Alone. Just you and me.' Celia opened her mouth under his and he stole the breath from her with a deep kiss. She moaned at the ache she had for this man and ran her hands up his arms, over his powerful biceps, sliding them along to his neck and into his hair. Arching her back, she pressed her body to his. Never would she be able to get close enough to him.

'Come here.' She pulled his head down and rose up on her toes, but he lifted her off her feet and she gave a surprised 'oh!'

He held her at his eye-level. 'Now this is better.'

'What, am I too short? Hmm, I might take offense at that. Does this mean you don't like short girls?' she teased, and nuzzled his cheek, enjoying the scent of his aftershave and the stubble rough against her skin.

Celia was comforted, aroused and more content than she had been in years, being in this man's arms. Plus, Landon's oh-so-casual mention of the 'L' word during their dinner conversation was a delicious memory she wanted to hang on to.

'I have no problem with short girls. And it's not that you're short, I'm just tall.' He chuckled and tightened his grip.

'You know what makes it fun when you're a short girl?' She wrapped her legs around his hips and he easily held her bottom with his other hand. 'This.' Locking her ankles together behind his ass, she tightened and squeezed until she felt his cock hard and insistent against her.

'I think I could get used to short girls.' He chuckled, and they came together with a ferocity that stole her breath away. It was a frantic tasting, a steamy clash of mouths. Their bodies crashed against each other and Celia was unable to breathe.

He carried her through the apartment, but she didn't see anything as they passed through all the rooms. It wasn't until he'd laid her down on a grand bed in an even grander bedroom that she got her bearings.

She rose to her knees and pulled her dress over her head. But she held it out to him, not wanting it to get crumpled. 'Hang it up, please.' She gave him her best puppy-dog eyes.

He took it from her. 'A little impatient, are we?' After doing as she asked, he followed her cue and shed his top, his pants coming off shortly after. 'Seeing you like that, kneeling in the middle of my bed, with those shoes on—'

'How about, rather than talk, you just get here and join me?' Celia reached her hands out, wiggling her fingers. 'Come.'

He was beside her in a second, growling, 'I plan to.'

She pushed him down and fell on top of him. The heat of their passion ignited her to a point where all she wanted was to feel him in her. On her.

She curled her fingers around the waistband of his briefs and yanked them down, freeing his cock. Tossing his shorts aside, Celia wrapped her fingers around him, stroking lovingly and watching the expressions cross his face. Straddling him and sitting on his thighs, her hand still wrapped around his hard cock, she looked at him lying there in front of her, his eyes closed and a look of desire and happiness on his face. What she saw filled her with love for him, and that realization tilted her world. Suddenly, she had the burning urge to tell him. But she decided to wait until after they made love.

'Landon,' she whispered, stroking his cock. His eyes fluttered open. 'I'll be right back, I have condoms in my purse.'

'There's some in the drawer.' His voice was husky with

passion, and she paused. She didn't want to use those. It wasn't entirely rational, but she felt like those condoms were a big reminder of the women he'd had before her. Why else would he have condoms in a bedside drawer? Clearly, they were for times like this. With other women.

Celia swung her legs off the bed and stood, shaking her head. 'No, I'd rather not use those. I'll get mine.'

Landon reached out with his hand and grabbed hers, staying her. 'Why don't you want to use the ones in the drawer?'

She hesitated and looked down at him. Could she tell him why? She decided that she should. If they had any kind of future together, she had to be honest. As much as she could be, anyway.

Celia sat on the edge of the bed and clutched his hand. 'Well, it may sound stupid to you, but it's very real to me. For you to have them in the drawer means that they were there for . . . uhm . . . other people.' She lifted her shoulder and, when he went to say something, she put her fingers over his mouth. 'I know you had a life before me, I'm not naive, but those condoms only remind me of that.'

'Celia—'

'No, let me finish—'

'No, Celia, let me talk before you go off on a tangent.' He raised his eyebrows and tilted his head toward her. 'Okay?'

'Okay.' She squeezed his hand tighter, wondering what he was going to tell her now. She wasn't sure she wanted to know. Yes, she didn't want to know.

'Those condoms in that drawer were put there two days ago. When I knew I'd be seeing you.' He reached forward and cupped her chin in his palm. 'So you see, Ms Celia, those there are for no one else but you.'

Tears pricked her eyes. 'Oh my God, I'm going to cry . . .

and over condoms.' Celia couldn't believe how wildly her emotions were swinging.

He smiled, and it brightened her world. 'You can cry with me anytime. I'll never judge you, or criticize you for the reason why you might be crying.' He pulled her into his arms and she snuggled next to him. 'I want to be your safe haven. Somewhere for you to run if you need to.'

She wasn't sure what to say, her heart was so full.

Landon cuddled her until he felt her move. Then he knew she was okay and over her moment of insecurity. She was complicated. It was one of her many endearing traits.

Landon rolled her on to her back, pressing her into the sheets. He was captivated by Celia and knew that he had to find a way for them to spend more time together. Knowing he wouldn't be able to see her every day after this weekend made him feel like his heart was being ripped out with a dull and rusty knife.

'My foxy beauty,' he murmured, and leaned down, sealing his mouth over hers. She softened under him and slid her legs wider. She wound her arms around his neck and held him in a vice grip.

He broke off the kiss, sucking in a breath, and moved to sit on the edge of the bed. 'I can't get enough of looking at you.'

Celia's eyes were half closed, her skin flushed, and it was the sexiest thing he'd ever seen. Landon smiled at her white cotton panties and bra. The closure at the front was easy for him to snap open, but he didn't remove it, loving the way her breasts stayed cradled in the cups, hiding the view of her from him. The temptation to take it off was huge, but he resisted.

He trailed the back of his hands downwards, between her trembling breasts, greatly enjoying how her nipples rose up to press against the fabric.

His mouth watered. He remembered all too well how good she tasted. How wonderful her heavy nipples felt between his lips. But he remained sitting beside her, loving how her eyelids fluttered as he touched her, and continued the track of his fingers lower, over her taut belly and to the edge of her panties. The innocence of the white cotton was such a dramatic contradiction to the passionate woman that lay before him.

He slipped his fingertips underneath the edge and she arched her back, causing her breasts to pull free from her bra, exposing the beautiful globes to his gaze. He leaned forward at the same time he slipped his fingers underneath her panties. Taking her nipple between his mouth and pressing his fingers into her folds, Landon brought out the passion lurking inside her.

She was wet, hot, and he couldn't resist any longer. Swiftly, he got a condom from the drawer and slid it on to his throbbing cock.

Her eyes were open and she was staring at him, the sea-green tumultuous with her arousal. He was getting to know her very well, and the look on her face right now was a look he wanted to put there for the rest of his life.

'Landon, don't make me wait. I've been waiting for you all day.' Celia reached her hands up to his shoulders as he slid her legs wider still and settled into the cradle of her thighs. They both fell silent as he reached between them and guided his cock into her opening.

Her legs snapped around his hips and her arms tightened around his shoulders. He gathered her to him and slowly thrust his hips. Tightness. Heat. He groaned as her body accepted him.

He pumped and she met him, and they fell into a steady cadence that carried them both higher. But Landon wanted to see her ride him. He rolled, taking her with him, and now she was on top, her hair wild around her shoulders. Her breasts bounced as she rocked her hips on him, and he reached up and cupped them.

Her eyes closed and her head fell back. He rubbed his thumbs across her nipples while her fingers reached between them.

Landon loved how she could be herself with him. Sexually, she was what every man dreamed of. Her breathing came shorter and a flush bloomed across her chest. His orgasm was close, but he bit it back. No way would he come until she had. Watching her now, he knew she was close.

He dropped his hands to her hips and held her tight. Thrusting up into her, she met him stroke for stroke, and then she seemed to pause, hovering on the edge. Her breathing stopped as she held it, then she fell across him with a cry and he felt her pussy throbbing around him and he was no longer able to hold back.

Landon growled as his orgasm crashed through him.

With quiet, ragged breathing, he and Celia lay in the aftermath of their pleasure. Slowly, he moved her off him and into the crook of his arm. She made a soft moan, one that told him more than any words ever could how satisfied and happy she was.

He lay staring up at the ceiling and realized he was the happiest he'd ever been in his whole life. And it was all because of this wonderful woman in his arms.

One thing crystalized in his mind: he would do whatever it took to keep her.

Chapter 34

The bright light shining into the room discombobulated an awakening Celia for a moment. She wasn't quite sure where she was until she felt someone next to her.

Her lips curved and she turned to look at Landon. She fully expected to see him sleeping, so was surprised to find him watching her.

'Have you been awake for a while?' She rolled on to her side.

'Yes, I have. I don't sleep much, as a rule.' He folded an arm behind his head and reached out to tuck a strand of her hair behind her ear.

'Insomnia?' she asked, as she wiggled a little closer.

Landon shook his head. 'No, not insomnia. My brain is very active and I spend a lot of time thinking.'

'Oh? About what?'

'You, as a matter of fact.' Landon looked at her, his eyes steady and clear, but she could see there was something he wanted to say.

'What about me?' She furrowed her brows and twisted the

sheet in her fingers as a little trickle of alarm grew low in her belly. Something told her she wasn't going to like what he said.

'I've been thinking about your situation. And you know I want to help you.' He sat a little higher in the bed, resting his head on the ornate carved wooden headboard.

She shot up into a sitting position, clutching the sheet to her chest. 'Landon, we talked about this. We had a deal.'

'I know, I know. I'm not trying to go back on our agreement. I respect where you're coming from. But I want you to know that I am here for you, should you need anything. I have so many lawyers – a huge legal team that could make your whole situation with Frank go away. They could crush him like a bug.' She could tell that Landon was leashing himself for her. The need to destroy Frank was practically vibrating off him.

'Thank you. I appreciate the offer. I've worked hard since my divorce, painstakingly so, to overcome my feelings of inadequacy. And you've really helped me these last few days. I want you to know that. You've brought me in touch with the woman I used to be, before I married Frank.' He lifted an arm and she snuggled into his chest, trailing a finger between his pecs and watching his muscles involuntarily contract.

'I'm glad. But I also want you to think about something else. I'm considering the possibility of permanently basing out of the San Francisco office of Bryant Enterprises. It's still a fair distance away from your home, but I would be nearby if you needed me and I could visit you and the kids. If you wanted me to.' Landon's voice had the barest hint of vulnerability and she raised herself up so she could search his face. The sun shone in the window, lighting his face, and Celia could see by his expression that he meant it.

This was a really big step, but it was also an incredible one.

She immediately wanted to cry out an agreement, yet her writing career hung over her head like a guillotine. She needed to tell him about *A Hot Vegas Night*, but now that Frank knew about her relationship with him it was even more likely that he'd get dragged into the legal proceedings. She really needed to talk to her lawyer and resolved to respond to yesterday's email with her questions.

Celia took too long to reply, and she could feel Landon's body stiffen. Pressing a gentle kiss to his lips, she said, 'I think it would be amazing if you came to visit. You'd be welcome any time you wanted.'

His eyes lit up and then he was hugging her, his arms clutching her tightly against him. Pulling back, he smacked a kiss on her cheek and she knew Playful Landon had returned.

'So, I have an idea. Go get dressed and I'll take us for a drive.' She quirked an eyebrow at him and he made a cute *oops* face. 'Okay, I can totally read your mind. I didn't mean to *tell* you we were going to do this but rather *ask* you if you'd like to go on another date with me. I was thinking we could drive over the Golden Gate Bridge, to a place that I really like called Muir Woods, and then head back up to the vineyard.'

Celia laughed and nodded her head as she climbed out of the bed. 'I think it's a wonderful idea. Before we'd go, I'd like to call Jilly and Colin, check in with the girls and post a couple pics to my Instagrams. But first it's shower time.'

She tossed a pillow at him and disappeared into the bathroom, laughing when she saw Landon was hot on her tail.

After extremely athletic shower sex Celia exchanged a few texts with the girls and complimented Ava on her pedicure after her friend sent her five pictures of her newly polished toes blinged out with sparkles. Then she had an all too brief conversation with her children, which left her feeling worried and unhappy while she posted some of the pictures from last night to her personal and authorial Instagrams. Landon attempted to distract her from her bad mood by tickling her, causing her to mess up more than one caption.

Now she was packed and they were off in the Bugatti as they headed to Muir Woods. The fog had rolled in from the sea and driving across Golden Gate Bridge was almost ethereal. However, Celia was rather disappointed that there was nothing to see except the great arching support of the bridge disappearing high into the mist.

'What a shame. I was looking forward to the view as we crossed the bridge,' she said, as she peered through the miasma.

'The last couple days have been good – it's lucky to have sunny days in San Francisco. Fog is normal. Chilly is normal. But there's just something about the city that calls to me,' Landon said, as he guided the car around slower traffic on the bridge.

She nodded in agreement. 'I feel the same. It has an energy, something different, that just seems to click with me.'

'We might drive out of the fog as we get further away from the city.' He flipped on the wipers at a spatter of rain on the windshield. It was cozy in the car with him and Celia fiddled with the radio so that light jazz was playing as they drove.

Landon was right. The further they drove up the highway away from San Francisco, the clearer it got. She turned around in the seat to see how the wall of fog just seemed to disappear behind them. 'It really is weird how it rolls in, isn't it?'

He looked in the rear-view mirror. 'Yes, it is. Sometimes you can see it swallow up valleys as it climbs over the hills. It can be kind of eerie.'

He slowed the car down and turned into an entryway. The

trees were magnificent here and she saw a big sign welcoming them to Muir Woods National Monument.

'Wow. This is magical,' she said, looking up at the forest as they drove into the parking area.

'And you haven't even gotten into the park proper yet,' Landon told her, getting his phone out and showing his parking permit to the attendant. 'They've made changes, and you have to reserve parking now. There's no cell service or Wi-Fi here either.'

'Oh, so no Instagramming from the park. How will I survive?' She snapped her fingers with self-deprecating humour. 'Wow, look at the crowd of people.'

'It's a very popular location,' he said. 'It's like this place holds the very essence of an ancient California. Some of these trees are almost a thousand years old and over two hundred and fifty feet tall. It's incredible.'

A few minutes later they were walking down a path and Celia was in awe as she craned her neck to look up. 'Oh my, this place is wonderful. Imagine what these trees have seen. It's heartbreaking so many were cut down.'

They wandered down the path under the majestic California redwoods. The cool of the forest bathed them and she breathed in deep.

'I like coming here.' Landon took her hand as they walked deeper into the forest, along the paths, both boardwalk and paved, constructed to keep people off the forest floor. 'See this tree, how it's hollowed out? Go stand in there and I'll take your picture.'

Celia did, and was dwarfed by the tree. 'It's all black inside.' She touched the wood and looked at her fingers, but no black rubbed off.

'This sign said it was struck by lightning and scorched on

the inside,' Landon told her while he took photos. 'Lots of the trees have been struck.'

'And they didn't burn down. Wow, that's amazing.'

'Come, there's more to see.' He took her hand again.

Celia felt the dream-like hush of the forest. Looking into the shadowed woodland, all shades of green with patches of sunlight that shone through the canopy, Celia was positive a twinkly faerie would fly by at any moment.

Suddenly, Landon pulled her into the belly of a huge tree and kissed her. 'You like it here?'

She nodded and returned his kiss with a fever that she was becoming addicted to. 'I do.'

'Me too. But mostly I love that I'm sharing it with you.'

'The forest is enchanting.' Celia gazed up into Landon's face, utterly smitten with him. Her belief that she was in love with him was becoming ever more certain. She could see in his face that he was feeling the same about her.

They held hands and wandered around the forest, enjoying the peace and tranquility as it washed over them. Celia barely noticed the people who rushed past them as they dawdled. There was only her and Landon and nature.

Chapter 35

Their forest adventure was over and the feeling of being connected stayed with Landon as they drove back to the vineyard. She didn't have to say a thing, and he felt good inside, a profound, satisfied feeling that was rare for him. He liked how they were becoming more and more comfortable with each other. It gave him hope that she was catching up to him, that if he moved to San Francisco, they could eventually figure out a way to build a family.

They made a stop along the way for lunch. It was quick, but they took the time to see if there was something he could buy for her kids at a roadside market that she could take back to them. She also checked her phone for any messages, swiping through a bunch of Instagram notifications to answer a series of increasingly cranky texts from Bonni, who wanted to know when they'd be back at the vineyard.

He'd caught Celia watching him more than once, and his heart felt full at the look in her eyes. He was a contented man with this woman by his side.

After a leisurely drive they arrived at the vineyard in early evening. He was almost reluctant to share her, but he knew the fast way to end their relationship was to try to keep Celia from her friends.

'What's going on?' Celia asked, after seeing many cars parked out front of the B and B.

'I have no idea. Maybe we ought to go in and see.'

He pulled the car into one of the reserved spots set aside for his family. He got out and walked around the car to open her door.

'Thank you, kind sir.' She stepped out and they walked hand in hand to the back of the building.

As they crossed to the terrace his first thought was they were crashing a private party. There was a big crowd, and he had no idea who most of the guests were. But then he spied Quinn.

'Hey, bro!' Landon called to him. He was standing next to a bar that had been set up under a market umbrella. His brother made a gesture to someone in the crowd and Bonni appeared.

Quinn and Bonni wove their way through the crowd to meet them.

'Glad you made it,' Quinn told him as they shook hands.

Bonni stepped forward and gave Celia a hug and whispered in her ear. 'The one day you are not surgically attached to your phone! You look great, by the way. Did you have a good time?'

Celia hugged her friend hard. 'It was phenomenal, except for Dickhead, but I'll tell you later.'

Quinn and Landon wandered off to get drinks, as Bonni nodded to the crowd. 'Fredi and Ava are over there holding court.'

Celia cackled at the sight. 'Good for them! Think Ava will

try to sneak one home as a souvenir?' Ava and Fredi were surrounded by a few men, all of them chatting and laughing, as the men seemed to fall over themselves trying to do things for them.

'Come on. Now that you're here, it's time.' Bonni stepped out of a waiter's way as he passed with a tray of empty champagne flutes.

'Time for what?' Celia was curious. Why *was* this party happening?

Bonni pulled Celia over next to the bar and, shortly, Ava and Fredi joined them. Landon came up behind Celia and gave her a glass of wine.

'Thank you. Oh, wow, I'm parched.' She guzzled back a few gulps and loved how Landon remained behind her, resting his hand on her hip. She smiled up at him and he dropped a kiss to her hair. Lord, this man had her feeling all the feels.

'Excuse me, folks, but can I have your attention for a moment?' Quinn and Bonni stood side by side, and Celia had a strange feeling. She looked at Ava and Fredi. Ava looked equally curious, but Fredi was grinning.

'I knew this was coming. I've got a sixth sense for it now,' she whispered.

Quinn continued: 'We'd like to thank you all for coming to our last-minute party. But we do have an announcement to share with you. Tonight, we're thrilled to share with you the news of our engagement.'

Ava screamed with delight, while Fredi and Celia eyed each other competitively. There could only be one maid of honour. A round of cheers and congratulations from the guests rose up on the night air.

'Please join us in our celebration with champagne and dancing. The night is young.'

Quinn swept Bonni into a hug, bent her back and kissed her soundly, which caused a riot of hoots from everyone.

'Oh my God. Bonni is getting married.' Ava had tears in her eyes.

Celia grabbed her friends' hands and pulled them through the crowd, abandoning Landon without a second thought. 'Bon-Bon! You sneaky thing, you! Congratulations, love.'

The women all fell into a group hug.

'I'm so glad you are all here to share in our news. I had a helluva time keeping it from you.' Excitement edged Bonni's voice.

'It's wonderful news,' Celia told her. 'Have you set a date yet or made any other decisions? Like the wedding party, just as an example?'

Fredi rolled her eyes and nudged Celia back, giving Bonni a sideways look. 'I guess this means a wedding-dress design is imminent?'

'Yes, of course! I'd only wear a Fredi original. And we haven't worked out the rest of the details yet, but we're thinking of a destination wedding.' Bonni laughed in sheer delight, and Celia thought she had never seen her friend look lovelier. But there was still the important matter of who would be the maid of honour to discuss. Before she could begin to campaign, a woman interrupted their celebration and they turned to her.

'Excuse me,' the stranger said, looking at Celia with a very weird expression on her face. 'I'm sorry to intrude, but I have to ask. Are you Jena Fox?'

Celia's heart dropped and she shook her head in helpless denial.

'I'm sorry, you're mistaken, this isn't Jena Fox,' Ava answered for her.

'Are you sure? She looks just like the picture.' The woman pulled out her phone, tapped the screen, then turned the phone to show them the picture of Celia and Landon the waiter had taken last night, posted on Instagram. 'The caption is gibberish, but that's you, isn't it?'

'Uhm, I – I . . .' was all Celia could stammer. She must have posted the picture to the wrong account. Here, of all places. At the worst time possible. She was going to be outed as an erotica author. She wasn't ready!

'I knew it! I told my friend it was you.' She turned around and yelled, 'Mary, it *is* her! I told you!' Then the woman rummaged in her oversized purse and pulled out a book.

'Oh God,' Celia groaned. She dared not look at her friends for fear of what she might see on their faces.

'Would you mind signing it for me?' The woman was fangirling all over Celia, and she didn't know what to do. 'This book is so good. I never meet men like Byron when I go to Vegas! He's just so . . . wow. I wish I could meet a man like him for a fling.' And then she giggled like a little girl.

'What? Vegas?' Fredi asked. Celia could see her stretch out her hand as if to snatch the book, before she thought better of it. 'May I see the book, please?'

The woman handed it over. 'It's amazing. I highly recommend it. I wasn't surprised at all when it hit the bestseller list. All the bloggers are talking about it.'

'Bestseller!' Ava squeaked, peering over Fredi's shoulder at the book.

Bonni crossed her arms and glared at Celia. 'What's going on?'

'Guys, I . . .' Celia was at an utter loss for words.

'It's called *A Hot Vegas Night*,' Fredi said.

'Holy shit,' Bonni said. 'What did you write?' She grabbed the book from Fredi and read the back-cover blurb. Celia watched her relax when she realized it wasn't about her and Quinn. Bonni raised her gaze. 'Does Landon know?'

Celia shook her head slowly.

'Does Landon know what?' His voice came from behind their little group and Celia spun around. She was sure panic was written all over her face, and the smile on his face froze. Icy fingers clawed their way up her spine.

'Oh Lord, Mary, look, it's Byron in real life! He looks just like I pictured him.' Celia's fan was ready to melt into a puddle at Landon's feet. 'Would you sign my book too?'

'Byron? Book? Celia, what is she talking about?' Landon's gaze searched the group and landed on the book Bonni was clutching to her chest. He held out a hand in an imperious demand for the book, and Bonni's gaze darted to Celia. She slowly nodded. What was the point in keeping it from him now? Bonni held the book out to Landon.

'Let me get you a pen. Mary, do you have a pen?' the woman said, rummaging through her purse again.

'Please, give me a moment, if you don't mind.' Landon read the back cover, then opened the book and flipped through the pages, stopping on one to read a few lines.

Celia's heart stopped when she saw the thunderous look on his face.

'This is us?' His voice was low. It held a tone she'd never heard before. And what it could mean scared her.

Celia nodded, her mouth dry and still unable to say a word. She wanted to tell him their relationship had merely been the inspiration behind the book. Everything they did wasn't transcribed on the pages, she had just used it as a launching pad. But she couldn't. She was tongue-tied. And she knew that only made it worse.

The woman offered a pen to Landon, but he waved it off,

handing her the book back instead. She turned to Celia, holding out the pen and book. 'Please sign it. Make it out to Joan.'

Celia kept eye contact with Landon while she took the book and pen being shoved at her. On autopilot, she scribbled something before giving the book back. The woman ran off to her friend, waving the book in the air.

Without a word, Landon turned and walked off. He left her behind, to wonder if this was it. All he'd ever asked from her was honesty and trust, and she still held this back. She started to cry, and she knew it was going to be an ugly cry. Her friends had her by the arms and literally swooped her off the terrace and up to their rooms. She hadn't even felt her feet move.

All she felt was her heart, the heart that had been slowly mending under Landon's care, shattering into a million tiny pieces.

Chapter 36

'Oh my God, I can't believe this is happening.' Celia wrung her hands and cried.

'Now calm down. There's no reason to get all crazy. You don't know what he's going to say or do.' Ava put her hands on Celia's shoulders, massaging them lightly.

'Bonni, I can't believe this is happening on the night you announce your engagement. What kind of friend am I?' Celia wailed.

'While I do wish the timing had been a little better, I have to say it's fucking amazing that you're a bestselling author!' She came over and took Celia's hands in hers, stopping her from wringing her hands together.

'Yeah, that is pretty amazing. I've already ordered my copy. But I do want to know why you didn't tell us,' Fredi said.

'We'll get to that later. I grabbed a couple bottles of champagne,' Ava said, as she stuck her tongue outside of her mouth in concentration and worked on the champagne cork.

'Here, let me do that.' Bonni took the bottle and had it open in no time flat, without a big spray of champagne.

'That's impressive,' Fredi said.

Bonni nodded. 'Quinn is an expert at opening champagne. He showed me how.' She filled up the glasses and handed them round. Celia saw that even Fredi took one, and she hated champagne.

'Now, this is a toast to us. Friends. To a night that went totally off the rails, but that was filled with some of the most joyous news!'

Bonni held up her glass, and the other women did as well. They clinked glasses. Celia smiled, even if it was a tremulous one. Her mind was running away with her about how she had just totally ruined everything.

'Let me see your ring!' Ava demanded, and grabbed Bonni's hand. 'Oh my.'

Celia looked at the beautiful ring. 'It's not a diamond?'

'No, it's a blue sapphire with triangle-shaped diamonds on the side.'

'Stunning,' Fredi said. 'I approve. I can almost see the dress for it.'

Music from the party downstairs continued to thump up into the room. 'Don't let me stop you guys from going down and having fun,' Celia said. 'I don't want to feel like I completely ruined the party.'

Bonni checked her watch. 'The music will be shut down in a little while anyways. I'm just going to dash out and talk to Quinn. I'll be right back.' She dropped a kiss on Celia's cheek. 'It's all gonna be good, don't you worry.'

When Bonni left Celia felt tears drip down her face. She should've told them about the book. All she'd wanted to do was protect them, keep them shielded from any of Frank's potential shenanigans. And now look what happened. She should have trusted her friends more. Should have trusted Landon more.

Once Bonni came back Celia explained her reasoning to her friends. She needed them to understand that her not saying anything wasn't meant to be personal. She explained about the custody issues and how afraid she was about it all, and the possibility of them perjuring themselves.

'Cee, I would perjure myself for you in a heartbeat. At least when it comes to this,' Bonni said.

'I couldn't ask you to do that. You'd be risking your freedom, your job! Besides, it wasn't like I planned on never telling you. I just wanted to talk to my lawyer first. Chances are, I'd have to disclose the income anyway,' Celia said, before draining another glass of champagne.

Ava tapped her fingers against her glass as she looked upward, thinking. 'Yes, you likely would, especially if you'd have to pay taxes on it, and there would be a paper trail. If you tried to hide it, it would only look really bad if the courts found out.'

'I can't believe Dickhead actually thinks Jilly and Colin would be better off with him and Baby Skank,' Fredi said, finishing off her champagne then refilling the glass with Jack.

'You guys are the best friends. I don't know what I'd do without you all.' Celia pushed herself up against the headboard of her bed and punched a pillow behind her back. 'I love how we can share our feelings, make each other feel better, without judging.'

Ava muttered out of the corner of her mouth, 'Fredi's being kinda judgey about Katarina.'

Celia pretended not to hear. 'Thank you for kidnapping me this weekend and forgiving me for keeping this secret.'

'We are in it, babe, through thick and thin,' Fredi told her, lying next to her on the bed, throwing her leg over Celia's in her version of an affectionate gesture.

'What Fredi said.' Ava winked at her, as she settled across the foot of the bed.

'So I don't start crying again, let's talk about something happier. Like who's going to be Bonni's maid of honour ...' Celia said. She, Ava, and Fredi all turned to Bonni, who looked taken aback by the sudden subject change.

After much discussion it was decided that Ava would be the maid of honour but Fredi and Celia could plan the bachelorette party. When the conversation naturally turned to Landon being Quinn's best man, Celia couldn't help but start tearing up.

They hashed it out and helped Celia come to a conclusion. She had to go talk to Landon in the morning. She needed to explain everything from her perspective. She'd be upfront, and open and, most of all, damn proud she'd written a bestselling book.

'You guys are the best. Don't ever think I don't appreciate you,' Celia said to her friends.

'Mm-hm,' Ava murmured sleepily.

'Yes, girl power, woohoo,' Fredi muttered sleepily, snuggled next to Celia's hip.

'We've got your back, friends for life.' Bonni puffed the pillow up beside Celia and curled into it.

Celia looked at her friends cozied up around her. She should really send them off to their own beds, because none of them was going to sleep well – Ava was a kicker – but she took solace in having her friends around her. They were circling the wagons, keeping her sane. She was so grateful that she hadn't permanently damaged her relationship with them, that she could fix things.

And tomorrow she would fix things with Landon.

Chapter 37

Landon was absolutely livid. How could she not have told him about her book? Especially the fact that she had written about him – them. She'd taken an intensely private moment, the start of everything they were, and published it for all the world to see. Thank God Quinn had the foresight to plan another party for family only, and that his mother wasn't there.

He sat at the kitchen island in the house, his brain working furiously at everything they'd done. Shared. He looked at the door to the wine cellar. Memories of them and their passion came rushing back at him. She'd kept something from him. Something that was very important. Was that any way to begin a relationship? If she could hide something of this magnitude, what else could she hide from him?

One thing he'd asked from her – one thing. To trust him. When she had opened up about Frank and the custody issues, he had felt like a real man. His woman was confiding in him, leaning on him. Not because he could make it all go away by throwing cash at it, but because she wanted his support.

Respecting her choice to go it alone had been a struggle, but he'd done it because she'd asked it of him.

But she couldn't do the one thing he'd asked for.

Picking up the glass of Scotch he'd poured, he drained it, then threw it against the wooden door, watching as it shattered into many sparklingly pieces. Just like his heart felt.

Quinn came into the room and whistled at the mess. 'Mom is going to kill you. You know that was part of a set.'

'Fuck off, Quinn,' Landon muttered, before raking his fingers through his hair.

'If you didn't want me to find you, then you should've turned off your Find My Friends app,' Quinn said cheerfully. Landon could hear his brother brushing the broken glass to the side with his foot. There was the opening of a cabinet, some clinking, then another glass of Scotch was slid between his arms.

Landon picked up the drink and looked at his brother. 'I suppose you know.'

'That our little Celia Fox is actually bestselling erotica author Jena Fox? I do now. Bonni texted me after they got Celia inside. She's kind of a mess right now, just so you know.' Quinn poured a drink for himself and pulled over another stool to sit on.

The thought of Celia being upset, probably crying, sent a pang of hurt through his chest. 'What am I going to do, Quinn? Why wouldn't she tell me?'

His brother got serious, clapping a hand on to his shoulder. 'I don't know why. But I do know her life's revolved around two things lately: her kids and her ex-husband being a dick.'

Landon took a sip of the Scotch, his anger subsiding enough that he could think. Thoughtfully, he said, 'She told me Frank had served her with papers. He's going for full custody.'

Quinn exploded off the stool. 'What? Are you kidding me? That bastard cheated on her and now he's trying to steal her kids? "Dickhead" isn't strong enough to describe him, he's an utter asshole.'

Somehow, Quinn's anger on Celia's behalf made Landon feel better too. He and his younger brother had always been tight growing up, because they were frequently the only emotional support each other had. Hearing him threaten to 'beat the ever-loving shit out of that cheapskate narcissistic jackass' for the woman Landon loved was positively heart-warming.

'I suppose,' Landon said slowly, 'that if Frank found out about the book, he'd use it as a reason to declare her an unfit mother.'

Quinn ceased his angry tirade at Landon's words, and turned to consider his brother. 'That seems likely to me.' Sitting back down on the stool, he said, 'You know, she didn't even tell the girls. Bonni had no idea until that woman approached Celia at the party.'

Landon tried to sort out his warring emotions. For Celia not to confide in her friends was serious. It meant that it wasn't that she hadn't trusted Landon, it meant she hadn't trusted anyone. Or maybe it wasn't a matter of trust. Maybe she had been trying to protect them from getting drawn into Frank's legal idiocy.

Celia had written a book, had it published, had it do well and had been unable to share her triumph with anyone. He felt a rush of pride and awe at her tenacity in doing something that could cause potential conflict. And respect. Respect that she'd gone for something she wanted and had achieved a goal.

'I need to talk to her,' Landon announced, standing up.

Quinn waved him back down as he finished the last of his Scotch. 'Look, I would give her the night. Let her work things out with the girls first, get a good night's sleep, and then talk to her in the morning.'

Go to bed without Celia? Not see her first thing in the morning? Yes, he really needed to ramp up his plans to move to San Francisco as soon as possible. He could also use the time to wake up his lawyers. He wanted information. There was also the small matter of his starring role in an erotica novel. Landon reluctantly nodded in agreement.

His brother stood, then looked down at the glass he held. Landon expected him to place it on the counter or in the sink, but instead Quinn threw it against the door.

'Bro, what the hell? Why did you do that?'

'I did it for you, of course,' Quinn said oh-so-innocently. 'Now it's a matched set of four.'

Quinn punched him on the shoulder before grabbing it and shaking it in a rough display of affection. As he left, he said, 'Good luck finding the broom.'

Landon flipped his brother off behind his back and surveyed the kitchen. He ran a multimillion-dollar business. Of course, he could find a broom. Didn't they have closets for that kind of thing? Once he got the glass up, so he wouldn't get scolded by the housekeeper in the morning, he had a book to buy.

Chapter 38

The ache in Celia's back woke her up. Her friends were still snoozing in a pile around her and she carefully extricated herself from a tangle of arms and legs. After a quick shower she threw on some clothes and went out to find Landon.

But he was nowhere to be found.

A housekeeper let her in to the main house, but told her that the oldest hooligan – whatever that meant – had left early this morning. She checked with the B and B next, but no one there had seen him either. She called his cell and left a voicemail, then sent him a text requesting that they talk, but she didn't receive a reply.

After grabbing a big mug of coffee in a travel cup from the B and B, Celia looked out over the hills. Yesterday, the forest had made her feel great; maybe a long walk through the vineyard would do the same. Its quiet ambience was a balm. Birds sang and the breeze was sweet. It was early, and no workers were in the vineyard yet, so she enjoyed the solitude while she could.

The walk through the vineyard brought her some clarity. It would be best if she left. She wanted to see her children. They were staying with their grandmother while Frank was on his honeymoon. Then she'd make an appointment with the lawyer and start fighting back.

She wanted to explain everything about the book to Landon and why she kept it from him. Even if he never forgave her, which made her heart hurt, she still owed him an explanation. Decision made, she headed back to the bed and breakfast and found her friends on the terrace, having breakfast.

'Celia!' Ava waved to catch her attention.

Sitting down with them Celia said, 'Landon's left. Since I'm unable to explain anything to him right now, I'm going home.'

'Do you want to leave right now? You're not listed as a driver on my rental car, but I'm sure Quinn could arrange something,' Bonni said.

Celia answered, 'I hadn't really thought about it.'

Ava reached over and covered Celia's hand with hers. 'Listen, I know this is upsetting, but we were all going to leave later today anyways. Just hang on and we can all go home together.'

Fredi sucked in a swift breath. The women looked at her. 'Are you choking on something?' Bonni asked, half out of her seat and ready to give her the Heimlich maneuver.

'Don't look now, but the man of the hour has just come on to the terrace.' Fredi tipped her head a few times in the direction of the door.

'Master of subtlety, aren't you?' Bonni said.

Celia turned to see Landon. Her heart burst and she stood quickly, the chair nearly flipping back with the force.

'Ladies.' He greeted them, before turning to Celia. 'Can we talk?'

She nodded and glanced at her friends. They waved her on

and made the texting motion to indicate they'd want details later.

Celia took it as a good sign that Landon put his hand out for her. She took it and he led her away. 'Where are we going?' she asked in a small voice.

'I thought we'd go over to the house. There's more privacy there.'

'Okay,' she said. 'I stopped by there, looking for you.' They moved past the beautiful gardens that she'd seen the first night.

'I know,' he replied. 'Donna, the housekeeper, she told me. I was out running an errand.'

Their feet crunched on the stone path. It was good to know that while she was desperately trying to find him he was out picking up monogramed cufflinks, or whatever errands rich guys did themselves.

She was being bitchy because she was scared.

She could take the fact that he was holding her hand as a good sign, couldn't she? Their time together this weekend had made her realize how important he was to her. And hadn't she planned to tell him after they made love the other night that she loved him?

But she hadn't.

Landon's silence on the walk back to the main house unnerved Celia, even though he didn't let go of her hand. Her stomach was in knots and her heart beat a staccato rhythm that was so out of tune she thought she might die. She would survive, though. This wouldn't be the first time a man had ripped her heart out and stomped on it.

Celia looked up at him, but he was still staring ahead. He hadn't made eye contact with her since he'd asked to talk. She drew in a shaky breath, trying not to let her worry take over. She would find out soon enough what the situation was.

'We can sit out here.' He let her hand go as he opened the wrought-iron gate to the private family patio that she'd seen from the kitchen the other night.

A table was set under a cabana that had linen curtains tied back, the ends of them fluttering in the soft breeze. Teal-and-red cushions sat on the white iron seats and the table had matching glasses, linen napkins and place mats. It all looked so very bright, happy and fun, which was a complete contradiction to how she felt at the moment.

Landon held a chair out for her.

'Have a seat here. I have a jug of sangria chilling in the fridge.'

Celia grabbed his hand. 'Landon, don't go yet.'

He looked down at her, and there was no trace on his face of the anger she'd seen on his face last night.

'Sit here for a minute and I'll be right back.'

Celia watched him walk to the outdoor kitchen. It was like something out of *Better Homes and Gardens* magazine. Watching him prepare things – actually *seeing* him – made her both happy and sad. Happy she'd met and spent time with him. Sad because that time could be over. She counted to ten in her head, forcing her breathing to be even and not to hyperventilate. She couldn't remember the last time she'd been this upset, not even when Frank told her he wanted a divorce because he wanted to marry someone else.

She heard the clink of glasses and watched as he easily hefted a laden tray and walked toward her. Celia let her gaze crawl over him. She took in every little detail, from his shaggy red-blond hair, the tan that had him nicely golden, his eyes so piercingly blue it almost hurt, to the power of his walk. Not to mention his kindness, his playful spirit, his strength of character and his compassion. She loved this man and she needed to tell him. Even if it wasn't returned, he had to know how she felt.

'I've prepared some snacks, to have with the sangria.' His voice seemed to have no emotion in it, and she swivelled her gaze up to meet his.

'Landon, I—'

He held up his hand. 'Celia, I want to talk first. I know you well now, so I just want you to relax and listen to me.'

He leaned forward and filled two glasses with sangria. He lifted a glass and held it for her and she reached out and took it, their fingers touching. Celia caught her breath at the spark she swore arced between them. Oh, how she would miss that.

Then he uncovered the plate to reveal a beautiful cheese platter, with deli meats, fruits, sliced Italian bread, pickles and chutney. 'Are you hungry?'

'I am, actually. I haven't eaten anything since our lunch yesterday.' The aroma from the food tickled her nostrils, and her belly growled. Loudly. So loud he heard it.

He looked alarmed and pushed the plate toward her. 'Good Lord, why haven't you eaten anything? Why didn't your friends feed you?'

Celia reached for a piece of cheese and a grape. The sharp Cheddar and the sweetness of the fruit exploded in her mouth. Under better circumstances, she would take a moment to savor the flavor. 'I was too upset last night to eat anything.'

He looked at her intently and she tried to remain silent so he could talk first, as he had requested. It was too hard, and they both spoke at the same time.

'Oh, Landon, I'm—'

'Celia, it was—'

They laughed, nervously, but it seemed to cut the tension tremendously.

'Landon, I'm so sorry about last night. I didn't want you to find out about the book like that.'

He frowned and tilted his head to the side, looking at her. 'I must admit I was a little taken aback to discover you'd written a book and you hadn't told me about it.'

'But you have to understand.' She leaned forward, pleading. 'You know I've always wanted to write, and our time in Las Vegas was an absolute inspiration. This book sprang from that. It's completely fictional. I kept it from the girls too. I didn't want Frank to find out about it, if I could avoid it.' She took a long drink and then put the glass down. 'They were shocked, and probably a little bit mad at me. We don't keep things from each other, usually, although Bonni's big announcement was totally unexpected.'

'Celia, stop. What I was trying to tell you is that I understand. I talked to Quinn and he helped me realize basically everything you just said. It's fine, darling.' She watched him select some meat and layer it with pickles, cheese and a dollop of a green chutney. He popped it into his mouth and Celia was mesmerized by everything about him.

'So you forgive me?' she asked, somewhat disbelievingly.

'I don't see there being anything to forgive, but if you feel you need it, yes, I forgive you. I know you would have told me if it hadn't been for Dickhead.'

Celia half laughed, half cried at his words, and the tension broke in her body under a wave of pure relief. At the sight of her tears he stood, rounded the table and scooped her up, before sitting down in her chair and arranging her on his lap. He made soothing sounds while building little mini-sandwiches of bread, meat and cheese, coaxing her to eat.

When she felt more like herself, she leaned back a little so that she could see his face and said, 'I was going to tell you something the other night. But it didn't happen. And then after last night I wasn't sure I'd ever get a chance to.'

He smoothed a hand down her hair, offering her another sandwich. 'So tell me now.'

Celia hesitated. Then, before she could change her mind, she blurted out, 'I'm in love with you.'

Air whooshed out of Landon, as if she had elbowed him, and he dropped the food on to the table. She watched his face, waiting, hoping for some kind of reaction. It seemed like forever before he smiled.

'Ah, Celia, my love, trust you to steal my thunder. I had this whole romantic surprise planned for you. I wanted it to be special when I told you that . . . I love you too.'

She fell against him, feeling like a ragdoll as a surge of relief washed through her. She clutched at his biceps. 'Really, you do?'

'Celia.' His voice was fierce as he stared down at her. 'We have something extraordinary. Not just the physical attraction between us, but something more. I felt it the first moment I laid eyes on you in Las Vegas.'

She drew in a shocked breath and blinked. 'I can't believe what I'm hearing.'

'Well, believe it. I love you, but I wasn't sure how you felt about me and, with the complications of your ex-husband, the last thing I was going to do was force you in any particular direction.'

'Oooh, I am . . . stunned, I can't even think. Really?'

'Yes, really. I want you in my life and I hope you want me in yours.' She was nodding furiously. 'Now, regarding my errand this morning, I want you to hear me out before you react.'

This didn't bode well, but she trusted him, so she knew it would be all right. Pulling her shoulders back, she said, 'Okay, where did you go?

He tightened his arms around her, as if he thought he would

need to keep her from leaving. 'I went and met with my lawyers.'

'Landon . . .' Celia wasn't sure she'd heard that right. 'What did you do?'

'I asked them to research how your writing career might impact the custody suit and if our relationship would help or hinder it. They said, in the politest and most professional way possible, that being with a man like me can only help you. Your writing career could be problematic, but they advised you not to hide anything and to be ready to produce character witnesses.

'I don't want you to misunderstand and think that I'm trying to take over or control the situation. But I have the best legal minds working for me – in my opinion, anyway.' He smiled a little. 'And I needed the peace of mind that being with me wasn't going to help that man take away your kids.'

Celia was silent for a moment, digesting what he'd just told her. When the reality of it sunk in, she swelled with emotion.

'I get it, and I'm touched that you looked into it.' Celia looked into his eyes, deep and clear and full of love for her, overwhelmed that she was sitting on the lap of this hot, charming guy who loved her and wanted to protect her family.

She took his face in her palms. 'I don't know what to say except thank you. This is great information and I will definitely pass it on to my lawyer later, but you've already made so many things better.'

He breathed a sigh of relief and Celia was overjoyed that everything seemed to be working out. Tilting her chin, she pressed her lips to his, aching to feel his touch again, and he kissed her back, their mouths meeting in a melding of joy and passion.

Resting his forehead on hers, he whispered, 'Can you stay a

little longer? I cleared my schedule so I could start moving out here, and I would really love it if you would stay.'

She bit her lip uncertainly. 'I want to, but I also kinda wanted to head back and check on the kids.'

'Then what do you think of this idea? We fly down there, take the kids out for ice cream, give them their presents, then fly back to San Francisco again and have a few days to ourselves. When it's your turn to have them again, we go grab your kids and take them somewhere fun. I'm dying to meet them in person.' He watched her intently, and Celia knew exactly how she would reply to that one.

'I think it's a perfect plan.' She couldn't contain her elation. 'I mean, it's crazy just to fly back home for only a couple hours, but if we can do it, why not? You, Landon Bryant, are re-establishing my faith in men. Loving you, I might not just be a lost cause after all.'

'Oh, I know you're not a lost cause. I think you're wonderful. I think you're a wonderful mother, and . . .' He gave her a sexy wink, '. . . you are a passionate and exciting lover. But most of all, I think you are an amazing author.'

She pulled back to search his eyes. 'What does that mean? "An amazing author"?'

'Well, there may be one other thing I have to tell you.' Landon pressed his lips together, playfully, and she gave him a little shake.

'Did you read my book?'

'I did. I downloaded it last night. It wasn't my usual fare, but I thoroughly enjoyed it. In fact, I think I picked up some pointers after reading about how Byron managed Adrianna,' he said teasingly. In a more serious tone, he added, 'But I want you to know how very proud I am of you.'

'I'm overwhelmed,' Celia said, brushing her fingers against

his nape. 'I can't believe all this is happening. It's like a dream come true.'

He kissed her then, again, and she wondered if he had read the dedication to her book.

To a man who has let me see
there are still knights in shining armor

Landon really was her knight in shining armour, one who was giving her the space and support she needed to be a warrior princess with a wild heart. Yet if she needed him, he'd be ready to slay the dragon.

'Landon,' she said against his lips. 'Promise me we'll live happily ever after.'

He reached to grab one of her hands, bringing it to his front. Brushing his thumb meaningfully against her ring finger, he stared deeply into her eyes, and said, 'Yes, ma'am.'

What Happens in Vegas

When the cop . . .
Meets the gambler . . .
The stakes have never been higher.

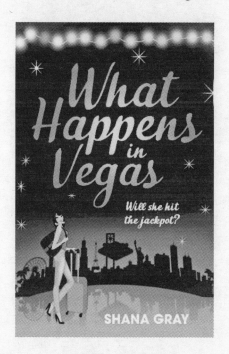

Available now from

HEADLINE
ETERNAL

WORKING GIRL

A sexy seven-day job interview.
Seven irresistible interviewers.
Who will she choose at the end of the week?

Available now from

HEADLINE
ETERNAL

FIND YOUR HEART'S DESIRE...

VISIT OUR WEBSITE: www.headlineeternal.com
FIND US ON FACEBOOK: facebook.com/eternalromance
CONNECT WITH US ON TWITTER: @eternal_books
FOLLOW US ON INSTAGRAM: @headlineeternal
EMAIL US: eternalromance@headline.co.uk